John Parsons Foote

Memoirs of the Life of Samuel E. Foote

John Parsons Foote

Memoirs of the Life of Samuel E. Foote

ISBN/EAN: 9783337415785

Printed in Europe, USA, Canada, Australia, Japan

Cover: Foto ©Raphael Reischuk / pixelio.de

More available books at **www.hansebooks.com**

MEMOIRS

OF

THE LIFE

OF

SAMUEL E. FOOTE,

BY HIS BROTHER

JOHN P. FOOTE,

——— I long
To hear the story of your life, which must
Take the ear strangely.
SHAKESPEARE.

——o——

He whom nature at his birth
Endowed with noblest qualities,
* * * * * is nobly born.
COWPER.

CINCINNATI:

ROBERT CLARKE & CO.
PUBLISHERS.

1860.

PREFACE.

This Memoir is a record of *industry, perseverance and success.* Of industry commenced at the earliest period of life practicable, and continued with unwearied perseverance until success was achieved.

It is a record of a life of moral purity, preserved amid extraordinary temptations.

Fortified by early instructions and examples, such as are the results of the influence of Christianity alone, many and strong temptations which could not here be recorded, were overcome, and a life that may be characterized as one "without fear, and without reproach," with more propriety than that of any *military hero*, was the result.

The occasion which called forth this record, was the desire expressed by a large number of friends and relatives, at the time of the funeral, to obtain a knowledge of the early life of one so beloved, and one whose youthful years had been uncommonly eventful.

The writer of the following memoir being known to have more power of communicating such knowledge than any other living person, was requested to undertake the task, and to place it in a permanent form, which could be transmitted to his and their descendants.

A compliance with this request was promised, and this work is the result. No other person possessed as much knowledge, not only of the events detailed, but of the motives, principles and opinions connected with them, as the writer: and whatever may be the character of the style and manner in which they are given, the facts recorded will possess peculiar interest to those for whom this account is especially prepared.

Biography ought to be the most instructive as well as the most pleasing department of our light literature; and a great portion of our novels and romances are based on the idea that—admitting this principle—imaginary biographies, as they are generally made more attractive, may be made better means of conveying such instruction, and illustrating such principles, as their authors desire to inculcate than correct accounts of the lives of individuals.

To works of this class, however, there have always been very strong objections, and genuine biographies have always been recommended as preferable means of giving instruction. But equally strong objections may be made to a great portion of the biographies of the eminent men of most countries, in which many, and those not the least attractive, instances are as demoralizing in their tendency as modern French novels; or as a great portion of the dramatic literature of our forefathers, or the Byronic poetry of the present day. Such works as most of the biographies of Napoleon, all those of Nelson, Parton's of Burr, etc., etc., throughout all of which runs a constant effort to disguise or hide the crimes of their heroes behind a veil of successful military exploits or public services of any kind, are dangerous to youth, by tending to inspire the idea that eminence and fame will atone for vice and crime.

Faithful biographies of many of our American merchants, engineers, inventors, artisans and artists would be a valuable portion of our literature, and they might be, and ought to be, made sufficiently attractive to neutralize, in some degree at least, if they could not accomplish, the hopeless task of superseding the taste for military detail, and the hero-worship of warriors.

Healthier sentiments than such details inspire would be engendered by the knowledge that might be obtained of the progress of refinement, and the spread of the arts that carry on the march of civilization. For to make improvements and discoveries, as well in the mechanic arts—in every thing connected with the physical progress of society—is no less a part of man's mission than to enquire and search out the sources and the means of obtaining happiness in that future life, to which all look forward with hope or fear.

Inventors of machinery and of the methods by which all the powers of nature may be made subservient to the improvement of society, and the

1*

advancement of civilization, and by which the results of human labor may be increased and multi-
plied—enquiries and researches into all the secrets
of nature and the resources of art—are the fulfillment of religious duties as certainly as the devotion of time and talents to the acquisition of the
knowledge of the will of God in the study of his
Word and his works, and in comparing and verifying the inferences drawn from each. Thus most
of man's employment in which mind and body
are engaged, if duly performed in a true spirit, are
the fulfillment of the duties and responsibilities of
men who are accountable for the employment of
their talents.

Not only private happiness, but public freedom
is connected with the combination of mental and
physical labor. The Northern serfs and the negroes of the South, have lost their freedom by
their neglect of this combination; and nations
that are under a despotic and arbitrary government are thus subjected, because easy pleasures
and thoughtless amusements have been made the
business of life, instead of its occasional relaxa-
tions, and of wholesome rest from its labors.

One of the earliest methods to be adopted by
our Missionaries for the conversion of the heathen
to Christianity, and one that would be most effective at the commencement of their operations,
would be the exhibition to them of the improvements in the comforts of life, made by civilized
men, through the combined effects of mental and

physical labor. The difficulties in commencing their labors may be lessened, and the results hastened, by sending with them, as our government did to Japan, those specimens of the superiority of Christian nations in the arts which exhibit the power of mind over matter; for it is certain that activity of mind is called forth, and its powers increased, by the researches to which Christian denominations are incited in order to furnish proofs for their peculiar dogmas.

Objects exhibited to the sight, according to Horace and other authorities, are more rapid in their effects on the mind than those addressed to the ear. And those savage people who exercise their bodies as little as possible, and their minds scarcely at all, cannot begin to receive instruction so easily in any way as by being shown specimens of the combined powers of each of these departments of labor.

Foreigners have been much in the habit of demanding from us an "American Literature," and we have seemed to think that this unmeaning and unintelligible demand required of us some thing to which our attention should be directed. It seems, however, chiefly to turn to the department of poetry, which has here little or nothing to inspire it different from the usual sources of inspiration of English poetry.

The only distinctive national literature—American, as distinguished from English—if such a distinction can be allowed—must be found in the biographies of those men who have given us whatever we possess of a distinctive national character. If we could obtain such biographies of eminent Americans as the delightful autobiography of Franklin—they would be as good contributions to American Biography as that department of literature could furnish. The contrast seen in the continuation of these memoirs with the commencement, is one of the best exemplifications of the difference in the interest excited by the different modes of telling a story.

Irving's Life of Washington, Spark's various biographies, particularly that of Gouverneur Morris, and some of Hunt's American Merchants, and others by different authors, are valuable portions of an "American Literature," and will have a good influence on the minds of youth. The tendency of such literature ought always to be to strengthen our love of free institutions, which cannot be maintained except in virtuous and enlightened communities. To contribute to such a result ought to be the chief end for which we should endeavor to establish a distinctive "American Literature." Many more biographies might be written with this tendency, and in such works the highest order of talent ought not to be confined to the memoirs of those in the highest stations. "Peter Parley's Recollections of his Life," are a more valuable contribution to "American Literature," than such "Lives" as those of John Randolph, Thomas Jefferson, and others who have held high political stations.

We do not need either the usual commemorative funeral panegyrics, or French "eloges;" nor is what is needed in our Literature mere attempts to rescue our sages and heroes from the fate of those who lived before Agamemnon; but it is to preserve for continual use those examples which exhibit human nature and human actions in their brightest light; in such a light, namely, as may show the path to progressive improvement in human manners and morals, and incite the young to tread that path. And the power to do this is not confined to the records of the great and powerful, but may be exhibited in those of persons in any station.

The greatest powers of narration have generally been devoted to the men of the highest political and military standing, and such can most easily be made to convey the sentiments of the biographer. It is, however, a lower order of genius and talents that can excite attention to, and interest in, those dazzling flashes of light that emanate from the records of victories and the triumphs of eloquence, than that which can give attractive records of those peaceful and quiet efforts of individuals in more retired life for the good of society —of lives which seem to flow modestly on in quiet obedience to the rule of our Savior, not to perform our duties to the sound of a trumpet.

The influence of records of characteristic human actions is great; provided such record be judiciously made, and the true light in which they should be seen made to illuminate them.

If it should be thought that in the following narrative greater powers have been needed to make it sufficiently attractive, in order to render it useful, I can only say, that "if to do were as easy as to know what were good to do, chapels had been churches, and poor men's cottages princely palaces. I can easier teach twenty what were good to be done, than be one of the twenty to follow my own teaching."

CINCINNATI, October 1st, 1860.

CONTENTS.

APPENDIX.

MEMOIR

OF

SAMUEL E. FOOTE.

CHAPTER I.

PARENTAGE.

———

"'T is to the virtues of such men, man owes
His portion of the good that Heaven bestows."—COWPER.

———

IN the ordinary intercourse of society, we occasionally meet with men whose genius and acquirements, regulated by sound common sense, and subjected to the control of rigid integrity, elevate them above their fellows, and command the respect and esteem of all with whom they associate —men in whose behalf we never invoke a consideration of their genius and talents to cover defects in their character and conduct. We love and esteem them, however, chiefly for their private virtues and genial natures, rather than from any consideration of their superiority to a large proportion of those whose biographies comprise the most interesting and useful portion of the history of nations, and whose names are memorials of important events in the annals of mankind.

When, however, we meet with such a character in private life, we cannot help, in consideration of its superiority, wondering how it happens, that in a country, under such a government as ours where personal character and not birth and favoritism are the qualifications looked for, (in theory at least,) in making choice of men to guide and direct its destinies—to watch over the welfare of its inhabitants, and to establish its standing among nations—that such men should not be called to assume higher duties than those of private life in its ordinary vocations. We are frequently disposed to regret the loss to our country of the services their superior talents might render it, for we think them to be men whose intelligence, good sense and integrity, might save the nation from the evils (to some of which we shall refer hereafter) to which it has been subjected from the want of such qualities in its rulers. We consider it a public misfortune, that the theory of our institutions in relation to the choice of public agents, has not been carried out in practice, and that the highest qualities in personal character have been too much neglected, or not appreciated. We observe, indeed, that these comparatively obscure persons, to whom we refer, contribute largely to the happiness of those connected with them by the ties of kindred or friendship, and to the silent, quiet, improvement of society in taste, in refinement, and in morality. The benefit of their examples of integrity and persevering industry in business—of their refusal to submit quietly to the domination of evil fortune, and of courageous renewal of their conflicts with adversity when it strikes them down, instead of endeavoring to drown the sense of their disappointment by intoxications or any other form of suicide, are felt by society, and speed the progress of civilization. Thus, though we regret the loss of the talents and labors of such men in cabinets and legislatures, we have reason to be thankful for the amount of private happiness, and of unostentatious aid to the progress of their country, in all those things that increase the happiness of domestic life, which they bestow on the community.

The substitution of such men for the demagogues and intriguers who so often usurp the places, which, according to the theory of our government, belong only to the most worthy and most capable of our citizens, would, as every one perceives, tend to the promotion of the public welfare and the stability of our free institutions. The domestic sacrifices thus required would, in many instances, be great, but the fact that our country has need of them, ought to overpower all merely personal considerations, for that this need is constantly increasing, is very manifest. The theory of political economy in relation to demand and supply, does not appear to be applicable to the demand of our country for an increased supply of wise and virtuous legislators and magistrates, which is constantly increasing, while the supply is diminishing.

The paramount want of our country is not a constant increase of territory, but an increase of men, competent to the judicious direction of the affairs of the territory we already possess, and an increase of knowledge and public virtue, sufficient to cause such men to be properly appreciated.

The true wealth and the source of permanent prosperity of our nation, as well as every other, consists in the possession of

> " Men, high minded men,
> Men who their duties know."

It consists in the possession of a competent number of such men as the subject of this memoir.

SAMUEL EDMOND FOOTE, the fourth son and eighth child of Eli Foote and Roxanna Ward, his wife, was born at Guilford, Connecticut, on the second of October, 1787. His Grandfathers, Daniel Foote, of Colchester, and General Andrew Ward, of Guilford, were both descendants of the early puritan, pilgrim fathers, of New England; whose principles they maintained, the former with that extreme "rigor and solemnity" which characterized that class of men who never did wrong (consciously) themselves, nor pardoned wrong doing in others; the latter, equally free from sin or crime himself, was of so kindly and benevolent a

nature, that he was as ready to grant forgiveness.
when asked, as to ask. as he did. for forgiveness.
in his daily prayers.

The former was the author of a treatise "on
Original Sin," written to edify his descendants in
the puritan faith, but was not published. The latter wrote and published a somewhat voluminous
pamphlet on the dissensions in the old Presbyterian congregation. in Guilford. which resulted in a
separation, and the establishment of a new sect,
denominated "New Lights." and the building of
a new meeting house. which. after a few years.
was suffered to go into a state of decay. the decline of the sect having commenced as soon as
their first pastor left them.

He wrote, also, a number of other articles, one
of which contained an account of the march to
Nova Scotia. of the regiment commanded by his
father. in which he was a captain. through a then,
fearful. savage wilderness. now a land of highly
cultivated fields. filled with beautiful towns and
villages. It contained also an account of the capture of Louisburg. which was the result of that
expedition. This manuscript was exceedingly interesting at that time, and at present would be
still more so, but unfortunately, it was accidently
destroyed.

The father and son were both in advance of
their age in relation to those principles, for the establishment and promulgation of which our modern temperance societies have been instituted. for

2*

they received in money that portion of their rations which consisted of rum, and this they converted into silver spoons, each of which was marked "Louisburg." These were left as mementos to their descendants, that the habitual use of spirituous liquors was unnecessary, under any circumstances; since, if any plea could justify such use of them, it would have been that of the fatigues and hardships encountered on that campaign.

One of those spoons was lately deposited with the Historical Society of Hartford, and in the notice of it which was published, it was remarked, that the descendants of those men (the Wards) had never been disgraced by numbering a drunkard among them.

The son and daughter of these puritans did not in their religious belief, tread in the footsteps of their forefathers, but became converts to the Church of England, at a period when a churchman in New England was in an enemy's country, especially in Connecticut, and more especially in Guilford, where puritanic testimony against the dangers of prelatism was declared in the strongest terms, and with the deepest feelings of determined opposition.

The purity of character, however, and the genial, kindly dispositions of the Footes, softened the asperity of religious intolerance as far as related to them, and acquired the friendship and respect of all who knew them, by whom their heresy was rather lamented than resented.

During the war of the revolution, Eli Foote, in common with all the Episcopalians of New England, adhered to the royal cause,* but in a quiet, orderly, peaceful manner, and so evidently from conscientious motives that he was never troubled by the zealous patriots of his neighborhood. His father-in-law, and his brothers Ebenezer† and John, served in the American army during the war, being, with all their relatives, except Eli, zealous Whigs. His father, also, in the civil service of his country, was a firm patriot. He was chosen one of the delegates to the State Convention to which the Constitution of the United States was submitted for approval or rejection, and strongly urged its adoption. Gen. Ward was also a member of the Convention, and opposed the Constitution on the ground, that by it the States surrendered too much of their power to the central government. They were both members of the State legislature for many years.

Eli Foote and Roxanna Ward, were married on the 11th of October, 1772, and at the period of the peace which established the Independence of our country, were the parents of six children.

The revolutionary war in its progress had impoverished the people of New England, not only by the loss of property already acquired, but also of the facilities they possessed of acquiring more, by the destruction of their commerce and naviga-

---

*Appendix No. 1.   † Appendix No. 2.

tion, in which almost all were concerned, directly or indirectly.

The change of the government of the country to an independent nation, would necessarily produce changes in the state of society and the course of business: but these were not as great in Connecticut as in the other States, and in commercial proceedings, the former system of operations was soon renewed, and the first resumption was in their navigation.

From the earliest period of the settlements of towns along the New England coasts, their merchants were engaged in some kind of navigation, and owned small vessels, in which they carried on their trade to the West Indies, to the Southern portions of America, and wherever else they were allowed to trade. A great portion of them was engaged in the fisheries, and supplied an important part of the cargoes of those employed in the West India trade. The other portions of these cargoes consisted of lumber and provisions, with deck-loads of horses and cattle. These were exchanged for the rum, sugar, coffee, pimento, etc., of the islands, and supplied the interior demands for those articles.

One of this class of traders was Eli Foote, who in connection with another person living on Long Island, had built a small vessel for this trade; but in this business he was unfortunate, owing to the mistakes or misconduct of his associate; and as his family was increasing, a decrease in the means of providing for it was peculiarly distressing. He, however, exerted his best efforts to repair his losses and to increase the profits of his business. as well as the number of individuals in his family.

It was at that period customary with many of the New England traders to transfer their business during the winter season to the towns of the Southern States, as most of the mercantile business of those States was transacted at that season, and commercial operations there were almost exclusively conducted by new England and Scotch merchants. It was the custom of New England traders to spend their winters at the South, and return in summer early enough to escape the deadly effects of a Southern climate on Northern constitutions, and as summer and autumn were the business seasons of New England, it was practicable to carry on business at the North and South to better advantage than to confine it exclusively to either of those regions.

Justin Foote, the youngest brother of Eli, to whose care he had been confided during his boyhood, had made a mercantile establishment at Murfreesborough, North Carolina, and had been successful, having fortunately formed a partnership with a young Scotchman, a man of excellent character, and a well educated merchant, who had resided in the West Indies long enough to consider himself acclimated to a Southern region. Being temperate, prudent and cautious, he escaped the prevailing fevers of that country. and lived to a good old age : the connection was dissolved only by death.

Those fevers, referred to, were so regular in their visits, as to be expected to return with the same regularity as returns of the season, which they characterized. With the natives they took the mild form of intermittents, or fever and ague, but with Northern visitors, billious fevers of a deadly type.

The course of trade in those mercantile establishments, was to furnish the Planters with every article they needed, which the plantations did not yield, and collect and ship their disposable produce of every kind, including corn, pork, naval stores, lumber, cotton in small quantities, with a number of smaller articles, and fish in large quantities, from the extensive herring and shad fisheries on all their rivers. The shipments were chiefly to the West Indies and the Northern ports, and their imports were from the West Indies, sugar, molasses, coffee, rum, etc.; and from the Nothern cities, not only dry goods and hardware, but hats and shoes, which were almost exclusively imported from England, together with millstones, millinery, medicines, and yankee notions generally, for there were no manufactories of any kind in the Southern States, and as few mechanics as possible. In Murfreesborough, at the beginning of this century, there was a considerable number of trading houses, but no mechanics exercising their trades, except a blacksmith and a

tailor. There was not a church, a clergyman or
a lawyer in the place; there was, however, a bar-
ber and two physicians. A masonic hall supplied
the place of all public buildings, except the office
of Surveyor of the port, it being a port of delivery. The offices of Surveyor, Inspector, Post-
master, etc., were held by Col. Murfree, the founder of the town, and afterwards of another of the
same name, in Tennessee. The town contained,
besides the masonic hall, a tavern, a boarding
house, and a race course, which completed the
number of its public institutions. Strolling com-
panies of comedians sometimes displayed their
talents in the masonic hall, and itinerant preach-
ers of the Baptist and Methodist denominations,
occasionally called the attention of the people to
the truths of Christianity, which to most of them
was like the preaching of St. Paul at Athens,
bringing strange things to their ears. Revivals
were occasionally awakened, the influences of
which, however, were not generally so permanent
as to superrede the necessity of frequent repeti-
tions.

The genial, kindly, hospitable and friendly dispositions of the inhabitants of all that portion of
the State, were very marked, and their social
gatherings were frequent, not only at regular hol-
iday periods, but at weddings, races, and all other
occasions which would authorize festive assemblages. The young men generally, however, seemed
to think that "a short life and a merry one," was

the maxim to live by, and, in consequence, old
men were as rare as young ones at Guilford, from
whence youthful emigrants were so constantly
flowing. that the proportion of old men among the
population was then, and has ever been, a striking
characteristic of the place.

The use of such quack medicines as whisky,
peach brandy, and alcoholic stimulants generally,
which were considered prophylactics for their fevers. produced the effects which quack medicines
generally do, rendering the first clause of the
above maxim. of a short and merry life, a practical doctrine, restraining over population as effect-
ually as any Malthusian could desire.

Justin Foote advised his brother Eli, to make a
trading establishment at Winton, the county seat,
ten miles below Murfreesborough, on the same
river, the Meherrin, and so much nearer to the
extensive herring fisheries of that river, and the
Chowan, of which it is a branch. The advice
was followed, and the business of the first season was so encouraging, that it was continued
another year, in the course of which the store was
broken open and robbed of its most valuable con-
tents: and some of the burglars being taken, he
was compelled to remain until the session of the
court in which they were tried. This was at the
commencement of the sickly season. of which he
became one of the earliest victims. He died on
the 9th of September, 1792, and through the losses he had sustained, and the difficulties naturally

attendant on a business left in such an exposed situation. the estate was declared insolvent. and though in a very small amount, it was sufficient to leave his widow destitute and pennyless, with ten children, the eldest nineteen years. and the youngest less than eight months old. Her father. however. who had no other living child. (his only other one. the wife of Abraham Chittenden. Esq.. of Guilford. having died several years previous.) took her. with all her children, to Nutplains. his farm, about two miles from Guilford. and during the remainder of his life was a father to her children. as well as herself. Her oldest son. Andrew Ward Foote, had been at his birth. adopted by him as his principal heir, with the intention of having his name changed by cutting off its last word, as soon as he should arrive at a suitable age. He died. however. before that period arrived. and his grandfather died a few years after, leaving to his daughter a life estate in his farm. together with the house in which she had resided with her husband in Guilford. and some lots in its vicinity in fee. Her two eldest sons died in 1794. at a period at which they had became competent to the management of the farm, and the third son having been adopted by an uncle. had gone to Williamstown for the purpose of being educated at the college. then lately established there. The two remaining sons. Samuel. aged nearly eight, and George. two years younger. although very precocious, were not qualified to do

the duties of men. They, however, improved
rapidly, and in a few years were men in power,
though but boys in age. In farm labors and
school attendance, they plodded along until circumstances enabled Samuel to enter upon the career in which he became distinguished at a very
early period of life.

CHAPTER II.

EARLY LIFE AND KINDRED.

———

"Who can find a virtuous woman; her price is far above rubies."*—SOLOMON.

———

THE value of female influence in forming the character of a young man, when proceeding from intelligent minds, purified by Christianity, and strengthened by the cares and labors imposed on those to whom afflictions have been sent from Heaven, cannot be too highly estimated.

In the blessings derived from this source, Samuel E. Foote inherited advantages which, in value, were "beyond the power of gold." His mother was an incarnation of the characteristics of charity as enumerated by the Apostle in the thirteenth

———

* A mercantile commentator on this motto might naturally, looking at it in the commercial point of view, suggest a doubt whether Solomon had not enjoyed a more extensive credit for wisdom than his capital of that article would give any one at the present time.

Such a quotation of prices as it gives would, in a modern mercantile circular, be considered very unsatisfactory to any person desiring to learn from it the fair value of virtuous women in the Jerusalem market in Solomon's time. At the present period, it requires no extraordinary amount of wisdom to give a much better quotation of the price of a virtuous woman (viz: one "sold for no fault") in our nearest markets. They may generally be quoted at from eight to twelve hundred dollars, according to quality. Some fancy articles in that line may be quoted at fifteen hundred dollars.

chapter of Corinthians.   His eldest sister, Harriet. was a zealous member of the Episcopal Church, well acquainted with its history and doctrines, and an acute and skillful controversalist in its behalf; qualities which were early called into exercise from the circumstance that Nutplains was much visited by young clergymen of the Presbyterian denomination,* who frequently exercised their controversial talents on subjects which were to constitute the pursuits of their future lives.

His second sister, Roxanna, was a woman of extraordinary talents and acquirements; and in that gentle, sweet womanliness of character, which is irresistible in its influence, could not be excelled. Her daughter, Harriet Beecher Stowe. has given a slight, but very graphic, sketch of her in her character of Aunt Mary, in one of her Mayflower tales.

The amount of the wealth of knowledge laid up "in the countless chambers of her brain," and her power of bringing it into use immediately when wanted, excited admiration, as well as wonder. How such extent and variety of knowledge could have been acquired in such an obscure village as Guilford. The attainment of this knowledge,

---

* Among the lay visitors at Nutplains at that period, Fitz Greene Halleck was one who excited much interest. He was a young lad of very modest and pleasing demeanor, and of remarkably precocious talents. His earliest poetical efforts were submitted to the critics at Nutplains and highly commended. Many pieces which he did not consider as possessing sufficient merit to be included among his collected works, were preserved, and some of them published many years afterward. They were more highly estimated by the public than by the author.

however, as far as could be obtained from books, was not so extraordinary as the power she possessed of combining in the various kinds of information acquired from books or conversation, those which belonged together or were sequent, and laying them up so carefully in her memory, that she could find and bring them together when wanted. The "Guilford Library" contained most of the standard histories and other works of the highest class in English literature. She had also the use of a valuable French library belonging to a Mr. Gomarre, who taught her the French language.

He was a venerable and intelligent gentleman, a fugitive from St. Domingo, who saved his library and some other property with his life, at the time of the massacre of the whites, of whom several came to Guilford, and the younger ones married there and became good Yankees.

Her grandfather, also, was in the habit of bringing, twice a year, the amount of his pay as a legislator,* in the newest literature of the time. And it was his custom at Nutplains, from the period of the close of the labors of the day till bedtime, to gather the family at the round table and read aloud, and make suggestive and judicious comments on such literature.

Roxanna Foote was married to the Rev. Lyman Beecher in 1799, and became the mother of eight

---

* The Legislature of Connecticut held two sessions annually previous to the adoption of a State Constitution.

3*

children, viz: Catherine, Edward, Mary, Henry Ward, Harriet, William, George and Charles, most of whom have made their names known in the literary and religious world.

The third sister, Mary, was endowed with fine talents and much personal beauty, but she married at an early age, and sunk under the circumstances which followed and were its consequence. The following lines, addressed to her brother on the commencement of his sea-faring career, are expressive of strong sisterly attachment, strengthened by circumstances that will be referred to hereafter:

TO A BROTHER.

A sister, anxious for thy fate,
With feelings most affectionate,
   Presents her parting prayer;
And—venturing forth life's dangerous road—
Weeping, commends thee to her God,
   And asks his guardian care.

'T is not alone that He would deign
To save thee from long hours of pain,
   And guard thy mortal breath,
When pestilence, in secret, blasts,
Or when around his fatal shafts
   At noonday scatter death.

For fond affection's anxious breast
For ills more fatal is distrest,
   And shrinks with fearful dread,
And fervent prays that grace Divine,
With brightest beams would ever shine
   Around her favorite's head.

She asks that Heaven's almighty Power
Would watch thee in temptation's hour—
    Thy erring heart defend.
And round thy yet unsullied youth,
His broad defence, "The Shield of Truth,"
    In mercy e'er extend.

And now to foreign lands you go,
Unconscious whether weal or woe
    Your future path attend,
Unconscious that you meet not there
A mother's or a sister's care,
    Or even a kindred friend.

When fever in a fervid clime
Rising upon thy youthful prime,
    Pours down his scorching ray;
Who then shall soothe thy aching head,
And, watching round thy painful bed,
    With fond affection stay?

But if thou own'st that "better friend,"
E'en there His comforts shall descend,
    Thy weary soul to rest.
And if perchance 't is His decree,
Thy friends belov'd with sight of thee
    Shall ne'er again be blest;

Yet in thy final dreaded hour,
His mercy of its bitterest power,
    Shall tyrant death disarm;
While in the last extremity,
Thy sure, thy firm support shall be
    His everlasting arm.

An older sister than Mary, Martha, died young.

His youngest sister, Catherine, died also at the age of nineteen. In her improvement he took great interest, making every effort in his power to strengthen her mind and increase her knowledge.

Such efforts for the improvement of a younger sister exert a favorable influence on the mind, as well as the morals, of a young man. He thereby both gives and receives good and useful lessons, and they are such as are most deeply and permanently imprinted on his mind and heart. This effect on the *heart* is generally well understood, but its influence on the intellect is not so much thought of, though it is very powerful, and a more general and just appreciation of it would be useful. A young man whose intellect *only* has been educated, and educated without reference to his heart, however great may be his genius and talents, will always display some obliquities of mind and crochetty characteristics that weaken not only his moral perceptions, but also those which appear to be exclusively mental. Before we send boys to male instructors for the education of their heads, we ought to be sure that their hearts are duly educated, or are in progress of education, under female influence, for, otherwise, their minds lose much of their power, in addition to the loss of strength in their moral character.

His sister Mary, two years older than himself, married, in 1803, John James Hubbard, a merchant of the Island of Jamaica, to which place she accompanied him in the same year.

He (Hubbard) was desirous to engage his brother-in-law in his service, and offered him a situation in his counting-house. His sister, also, was very desirous of his company in the strange land to which she was going. He therefore accompanied her, intending to qualify himself for a mercantile career. He remained there, however, but about a year, and during that period displayed that extraordinary aptitude for the acquisition of knowledge, and that quickness of apprehension which distinguished him throughout life. His knowledge, not only of book-keeping, but of the manner of transacting business generally, together with a hand-writing which was a model of easily legible and elegant penmanship, would have been sufficient recommendations for a good situation in any counting-house.

He returned with his sister, whose health had become so feeble, that her physicians could only prescribe for her a return to her native land, as offering the sole hope for a prolongation of her life. Her mind had first been shocked by the contrast of manners and morals in the Island (a state of society prevailing there of the existence of which she had never conceived the idea) with the rigid and pure style of morals in her native village, which, at that time, was one of the most primitive of the Puritan towns of New England, where a course of life considered harmless and not disreputable in the West Indies, would have been thought one of extreme depravity. Her physical system. also, was shattered from the influence of a West India climate on a New England constitution. And she who had left home a year before in the full bloom of beauty, glowing with health. and full of the hopes, so natural to a young bride, of a life of wedded happiness in the fairy isles. whose delicious fruits and mild. genial climate, made it seem to the youth of the cold north like the enchanted regions of the Arabian tales. returned to linger and die: her hopes changed to bitter disappointment. and her prospects for the future only those of mental and physical suffering sufficient to carry her to an early grave. To a rest there, in the belief that it was the entrance to an existence in a better. brighter world, where hope is not killed by disappointment, but changed to joyous fruition. she looked forward: and, purified by affliction and suffering, she found that haven of rest for the weary and heavy laden, which her Savior had promised to all that should come unto Him. Her sister Roxanna, who had the power of conferring comfort and happiness on all within her influence. beyond that of almost any other human being. aided by her excellent husband. smoothed her path to the grave and cheered her in its progress.

Samuel, on his return from Jamaica, determined to continue his mercantile education, and, at the same time, qualify himself for a navigator, a vocation for which the two passages he had made strengthened the desire and fixed his determination. For this purpose he entered the trading establishment of Andrew Elliott, of Guilford, who occupied the store that had formerly been that of his father, Eli Foote, and whose daughter (then unborn) he married twenty-four years afterward.

For the purpose of obtaining the mathematical knowledge necessary to a navigator, he placed himself under the tuition of a person then residing in Guilford, a surveyor by profession, and Nathan Redfield by name. This was one of those men to whom the mathematical sciences afford all the pleasures of life that they desire to enjoy, and who never are, and never can be, any thing but mathematicians, having no room in heart or mind for any other guest. The following anecdote will illustrate his character.

One morning early, Foote saw him passing along the street, and called to him, saying he wanted assistance for the solution of a problem. This was an attraction which it was impossible for him to resist, and the two immediately began chalking diagrams on the floor until it was nearly covered, when, suddenly, Redfield started up, saying that he could not wait any longer, as he was going for the doctor to come to his wife, who he feared was dying.

The wife died indeed, but the problems survived, and the mathematician was comforted.

Messrs. Samuel and Andrew Elliott were owners of several vessels employed in the West India trade, and as soon as Foote considered himself sufficiently learned in the theory of navigation, he set about qualifying himself in the practical knowledge, by shipping as a foremast hand on board one of their schooners. He made his first voyage in that capacity to the West Indies. On his second voyage in the same vessel, while lying in port, a brig from Philadelphia belonging to her captain, lost its chief mate, and Foote was recommended to fill his place. Although he (Foote) had some doubts as to his qualifications for that office in a square-rigged vessel, as his experience had been only in those of fore-and-aft rig, yet as he had, while a boy, built a ship of about two feet in length, and rigged her complete with every rope, spar and sail, he concluded that he might rely on his knowledge thus gained, and accepted the berth. He went to Philadelphia and returned to the West Indies, where Captain Chase determined to remain until the brig could go to Philadelphia and return, and gave the command of her to Foote, although he was at that time but eighteen years of age. He made a short voyage in her as master, to the West Indies and back to Philadelphia. He then, although Captain Chase desired him to remain in command of the brig, determined to seek further experience in a subordinate situation. The difficulties he experienced in consequence of his extreme youth—among them the apparent incongruity of seeing men of twenty and thirty years experience in navigation placed under the command of a lad of eighteen years* and of very little experience—induced him to make this determination, and he went with Capt. Chase, as chief mate of the ship Cotton-Plant, to Rotterdam.

While in Holland, he made inquiries and observations (according to his custom in relation to whatever belonged to the pursuit in which he was engaged) respecting the progress of improvement in navigation, and the construction of merchant ships, in that country in which commerce, in the style in which it is conducted in modern times, may be said to have commenced earliest and been most successful.

Although at that time Holland could not furnish specimens of fast sailing clipper ships,† her progress in that respect from the time of the "Goede-Vrouw" not by any means resembling Yankee progress—yet the examples furnished by her ships of extraordinary neatness, good and useful arrangement for economy of room, good discipline and regularity, were useful to a young man

---

*While getting his brig into her place in the dock at Philadelphia, he overheard two old East India captains, whose ships were lying near by, discoursing on the subject of "modern degeneracy." In exemplification of its alarming progress, one of them remarked, "Why that boy there is master of that brig!" "Ay, ay," says the other, "they make captains of babies now-o'-days as soon as their clouts are off."

† The French navy—mercantile as well as warlike—at that period furnished the best specimens of fast-sailing vessels, and at the same time the worst examples in discipline and in the neatness, &c., in which the Dutch vessels excelled.

4

seeking information relative to every detail in all the departments of his profession, and he profited thereby. Yankee vessels, at that time, were very apt to be deficient in the above-mentioned particulars, the Yankee characteristic of doing every thing in a hurry causing such matters to be too much neglected.

He then returned to New York, and placed himself under the command of Capt. Chase, one of the best navigators of that port, as mate of the ship Golden Fleece, and made two voyages to England, after which, in compliance with the solicitations of his uncle and brother, (the firm of J. & J. P. Foote), he took command of one of their vessels trading to the West Indies, taking an outward cargo from North Carolina, and bringing the returns to New York.

This trade, however, did not suit his taste, and he continued in it but a short time.

CHAPTER III.

EDUCATION.

" Dull conceited clashes
Confuse their brains in college classes."—BURNS.
" Travel in the younger sort is part of education "—BACON.

THE pursuit of knowledge under whatever circumstances might surround him, was a strongly-marked characteristic of Samuel E. Foote. It was a pursuit begun at the earliest period of life, and continued until he became one of the best educated men of his time.

In attributing to him this endowment, the idea intended to be conveyed by it is not based upon the generally received opinion in relation to the constituents of the best education, but upon the belief that it consists in the acquisition of the greatest amount and variety of the knowledge of such facts in nature, and such truths of science, as may be, and are likely to be, requisite and available for his aid and success in the course of life before him. The course, namely, which circumstances or natural disposition may require him to adopt. It embraces a just appreciation of the results of the experience of others, divesting them of the prejudices under which they are often stated, and combining various statements and opinions in such order that the truth may be drawn from them, whether in accordance with the opinions of their authors or not.

His course in acquiring knowledge was not in conformity with any established system of education, nor in accordance with the prescribed methods of any seminary of learning; neither was it conducted, in its details, upon such a plan as could be generally adopted.

The knowledge which requires for its attainment of such deep and exclusive attention to any one or two departments, as to make it impossible to acquire a competent acquaintance with the various matters requisite to enable a man to make the best use of his faculties and talents for the benefit of the community, and of himself and those dependent on him, is not what ought to stand in the place of a good education. Parrs and Porsons may be reckoned among the "Curiosities of Literature," but they would not be very well qualified for American citizens. It may, perhaps, be well enough to have such "curiosities," but it is not good judgment to place them among the highly educated. On the contrary, *they* are best educated who are best prepared by their education to meet and to control circumstances. They are such as possess so much, and such various kinds of, knowledge, that may be made practically available in the active pursuits of life, as constitute an accomplished man of business. prepared to act promptly in every emergency. Such were the attainments which authorize us to place Samuel E. Foote so high in the ranks of men of education.

It is with mental, as with physical, endowments, in which a man with duly proportioned powers in each of his bodily faculties, is a more perfect man than one with uncommon developments and powers in one or two of them. The well balanced character, however, does not excite extraordinary attention, and yet it is sufficiently rare to be offered to our consideration for an instructive example.

The method of education adopted by Foote at a very early age, was to direct his attention rigidly to the acquisition of the branch of knowledge which was first in importance to him—as instanced, previously, in the case of his mathematical studies—and. having obtained a competent teacher, to devote his time to that subject until he understood it as well as his instructor. Having made one acquisition, and secured it well in his memory, he turned his attention to the next in importance to himself. and followed the same course. By this means his knowledge in each department was more perfect than is generally obtained by young men. especially as, in most cases. they adopt studies prescribed by others rather than those to which their own choice would lead.

3*

Under the tuition of one of the best teachers in New York, he extended his knowledge of the physical sciences, taking the time necessary for his studies whenever he pleased. The science of chemistry was then in its infancy, as compared with its state at the present time. Chilton delivered lectures on this science, which he attended, and studied the works of Black, Chaptal, Priestly, and others, until he understood its principles and its progress up to that period. The knowledge of the scientific principles of mechanics was made of practical utility throughout life.

With the progress of improvement in all the sciences and arts, his knowledge of their principles enabled him to keep pace, and to derive that gratification from that progress which is among the purest enjoyments of life, and which is the paramount advantage of any system of early education.

Political economy he studied rather as a matter of amusement than otherwise. Beginning with Adam Smith in a dry French translation, was a proof that amusement could be derived from a study the least attractive in appearance. He understood his principles thoroughly, and continued through the works of Say, Ricardo, Malthus, Sismondi, and the rest of the writers on that science, down to Raymond, an esteemed cotemporary and friend of his early days.

Geology was not then the science that is now designated by that term. but was chiefly devoted to giving instructions, derived, for the most part, from imagination, on the subject of world-making—in attempts by learned speculators to show how the world had been, or might have been, or ought to have been, made. Hutton and Werner, the champions, one of fire, the other of water, as agents employed in the formation of the world, were the leaders, under whom the savans contended for doctrines which did not tend to increase the utility of the science. La Place had not invented the theory of world-making out of nebulous matter (what kind of matter is that?) and thereby contributed another useless subject of contention to the learned; but there were many " guesses at truth " in relation to the " cosmogony or creation of the world " besides those quoted by the famous Mr. Jenkinson, and they were proclaimed then with as little diffidence and modesty as they are now.*

---

* The science of Geology, into which an economical department has been admitted during the present century, constituting it thereby a new and useful science, has not been delivered from the dreams of the early geologists, nor closed against those of the more modern savans. The cultivators of this science still continue, as Hugh Miller said of Lamarque, to "call their dreams philosophy," and to publish "guesses at truth" for deductions of science, and it is quite edifying to see with what trust and confidence their guesses and dreams are adopted. The Mosaic account of the creation is not considered by modern savans sufficiently philosophical, and the old "fortuitous concourse of atoms" has been replaced by "nebulous matter," for the purpose of lightening the labor of creation. The efforts of modern skeptics in endeavoring to discredit the first chapter of Genesis, are stimulated probably by the idea that, in case of success, they will be relieved from the duties imposed on them in the twentieth chapter of that book. and the fifth chapter of Matthew. The stupidest fables of the East, as well as the equally stupid conjectures of modern skeptics, have been re-

Pseudo-philosophers have always been zealous deifiers of chance, and anxious to justify its ways to men. The author of the "Vestiges of Creation," and Mr. Darwin, have constituted them-

lied on for aid with a coolness that is quite edifying to contemplate. The incalculable millions of years appropriated by them to their different eras of creation, have been adopted by their disciples with the same unhesitating confidence with which school-boys used to receive the accounts of Romulus and Remus, and their nursing mother, the she-wolf.

The belief of the transmutation of vegetables into mineral coal has been received with more unanimity than almost any dogma in science or religion. Having set aside the account which represents the Creator as accomplishing his work by the fiat, "Let there be," &c., modern savans seem to think it necessary to help him work in a different and easier mode in the establishment of the coal measures. This is by the collection of such quantities of vegetables together in a heap, as could not possibly be so collected, then squeezing and melting them into coal, then covering them with a stratum of earth or sandstone, repeating the process at various times, at the same places, which would be quite as difficult as to bring forth light by the fiat, "Let there be light." Why it should be more difficult to create coal than granite, has not been satisfactorily stated.

The old discoveries of Asiatic histories and astronomical calculations, going backwards thousands of years beyond the Mosaic period of creation, the calculations of similar periods of time from beds of lava, and the discovery of human bones in caves, which must, by geological calculations, have belonged to pre-Adamites, have had their day, and new fooleries are constantly succeeding them. It seems to be an inevitable tendency of geological science to generate theories and hypotheses. The impossibility of establishing their correctness, and the detection of the fallacies on which they are based, do not seem to serve as warnings of the necessity of laying a foundation before beginning to erect a superstructure. On the contrary, they seem to imagine they can commence at the top and build downwards, as Gliddon says the Egyptian pyramids were built.

The progress of geological discovery has been very rapid during the present century, but the progress of the application of sound judgment, founded on common sense, has been proportionably tardy. Some geologists, however, use this quality—for instance, Sir Charles Lyell, in England, and Prof. Christy, in America—whereby they discover that there is no necessity for the millions of years assumed as necessary to geological phenomena, and that there is not at present any particular need for making a theory for the purpose of adapting to it old or new facts.

selves high priests of that idol, and seem to be endeavoring to introduce some kind of order into the temple where they worship. Their mysteries, however, when brought to the light that men of science—and not of notions—reflect upon them, make them appear ridiculous, looking like a heavy superstructure built on a foundation of mud, straw, stubble and weeds.

Palæontology had not yet received its name, and when Foote, while engaged in the trade with Mogadore, brought from that port a collection of fossils, no one could name them. He gave them to Dr. Archibald Bruce, the most eminent mineralogist in the United States, who had commenced the publication of a Mineralogical Journal, which was highly commended in Europe, and so totally neglected in America, that not more than one or two numbers were issued.

Dr. Bruce seemed to value these fossils chiefly as specimens of the classical region of Mt. Atlas, from a spur of which—the Iron Mountain—they were taken.

They had been collected by Roentzen, a traveler in the service of the African Association, who had spent most of the year 1809 at Mogodore, qualifying himself to follow the footsteps of Mungo Park in search of the sources and mouth of the Niger. He began by acquiring a knowledge of the Arabic language, gaining information respecting the interior of the country, and making the necessary preparations for his journey generally. Taking with him two guides, he set out to join a caravan for Soudan, but was murdered by his guides soon after leaving Mogodore; the temptation to the commission of this barbarous murder being the covetousness awakened by the property he carried with him, which, although of no very great value to a European, was to them more valuable than the life of an infidel.

Such of his fossils and minerals as he had collected and left behind, were presented to Capt. Foote by the friend in whose care they had been left. The fossils were given, as above mentioned, to Dr. Bruce; the other articles, which consisted chiefly of agates, carnelians, &c., to various friends.

A knowledge of the most useful modern languages was among his early acquisitions. His method with them was to acquire a perfect acquaintance with the grammar of one, and then go to the country where it was spoken, and begin to speak it, undeterred by any awkwardness or blunders into which he might fall, until he could think in the language, and speak it like a native. During a residence at one time in St. Jago de Cuba, he was domesticated in a family, the children of which, he remarked, acquired without any effort three languages which had cost him much study and labor to acquire. The father being a Frenchman, the mother an Italian, and the children Spaniards, the three languages were used so impartially, that the children could not tell which was their native tongue.

While perfecting himself, at previous periods, in the Spanish language at Cadiz, and the French in the West Indies, he remarked, as others have done before and since, that a Frenchman will correct any errors of a learner with a kind politeness, and will understand his meaning, if possible. If he should say, in that language, that he had swallowed his physician, when he intended to say that he had swallowed his medicine, (a mistake that might easily be made by a novice), he would not be ridiculed, but politely corrected. The Spaniards, on the contrary, allow no indulgence to the errors of a foreigner, but require strict correctness of language, and without it will not seem to understand in cases in which a Frenchman would compliment a learner on his progress. They hold their language in so high respect, that they will not, like the English, introduce words or names into it, and allow them to retain their original orthography. Phœbus and Achilles are Febo and Aquiles, when they are admitted into the Spanish language, and all other foreigners are subjected to the same process of qualification for the lofty Castilian speech.

Although Foote spoke and wrote each of these languages with grammatical correctness, and with so little of foreign accent or idiom, that he was frequently taken for a fellow-countryman by natives of each of those countries, he preferred the Spanish for conversation, when he could make a choice. The Italian and Portuguese he was never in the habit of using in conversation, though he relished their literature. Of Latin, as he had no temptation or desire to explore the depths and excel in scholarship, he was content with knowledge enough to understand common quotations.

The library which he carried in his cabin occupied a space so much larger than we were accustomed to see devoted to books in ships' cabins, at that period, as to be the subject of frequent remark, and, among the old sea captains, of suggestions respecting the tendency of modern innovations to corrupt the manners of the rising generation. These were similar to those which attended the various departures from primitive manners and customs in other matters among our forefathers.

Such authors as Hamilton Moore, Bowdich, and other nautical instructors, with, perhaps, Pilgrim's Progress, Robinson Crusoe, and some stray volumes of travels or novels, generally constituted the whole of a shipmaster's library in those early times, which preceded "modern improvements" in ships and in dwellings.

Foote's library comprised the standard histories, scientific works in English and French, with a cyclopædia, and the best English poets, essayists and novelists. Of the latter, Miss Edgeworth was his favorite, and he always considered it one of the misfortunes of his life, that he was prevented from accepting a very polite invitation to pay her a visit when at Dublin, on one of his voyages, where he was somewhat of a lion by reason of his attainments at so early a period of life. aided, perhaps, by a remarkably fine face and person.

A letter to the writer from the captain of a British ship in the trade between London and the West Indies, speaks of Capt. Foote as one who had aided greatly in raising the character of ship-masters in the merchant service, and thereby increasing the respectability of his profession. for which he felt grateful, and desired to express his thankfulness.

The idea of his extraordinary learning entertained by his sailors was such, that if the age of magic had not passed away, he might have been taken by them for a potent enchanter. His rigid discipline on board his ship was submitted to with as implicit obedience as if his commands had been the laws of nature, and his care of his men was proportionate to their trust in him. On an occasion of an attempt, while at sea, by a lieutenant of a British frigate, to impress one of his men, Foote told him that he might capture his ship and send her in for adjudication, but that he should not take one of his men without taking him and his ship also. The lieutenant, finding him so determined in his resistance, allowed his man to remain, and during the whole period in which impressments of seamen from American vessels were such frequent and just subjects of complaint. he never had a man taken from him.

5

If the government of our country had displayed a similar bold and determined resolution not to submit to the overbearing encroachments of unscrupulous belligerents, the war into which we were forced would either have been avoided, or commenced at an earlier period, before unwise statesmen had blunted our energies and crippled our resources.

A well stocked and extensive medicine chest was always one of the indispensable means and appliances of Capt. Foote's ship, and the idea of his universal knowledge, entertained by his men, made them apply to him in cases of sickness with perfect confidence in his power to relieve them. This confidence formed a most important element of success in his medical practice, which was such that it might have been envied by most practitioners, for he never lost a man. His men also felt safe, under his protection and government, from the dangers of the sea, being confident that he could foresee and avoid all the dangers to which they were exposed. Their superstitions, so prevalent from time immemorial, were treated with little respect, and never suffered to interfere with their commander's orders, and they understood that prompt, unhesitating obedience was the course of safety; a truth in relation to the commands given to all men by their Creator, which it would be well for them to consider.

To the increasing vigilance and attention exercised under all circumstances under which any increase of useful knowledge could be obtained, whether from books, observation, and especially conversation, he was indebted for the various and accurate knowledge acquired at an early age, of many subjects that most persons consider as incompatible and impossible to any but a laborious German student. It was not only a mind originally of strong and varied powers that enabled him thus to acquire knowledge, but in addition a body capable of affording those changes from a mental to a bodily labor, by which both body and mind are invigorated and strengthened. Each was rested in its turn by the labor of the other, and the diseases which destroy so many ambitious students are by such a course avoided. Such a sound mind in a sound body is not an endowment of every one desiring to attain excellence, or success in any line of life; but minds of every class may imitate this example. They may not be able, indeed, to follow its details, but to adopt the general principle of dividing the time between labors that keep the body in health, and those that promote the growth of mind, is in the power of all.

A young man, by giving the preference to those studies which are most likely to be called into use by the course of life before him, will acquire that confidence in his own powers which is an important element of success. The self-conceit which is generated in weak minds by superficial acquirements may for a time impose on his associates, but, like alcoholic stimulants, it eventually lessens his powers and his influence. The cultivation of a taste for mathematical investigations, at the commencement of his studies, will benefit him in any course of life. Even in cases in which a taste for pursuits that seem not to require a knowledge of them—the natural sciences for instance—they will be found useful. Their direct utility in the ordinary pursuits of life is not the only advantage they confer, but they are found to be useful in acquiring an accurate knowledge of things which are supposed to be entirely beyond any need of their assistance. Music, for instance, the theory of musical temperament and the mathematical doctrine of the relation of sounds, is among those recondite studies that few ever attempt, and of which few musicians have any comprehension Although Foote had no powers of voice which would enable him to cultivate vocal music, nor did he ever attempt to play on any musical instrument, yet he was a lover of music. and was desirous to understand the recondite principles by which they are regulated; and, on one occasion when he was detained in the West Indies, being compelled to wait there several months for the termination of a business that occupied very little of his time, he became acquainted with a mathematician as devoted to the science as his first instructor. This gentleman, however, was not so exclusive in his devotion, but was accomplished in many other matters. Under his tuition Foote acquired that acquaintance with this department of science, which many would characterise (to him) useless knowledge. If it were really so, it would scarcely derogate from the commendation he deserved, of not wasting any portion of his time for such acquisitions. This knowledge, however, although not precisely utilitarian in the technical sense of the term, cannot with propriety be considered as useless to any young man. Its acquisition may possibly, in some cases, exclude something more practical, but that was not the case in this instance.

Another branch of the fine arts, painting, was one of his enjoyments, though he gave no part of his time to any attempt to practice any department of it, nor suffered it at any time to interfere with his business. On one occasion, he happened to have in company with him at Seville, a man (the carpenter of his ship) who was remarkably uncultivated and uneducated: he had a curiosity to witness the effect which the first sight of some of the finest specimens of high art would produce on such a man. For this purpose he took him into the celebrated Cathedral of that city, and showed him the famous pieces of Murillo, and other great masters, which it contains. After looking at them all with much attention, but without any display of their effect on his feelings, Foote asked him what he thought of them, he said he "didn't know much about such things, but he did not think any of them was as good as a picture he saw once outside of a showman's booth, representing a tiger

5*

with a child in his claws, and the blood trickling
down in a stream as natural as life."

The want of a knowledge of many things peculiarly useful and necessary to an agriculturist,
he considered the prominent defect in New England farmers generally, and one which was worthy
of more attention than has hitherto been given in
the education of young men, and especially so in
a region which is annually sending forth such
numbers to introduce cultivation into new regions.
The deficiency in this respect, among farmers,
was remarked by him at that early period of life
when he was one of them; and he, in all his
wanderings, paid attention to every thing which
would be made to exert a beneficial influence on
the agriculture of his native country. This he
thought susceptible of much improvement, and he
always looked forward to a period when he should
be able himself to exhibit a good practical example.

This is a not uncommon anticipation among
commercial men, but few of them, when they have
the opportunity, display the patience and perseverance which Foote exhibited during the period
of his residence at New Haven.

In a letter from Buenos Ayres, in 1817, he says:
"Tell G. this is one of the finest countries in the
world for a farmer. The land produces 100 and
120 for one, and that with one fifth of the labor
required in Connecticut to obtain 15 or 20. * *
The laziness of this people is almost beyond con-

ception, and I believe a Connecticut farmer does more work than a regiment of them." "It frequently happens that the owner of 1000 oxen and horses. and five times as many sheep, has not a bed in his house. and is too lazy to take the wool from his sheep's back, to spread on the ground beneath him. The skull of an ox serves him for a seat. and the horn for a cup—and this is all his household furniture."

In Peru he was particularly observant of the effects of guano, and thought the importation of it to this country a great desideratum : but did not suppose that such importation would ever be made a source of profit—an opinion which he was glad to see proved erroneous. Most of his observations of the state of agriculture in other nations, furnished him with warnings rather than examples for the benefit of his own country. In the latter part of his life he saw. with much satisfaction. in the establishment of institutions expressly for the education of the agricultural classes, the commencement of a realization of his wishes. "The Farmers' College," near Cincinnati, had not been established when he left this city. It would have gratified his hopes had he lived to see its success. The establishment and the constantly increasing circulation of agricultural periodicals, however, evinced a great improvement on the part of the farmers, not only in knowledge, but in their estimate of the value of the knowledge of the sciences connected with agricultural pursuits.

It was somewhat remarkable that of three accomplishments which he admired exceedingly in others, he never attempted to acquire any practical skill in them himself. He never attempted drawing or painting—except architectural and mechanical designs, and diagrams; nor did he ever attempt to make vocal or instrumental music, and, although a great admirer of graceful movements and bearing, never attempted to dance, and never attended a public ball.

CHAPTER IV.

MOGADORE.

" Many shall run to and fro and knowledge shall be increased."
                                        Daniel xii, 4.
" The race is not to the swift, nor the battle to the strong."

The love of adventure and the desire to see foreign countries where those strange people live, and where those strange sights are to be seen, of which they have heard or read, is a general characteristic of youth, and one which is strongly developed in those of the sea coasts of New England.

Visits to the West Indies are generally the first steps taken for the gratification of this propensity: those in Foote's case stimulated it more strongly, his disposition being one of those which are not discouraged, but invigorated by the necessity of submitting to unaccustomed dangers, privations and labors. After a few voyages to the West India Islands, finding them not sufficiently profitable to repress the desire of more adventurous roving, and of a wider sphere of observation and better fields for increasing his knowledge of the world and its inhabitants, he sought for a traffic better suited to these objects.

A proposition being made to him to conduct a business which gave fairer promise of profit and of the means of extending his knowledge of the world and of commercial operations in different regions, among, to him, a new and strange people, he accepted it. This was the importation of various African products from Mogadore. Goat skins constituted the bulk of these products; they included, also, gums and drugs of various kinds. The merchandise with which they were purchased consisting chiefly of dry goods of thin, light kinds, furnished but a small portion of the outward cargoes. These were made up of articles suited to the markets of Lisbon, Cadiz and Teneriffe, from which ports the run down to Mogadore is easy.

In this trade the parties concerned were, besides Samuel E. Foote, the firm of J. & J. P. Foote, and William Radcliff, a very intelligent, highly educated gentleman, possessed in an eminent degree of those qualities which will generally insure success in any line of life; such as unwearied industry, economy without meanness, unshrinking perseverance, and unquestioned integrity. These qualities of the "strong" did not, however, enable him to win the race or gain the battle. The latter portion of a career marked by these qualities, was so unfortunate that he was willing in his old age to accept of banishment from friends and country for the poor consulship of Lima.

At the period of the renewal and expansion of the foreign commerce of the United States, conse-

quent on the establishment of our national independence, a feeling of freedom from the restraints
of colonial restrictions, was generally experienced
among our merchants. This led to many losses
from the gratification of an instinctive love of
trade, without the knowledge necessary to its
proper management. On the other hand many
adventurers succeeded by the mere aid of fortunate
accidents, and among these were many which occurred in the commercial countries of Europe
through the changes brought about by the French
revolution. This revolution gave success to, and
consequently increased, American enterprize during many years in which our country was little
thought of by the belligerents of Europe.

The attention, however, of these belligerents
was awaked by perceiving that they were not
only engaged in "burning, sinking and destroying" each other, and making themselves poor
thereby, but that they were making another
nation rich. The bone of commerce for which
they were fighting, was picked up by a new people, and when its success became remarkable,
excited a degree of envy and jealousy which annoyed our merchants, and eventually influenced
our government to the adoption of measures
which annoyed them still more.

The hazards attendant on commercial adventures had never seemed to exert much influence
in restraining them. On the contrary they seemed
rather to stimulate than repress, and every por-

tion of the globe was put to the question and made to reveal its capacity for increasing the commerce of the United States.

The continent of Africa furnished very few articles for traffic except human chattels, and our imports from the middle and southern portions of that continent, consisting of beings "found guilty of a skin not coloured like our own," was continued for many years after we had proclaimed to the world our belief in the self-evident proposition, "that all men are born free and equal," and alike entitled to enjoy "life, liberty and the pursuit of happiness."

The inhabitants of the north of Africa were more consistent in their practice of making slaves of the infidels of Europe and America, and giving them the opportunity of saving their souls by becoming "true believers" in Allah and his prophet.

But, with an inconsistency very common in the morality of nations, *we* considered slavery, when *our people* were the subjects, a horrible enormity. and after disgracing our nation for awhile by paying tribute to the African barbarians, to avert it we acquired glory by chastising and compelling them to abandon their practice of enslaving Christians.*

---

* The resolute daring and enterprising courage displayed by the officers and men of our navy in the course of the brief war with Algiers, gave the Americans a fame—a prestige—along the whole coast of Barbary, as well on the Atlantic as the Mediterranean, which no nation had ever acquired.

The powerful armaments of Christian nations had failed—that of Charles V most signally as it was the greatest—in their efforts to repress the piracies

The inconsistency of our professed belief on the subject of slavery, with our practice, was not quite so outrageous after the law prohibiting the slave trade was passed, but we have never been able to exhibit real consistency on this subject.

After men and women had ceased to be articles of traffic with Africa, other articles were sought for, and palm-oil, ivory, goat skins, gums, drugs, and a few other articles supplied a small amount of commerce, but it was very small in proportion to the very extensive regions embraced in that continent. The strong desire to discover the course and mouth of the Niger, which has cost the life not only of Mungo Park, but of many other valuable men, was due as much to the desire of increasing a trade with Africa, as for discovering its geographical features. In that with Mogadore, the above named parties had at that time no American competitors, nor has it ever been very attractive to our merchants. The foreign commerce of that port was transacted chiefly by

of the Mediterranean Barbary States. The small naval force of the United States, a young and weak nation, achieved a success where old and powerful ones had failed. The cause is seen in the different character of the men employed. Every American engaged in that war seemed ready to perform any act of heroism required of him, totally regardless of any danger by which it might be attended.

Capt. Foote became acquainted with the commander of one of the Algerine vessels, who spoke of Decatur and his associates with that respect and reverence which undaunted courage inspires—when successful. He verified many of the statements published at the time, and gave others which we regret to have forgotten.

William Willshire, the British Consul, and Wm Court & Co., an English house of extensive commercial talents and experience.

It was necessary that every vessel going there for a cargo should carry some merchandise: for the Emperor, on one of his visits to Mogadore, seeing a foreign ship lying there, inquired what cargo she had brought, and being informed that she brought nothing but money to purchase goat skins, made a decree that no vessel should be allowed to take away the products of his Empire without bringing some of the products of foreign countries to exchange for them. This trait of paternal solicitude for the welfare of his subjects, resembles those of despotic rulers generally, who are very apt to consider themselves the best judges of what will conduce to the welfare of their subjects, with a special regard to their commercial operations. This, however, is not an exclusive characteristic of despots, as we shall find in the case of Jefferson and the American embargo.

The decree of the Emperor of Morocco was rigidly enforced, as he was in the habit of cutting off the hands of some of his subjects, and the heads of others, if his decrees were neglected or evaded; and if he could not discover the guilty, he substituted for them vicarious subjects: upon the same principle that dictated the laws of ancient Rome, by which all the slaves belonging to a master were, in case of his murder, put to death without any reference to their guilt or innocence.

The surgical practice of cutting off hands was very simple, being that of merely severing them from the wrist by the blow of a cleaver, and dipping the stump in boiling pitch as a substitute for tying the arteries. The excision of heads was a still more simple operation, requiring no care of the arteries. Both of these operations were so frequent as to cause no great excitement.

An illustration of our second motto was exhibited in some incidents connected with the Mogadore trade. Among the imports from that port, was included a variety of gums and drugs, and these included at one time, a quantity of *semen santonicum* (worm seed) so large that it completely glutted the market. The manufacture of worm seed oil had been commenced, and it was supposed would require a large supply of the raw material. This expectation was not fulfilled, and the article remained on hand longer than the patience of the owners could be kept under due restraint. They therefore resolved to make experiments with it in foreign markets, which they did with very discouraging results, except in one instance. At Havana the bales were thrown overboard, that being the easiest way of paying the custom house duties; in one or two other ports the market was little better, but at St. Petersburg the profits were enormous, and the proceeds being invested in Russia linens, arrived at New York at a period when the market was very bare of those articles, and gave another

handsome profit. This extraordinary success encouraged the shippers to hope that the Russian
market would be a very important one for increasing the profits of their Mogadore trade, and
they were thereby induced to make a much larger
shipment to that market, including other articles
of African produce. which were lying heavy on
their hands in New York. This adventure was
peculiarly unfortunate. It went to so bad a
market at St. Petersburg, that the consignees in
the hope of being enabled to give a better account
of it than their market would afford, determined
to try that of Moscow, hoping to be able not only
to give a good account of this adventure, but to
open a new market for African products, by which
the profits of the Mogadore trade might be increased. The account of sales, however, was
superseded by the account of the burning of
Moscow, after its capture by the "grande armee
of Napoleon le grand," the adventure being among
the merchandise destroyed.

The return of this army after the conflagation
was an exemplification of our second motto on a
large scale; the snow and ice of Russia being more
powerful adversaries than man. Like gentle.
quiet female influences, stronger than masculine
powers, the soft gentle snow and quiet ice of
Russia performed greater feats of conquest than
the greatest and best army, led by the most skillful and experienced generals of modern times,
could accomplish. although fresh from the work

of desolation which they had spread over the fairest countries of Europe. "Havoc, spoil and ruin are my gain," seemed to be the appropriate motto for the advancing armies, and "the spoiler spoiled" for the same armies on their retreat. No event of history "points a moral" more emphatically than this retreat from Moscow. It includes, also, many scenes and events, not only among the rich and powerful, but among those in the humbler walks of life, that would exhibit more intelligibly to common minds, the keenness of the point and the applicability of the moral, if they could be displayed.

At the period of one of Foote's voyages to Mogadore, the merino mania was prevailing in the United States, as extensively as the "hen fever," and the morus multicaulis excitement, have prevailed at subsequent periods. Search was made, at that time, in all parts of the world, for wool-bearing animals that would furnish the fine kinds of wool neccessary for the manufacture of the finest fabrics. He was at that time informed, that in the province of Tedlah, there was a breed of sheep with fine silky fleeces, superior to those of the merinos. Of course he could not fail to be anxious to obtain so valuable an addition to our American flocks. Although the exportation of animals, of every kind, was strictly prohibited in Morocco, yet permission might be obtained to take a certain number of sheep for ships' stores, provided they were males, no females of any kind being allowed to be exported on any consideration. Of this he intended to take advantage by sending an agent to procure some specimens of these sheep. As all commercial operations with the interior are, in that country, transacted by the Jews, he employed one of them to go to Tedlah. and procure for him some of these valuable animals. He went there and purchased the number wanted; and the only mode of transportation of merchandise, in that country, being on the backs of camels, he had boxes made of the proper dimensions and form, for containing his live merchandise, and swung them. as John Gilpin did his bottles, a box "on each side to make the balance true." But the result was far from any resemblance to John's comic adventure. In his journey towards Mogadore, his course was through an intermediate province. the governor of which chanced to notice his novel method of transporting animals. and being. like all barbarians, a strict conservative, was, of course. strongly opposed to any innovation in the habits and practices of true believers. especially if made by a Jew, at the instigation of an infidel. His principles of jurisprudence were so simple, that Jeremy Bentham could not easily have suggested any mode of simplifying them. though he might have found "fallacies." as striking as in more complex systems. The mode of proceeding in this case was, to administer the bastinado to the Jew, confiscate his cargo, and put him in prison. until the Emperor's pleasure in the matter could be made known. This, which always partakes of the simplicity of the criminal jurisprudence of that region, was expected to be shown in an order to cut off the Jew's head, or dismiss him with the loss of his cargo, and the lesson of instruction given by the bastinado he had received, warning him against the introduction of any novelty in the mode of conveying animals in Morocco. The life of a Jew was of so little consequence in that country, that Capt. Foote could not learn his fate.

The loss of the money, entrusted to his agent, was not of sufficient importance to discourage further attempts to obtain some of these valuable animals, but the risk of life, or even of bastinado and imprisonment, was too great a price to pay, even for finer wooled sheep than merinos.

These animals were afterwards supposed to be Angora, or Cashmere goats, some of which were, at a subsequent period, imported from Asia, and are now propagated in Alabama and Georgia. They probably do not furnish so profitable an article of cultivation as cotton, and as "Cotton is King," in those regions, it, like other kings, tolerates no other rival near the throne. It is probable, however, that at no very distant day, Cashmere goat's wool, will be included among the valuable products of our Southern States, and perhaps may, when the efforts to give success to the cultivation of cotton in Asia and Africa, take from

the United States their monopoly of that cultivation, give us a new staple, equally valuable.

Capt. Riley was heard of as a prisoner and
slave, among the Arabs of the desert, at the time
of one of Capt. Foote's visits to Mogadore, and
much interest in his fate was excited among the
few Christian inhabitants of that place. Efforts
for the rescue of him and his companions were
planned, but the British Consul, William Willshire, had the happiness of being the agent of
their redemption, and giving them, with the most
kind and friendly liberality, the aid and comfort
they needed. The town of Willshire, in Ohio, is
named in honor of him, and if all honors bestowed
on cotemporaries, were as worthily bestowed, it
would be better for mankind.

The United States, at that time, had no Consul
at Mogadore, but Mr. O'Sullivan was soon after
appointed to that office, and held it many years,
with credit and with abilities worthy of a better
station.

The Moors of that part of Barbary take but
little interest in commercial affairs, which, in the
seaports, are in the hands of foreigners, and in
those of the Jews in the interior. The native
Moors are as averse to degrading themselves by
productive labor as our southern planters, or the
aborigines of our country. The Jews are there
an oppressed and despised race, treated with obloquy and contempt, by a people that, like themselves, has sunk from a higher to a lower state of

civilization and refinement, in which state men lose their best and retain their worst qualities. They are superior in character to their superiors in station and national standing; for they possess some degree of commercial enterprise, a quality which will always elevate any people when the government does not restrain and limit it, as in China, and other semi-civilized nations; but on the contrary, encourages it, as the British government has done, since the commencement of the career of that nation, in civilization and social improvement. Having neither the stimulant of commerce, nor of the necessity of contending against a wintry climate, for the means of subsistence, they are in a state of society, in which their good qualities being such as are generated by indolence, and their evil ones not untimely developed, or intensified by alcoholic drinks, they vegetate rather than live. For they have no amusements in which females can share, and are therefore condemned to live, "in dull repose."

"No joy that sparkles and no tear that flows."

This state of society was so intolerable to Capt. Foote, that he purchased an "Arab Steed," on whose back he could race at full speed over the sands, and thereby soothe his impatience, his horse seeming more intelligent and capable of understanding the feelings of his master better, than the lazy Moors, who lived without excitement, and could not comprehend how anything but fighting could rouse or need that quality.

The measures of our government put an end to this and all other foreign commerce, in the year 1807, and it was never renewed.

CHAPTER V.

THE EMBARGO.

"It cannot be but a matter of doubtful consequence, if States be managed by empiric Statesmen, not well mingled with men, well grounded in learning."—BACON.

In the year 1807, an embargo was laid on all the shipping in the ports and harbors of the United States. This measure was not in accordance with the generally received meaning of the term. a mere prohibition of the sailing of our ships for foreign ports, during a limited and specified period of time, but an entirely novel experiment in national policy. It was proclaimed to be intended as a measure. both of offense and defense, in relation to the European belligerents. by cutting off all commerce. not only with them, but with the whole world. Their insults. piracies and robberies of neutrals on the high seas. and in their own ports. had been so flagrant and outrageous. that our country had become despised and disgraced by submitting to them. after an armed resistence to those of France.

The party in our country which assumed the name and style of Republican, in lieu of that of anti-federal, consisting of the anti-commercial slave-owners of the south, and the discontented, restless and ambitious politicians of the North, had succeeded in obtaining the control of the government. The measures adopted under the administration of Washington and his successor, John Adams, for obtaining redress for past wrongs, and security for the future, had furnished a theme for clamor against their policy, under the pretense that it was ruining the nation by extravagance, in building ships of war, and fortifying our harbors. The ill-advised measure of Adams, in raising a land-army, had intensified this idea and carried its ramifications deep into the feelings of all classes, who were, some of them, ashamed, and others maddened, by a sight of the parades of soldiers in their towns and villages, without any apparent object or necessity. The "alien and sedition laws," also, were so wrested, by party zealots, from their true intent, as to give great force to the denunciations of the Federal party, by demagogues.

The Anti-Federalist party adopted Jefferson as their leader, and succeeded in wresting the reins of government from the hands of those who had been the most active and efficient agents in achieving our independence and establishing our system of government. In order to justify the change of men, it was necessary to adopt a change of measures, and under new auspices, to preserve the nation from retrograding towards those of the old monarchies of Europe. Jefferson, being considered by his supporters and himself, a philosopher,

he thought it proper, in this new country, which
had established an entirely new system of government, to introduce a novel and philosophical system of statesmanship. This he commenced by
removing from office such of the wise and experienced officers in the civil department as he supposed might embarrass his system of reform, by
their common sense view of measures, and then
inaugurating his foreign policy by prohibiting
foreign commerce. The course pursued thence-
forward, until the country could endure it no
longer—it being a course of embargo, gun boats,
dry docks, and French philosophy generally—was
an exemplification of the dangers—referred to in
our first chapter—to our country and to freedom
generally, which arise from giving empirical, incapable statesmen, the control of national affairs,
and investing them with the power of controlling
the political progress of their country.

These measures were not merely ridiculous,
but—the embargo specially—more unjust and unequally oppressive than could have been forseen
or feared by any of the founders or advocates of
our system of government. It, (the embargo,)
was a measure which might have been considered
as perfectly in character, if adopted by such statesmen as those of China, Morocco, Japan, and other
nations of similar repute and standing in relation
to the knowledge and practice of political science.
It was. if characterized by its influence and causes, a declaration of war against our own commerce,

in retaliation for the insults and injuries inflicted upon it by the European belligerents. Comparing great things with small, it was like the conduct of an individual beating and abusing his wife and children at home, to gratify his resentment for insults received abroad. Its disastrous influence on the prosperity of our country can scarcely be realized, at the present time. Even the subsequent declaration of war against Great Britain—after a course of measures, of which the tendency was to deprive us of the power of making offensive war—although equally impolitic, was not quite so silly a measure. It was not so disastrous in its effects on our country's prosperity, and it gave us an opportunity of retrieving the reputation we had lost, among other nations, by the inappropriate measures of weak, conceited statesmen.

There was this difference in the inception of the measures, and they exhibit the empiric, and the experienced and sagacious, but weak statesman. Jefferson forced the embargo upon his party, Madison's party forced the war upon him, for it was a measure he dreaded, because he possessed sufficient political sagacity to understand the danger of making war without being prepared, or counting the cost. For he had belonged to that band of profound, wise and experienced statesmen, who conducted the affairs of our revolution, established the constitution of our country, and organized, under it, the system of conducting the various departments of government. Washington, as a leader, had associated with him such patriots as Hamilton, Jay, Rufus King, the Morrises, Pickering, the Adamses, and other heroes and sages of the revolution, possessing talents to plan and carry into effect a republican system of government, upon a federal basis. These men laid the foundations of our government so deep and strong, that although many checks and obstacles have been placed in the way of its progress, they have not been able to arrest its course of prosperity. No other attempt to establish a federal republican system of government has succeeded, because no other nation was founded by men, who made the establishment of the Christian religion in its purity—according to their belief—an object paramount to the acquisition of wealth.*

Madison's defect was a weakness of will, which caused him to submit to the dictates of party leaders, inferior to himself in talents and experience.

Jefferson's defect was that of supposing himself qualified to become a statesman, for which he was specially *disqualified.*

A permanent embargo as a measure of retaliation for national injuries and insults, was an original idea with him, of which no one has ever disputed the merit of the invention, unless, indeed, it may have been borrowed from the course of policy

---

* The Huguenots, at the South, and the Puritans, were alike governed by this principle.

adopted by Japan, some centuries ago. He was a man of amiable manners, and possessed an extensive superficial knowledge of the literature and science of the day. He was qualified to be a philosopher as philosophers went at that period, and it was particularly unfortunate for the country that he did not possess a juster appreciation of his own qualifications, as well as the duties of a chief magistrate.

Short as has been the period of our history, it furnishes useful lessons in that philosophy which teaches by example, and gives warnings which are seen, acknowledged, and—neglected.

Politicians who experience a call to assume the duties and functions of demagogues, are as averse to useful lessons as truant school boys, and as heedless of warnings as railroad officials. Thus instructions and warnings are wasted, and the community pays the price of its neglect of the earliest duty of a people under a free government, that, namely, of a rigid investigation of, not merely the reputation, but the characters of those to whom the management of their national affairs is committed, and a judicious selection of agents, best qualified to conduct them; for reputations often are made or destroyed by interested political partizans.

When the embargo was laid and proclaimed to be intended as a permanent institution—permanent at least, until it should bring the European belligerents to our feet, humbly to beg for supplies of cotton and flour—the commercial cities and states submitted to it for awhile, in moody quiet and silence, apparently stunned by such an unexpected and sudden destruction of the means of subsistence to thousands of the poorer classes, and of a sudden paralysis of the efforts of the enterprising and industrious. The impolicy of totally destroying our commerce ourselves, because foreign nations were trying to destroy certain portions of it, was very manifest to the immediate sufferers; but those whose experience of its effects was more remote, had not that realizing sense of its tendency, not merely to impoverish. but to demoralize the citizens, which was requisite to unite them in adopting the means of obtaining relief by transferring the government to wiser men.

There was, however, among them, so large a portion of believers in the doctrines of freedom, which, since the establishment of our independence, had been constant themes of writers and orators, that freedom of speech, in relation to a measure so oppressive. was freely indulged, and freedom of action was so ardently desired as to excite the proverbial inventive faculty of the universal Yankee nation. The law establishing the embargo was considered impolitic, unequally oppressive. and its character as a permanent institution unconstitutional. Submission to an oppressive act of tyranny, adopted for the purpose of enabling a weak minded ruler to make a foolish experiment, was not considered a patriotic duty. A belief in

7*

the maxim, that "the king can do no wrong,"
even when the king is a party leader, with the
title of President, was not so general as in the
contrary maxim, that "resistance to tyrants is
obedience to God." The contest between the two
parties which resulted in the election of Jefferson
to the presidency, was so severe and bitter, that
the victors bestowed—as usual in such cases—unlimited power on their leader, and received his
commands with unhesitating obedience, and thus
he was enabled to make those experiments which
demonstrated his want of the qualifications of a
statesman.

Resistance, by force, to an oppressive party measure, however, was not, although advocated by many
of the discontented, seriously thought of, since a
civil war, whatever the result, would be the greatest
of all evils, however justifiable it might be considered under intolerable oppressions. The system
of misrule, through party tyranny, under which
they were suffering, arose, in part, as was supposed, from the jealousy of the southern nabobs—
the negro-slave aristocracy—of what they styled,
"the cod-fish aristocracy." It was excited by
seeing that prosperous commerce would enable
some northern merchants to dash as extravagantly,
and spend money as foolishly, as those planters
who could exercise lordship over gangs of negro
slaves, and who exhibited their love of liberty by
taking it from as many of the African race as
they could get in their power. The idea of the

savages, that they could inherit all the desirable qualities of every enemy they killed, appeared to be modified by them into a belief that their own freedom was increased by taking it from others.

The southern aristocracy who then, as now, constituted the leaders of the Democratic party, understood the character of negro slaves better than that of Yankee freemen—the former having necessarily claimed much of their attention. while the latter were considered unworthy of it, because obliged to labor for themselves.

Yankee contrivances have long been proverbial; their situation from the time of the first settlement of their country having required a frequent exercise of the talent of invention, to supply wants originating in an old and highly civilized country, which, in a new and savage region, could not easily be gratified. Under the pressure of the embargo. regarding it as they did in the light of a tyrannical and ruinous measure, they exercised their inventive faculties in contriving methods of evasion. The transfer of cotton across the southern frontier, to Amelia Island, and shipping it in British vessels, and of various articles from Passamaquoddy, and across the lake, were among the earliest operations for nullifying the embargo law; subsequently it was found practicable to obtain the connivance of government officers for open violations of it.

Soon after its effects began to be felt, Foote had been commissioned by two merchants in New

York, to conduct some mercantile operations abroad, and sailed in the Echo, Capt. Bates, for Europe. His business was commenced at Liverpool, and gave promise of prosperous results. But the arrival there of the ships, which, through the connivance of custom house officers, had evaded the embargo, reduced the profits ot his speculations to a moderate percentage, after having given promise of a very great profit. These ships, fitted out by G. M. Woolsey, and other New York merchants, produced effects beyond the calculations or intentions of the owners, on the permanence of the embargo, as well as of the price of cotton. In England it gave new proof of the weakness of the government of the United States, and caused their new invented plan of making war to be regarded as a burlesque. And it was the more disgraceful from complicity of government officers, some of whom were changed in consequence, and were succeeded by others still more corrupt. It was treated with ridicule in the British parliament, when it was proposed to abandon it, upon condition of the abandonment of some of their high-handed, arbitrary proceedings on the high seas, such as impressment of seamen, paper blockades, etc., authorizing acts of piracy, and subjecting neutrals to intolerable insults. By our own government it was felt that the embargo war was undergoing a disgraceful defeat, and that some new course must be adopted. Non-intercourse and non-importation substitutes were tried, and failed signally and disgracefully.

After the termination of Foote's commercial operations at Liverpool, he went to the West Indies for the purpose of transacting some business there, which yielded some small profits, and gave him an opportunity of visiting nearly all the islands, and acquiring much knowledge, which was afterwards of practical usefulness.

Upon the repeal of the embargo law, he returned to New York and resumed his business there.

Appendix No. 2.

CHAPTER VI.

THE WAR.

"So war untired, his crimson pinions spread."—HEBER.
"Whence come wars and fightings?"

The Jeffersonian experiment of making war upon the commerce of our own country, as a substitute for the old fashioned modes of attacking its enemies, having been fully tested and found wanting, some new experiment in statesmanship was thought necessary. The first trial was made by the non-intercourse and non-importation law, prohibiting the introduction of British goods into the United States, substituting thereby as enemies, the English manufacturers for the American merchants. This was a mark of improvement in knowledge acquired by our statesmen, who had begun to discover what would have been the result of the embargo experiment, if it could have been carried into effect in conformity with its intent and meaning. It might, in such case, have rendered us as independent of foreign powers as was a governor of Mogadore, who, when a British admiral threatened to batter down his town, if a certain demand on him was not complied

with, returned for answer, that if the admiral
would pay him half the amount of the cost of bat-
tering down the town, he would order it pulled
down himself.

Mr. Jefferson, the inventor of cheap substitutes,
had retired to private life, and those upon whom he
left his mantle, had begun to feel restive from observing that his measures rendered us ridiculous
and contemptible. The non-intercourse law, if it
had been tried before the embargo, might have
produced some effect, but all the measures of the
Jeffersonian democratic party had been so much
more calculated to sink, than to raise, the reputation of our country, that they began to feel that
the old-fashioned method of settling disputes between nations, "by trying which could do the
other the most harm," could not be made effective
by embargoes, non-intercourse, and gun-boats, but
required a return to the old fashioned system of
opposing our enemies with force and arms, on a national scale. After long and wearisome debates it
was finally determined that nothing remained but
to rush headlong into a war, for which, instead of
making due preparations, the Jeffersonian party,
from the time they got into power, had been engaged in destroying the preparations made by
their predecessors.

This return to first principles, in national affairs,
included the laying of a temporary embargo, in
order to allow vessels abroad to return, and escape capture before the war, and thereby save

them from being exposed to the hazards of war, without being aware of them. When war should be proclaimed, every one would be, in such a case, at liberty to judge for himself of the risk he might encounter, and be governed thereby, according to his own discretion.

The intention of the dominant party to lay an embargo, was communicated to J. P. Foote, by a friend of his in that party, but it was not stated that it was to be a preparation for war measures. The idea, that our government would declare war against Great Britain, after so long a period in which its policy had been chiefly directed to destroying the means of carrying on a war, was too monstrous an absurdity to be considered a supposable case. For besides the reduction of our navy, the means of procuring "the sinews of war," had been among the destructive operations of the party in power. They had destroyed the Bank of the United States, which, as a financial agent, was absolutely necessary, as the war of the Revolution had taught them, and they had insulted, and abused, and alienated most of that class of men from whom they could expect to obtain loans on the most favorable terms, so that they were obliged to submit to new humiliations in their efforts to procure pecuniary aid.

The brothers, on receiving information of the intended embargo, were fitting out the ship Passenger, which they had purchased for the Cadiz and Mogadore trade, and supposing that our government was returning—like the sow to her wallowing in the mire—to the Jeffersonian system of making war, not on our enemies but on our commerce, labored night and day for several days and nights, abandoning the Mogadore department of the adventure, to get her safely beyond the reach of custom-house officers and revenue cutters, in which they—unfortunately, as the event proved—succeeded.

The Berlin and Milan decrees of Buonaparte, which denationalized and rendered liable to capture and condemnation, any American vessels which should be found on the high seas, going to or from any British port, and the British "Orders in Council," prohibiting all trade by neutrals with France or her dependencies, professedly in retaliation for these decrees; the impressment of our seamen and the capture of the Chesapeake, furnished sufficient ground for a war with Great Britain. By these outrages both nations were disgraced: the one by the piratical insults which they inflicted, the other by their tardy, weak and inefficient measures adopted to check and obtain redress for them. The measures inaugurated by the Democratic party had proved so inefficient, and displayed such a deficiency of talents and of knowledge of their duties, in our statesmen, that the reputation of our country sunk so low in the estimation of the European belligerents, that they did not seem to think it necessary to keep up the ordinary appearances of respect for us, or for the laws of nations.

How much they were mistaken, in supposing that the character of the American rulers was that of the American people, they had opportunities of discovering thereafter. Thus far all their insults and indignities had been met by no other measures, on our part, but such as weakened ourselves and rendered us less capable of retaliation or resistance by force. It was, therefore, a very natural supposition, that the party in power had adopted the policy of submission to insults from stronger powers, and consoled themselves by heaping insults on those over whom they had obtained the victory; on those, namely, who had achieved our independence, including Washington and all his officers, with two or three exceptions.

Governed by such suppositions, the owners of the Passenger dispatched her for Cadiz, with a a view of keeping her in the Mediteranean and North of Europe trade, as long as the measures of our government should deprive our ships of the power of leaving our own harbors. She was insured to Cadiz, from whence intelligence was to be sent in relation to her future course, and new insurance was to be effected in conformity therewith.

The Passenger arrived at Cadiz during the siege of that city, by the French troops, under Marshal Victor. The greatest part of the Peninsula had been subdued, and the patriot Junto, with all the government officers of their party, had taken refuge in the only city that was able to withstand the power of the French armies. In a letter from Capt. Foote, announcing his arrival, he says, "The French are in possession of the opposite side of the bay, and are constantly throwing bombs and shells into the town, which, passing over our own heads, have a very fine effect, particularly in the night, when the arch of fire which they form appears to great advantage. The batteries on shore, and the bomb ships generally, answer shot for shot. We do not, however, apprehend any danger to the shipping; nor, indeed, does the town receive much damage, as only about five shots out of a hundred take effect, and as long as the Spaniards are assisted in defending the place by the British, there is no fear of the French being able to get possession of it." Great distress and misery was suffered in the city, during the siege, increased by the numerous fugitives from the places which were exposed to the cruelties of the French soldiery. These were so great, that they would justify the supposition, put by Dr. Franklin in the mouth of an inhabitant of another planet, that this earth was inhabited, not by men, but devils. But the distress which these fugitives were obliged to suffer, in their state of destitution, at Cadiz, were not so much dreaded as the atrocities committed by the French armies. These cruelties resembled those inflicted more than two centuries previously on the wretched inhabitants of Flanders, by the Duke of Alva, and the other commanders of the Spanish armies, sent out by the bloody tyrant, Philip II, to bring heretics to acknowledge a belief in the Christian doctrines of love, forgiveness and universal charity, as taught by the doctors of the holy inquisition. The accounts of the cruelties which Capt· Foote heard at this time, he considered as much exaggerated, not thinking it possible that such outrages could be committed in the nineteenth century by the inhabitants of any civilized nation; but their truth was confirmed to him several years afterwards, by some French officers, who gave details of deeds which they saw, and in which they participated, that, like the crimes charged by Burke on Warren Hastings, might have been characterized as "cruelties unheard of, nad crimes without a name."

The state of affairs at Cadiz checked all commercial operations, and intelligence of the repeal of the British "Orders in Council" having been received, while the Passenger was in that port, it was judged best to change her destination, and return with her to New York. The expectation that an adjustment of all matters in controversy between the two nations, would follow this repeal, gave reason to expect a renewal of American commerce, to an extent that would give our merchant ships better business there than they could find elsewhere. The measure of repeal was undoubtedly intended to be introductory to the termination of the commercial hostilities between England and the United States, but it was too late.

The change of destination of the ship being determined, Capt. Foote wrote to his brother, giving the necessary advice for effecting insurance: the letters however were never received, the vessel by which they were sent having probably been captured.

The Passenger sailed from Cadiz, and had a favorable time until near the banks of Newfoundland, when she met with the British frigate Belvidere, commanded by Capt. Byron, whom Capt. Foote had met with on a former voyage, and who sent for him to come on board the frigate, and invited him to dine—treating him with marked politeness and hospitality. The invitation was accepted, and they passed some time at table very pleasantly, with good wine, agreeable chit-chat, and all the "delicacies of the season" that could be obtained at sea.

When it was time to break up the party, Capt. Foote being about to return to his ship, expressed his gratification at the repeal of the " Orders in Council," adding that all matters in dispute between the two countries would doubtless now be settled, and friendly feelings restored. "Why, yes," said Capt. Byron, "your country has taken measures to settle them all by a declaration of war." Then calling to a subordinate officer, he said, " Go and set fire to that ship." This order

8*

seemed so little like the restoration of friendly feelings, that Foote was astounded and looked in Byron's face with a doubtful feeling, hoping that it might be a joke, or some unintelligible mystification; but being assured that it was serious earnest, he begged permission to go on board his ship, and bring off his baggage, which request was very politely granted. On going aboard, he found his cabin looking, as he said, as if a carpenter's gang had been at work cutting up the lockers, and tearing the wood-work apart to search for hidden treasures, some of which they had found, and dollars were rolling about the cabin floor. He was able, by the aid of the officer who attended him, to save about two hundred of them, which Capt. Byron allowed him to keep, and which served to pay his expenses, and make some necessary provisions for his men, while a prisoner at Halifax, a station which he soon after occupied.

After the sailors had cut as many trousers patterns out of the sails as they wanted, and taken whatever else was portable and desirable, they set fire to the ship, and as it was a calm day, she drifted towards the frigate, threatening her with a fate like her own. This, however, there was men enough on board the frigate to prevent. Foote stood on the deck, feeling a grim satisfaction in the danger as it increased, thinking that he would be willing to risk his life in his boat, for the gratification of seeing his wrongs avenged. by a ten-fold retaliation.

This, however, was but a transient, involuntary feeling, for he knew that Capt. Byron's instructions were to burn, sink, and destroy enemies ships when he did not send them into port for condemnation, and that he was willing to show any kindness consistent with such duties. Foote always bore testimony to the polite and gentlemanly demeanor of the English naval officers, in their intercourse with him, with the exception of the captain of the La Hogue, who supposed him to be a Spaniard, and treated him with the haughty disdain which the British were too apt to bestow on their Peninsular allies, and which disgusted the Spanish people so deeply that they seemed to be considered by them as enemies rather than allies.

Of Commodore Hardy, who commanded the squadron on the American Station, Capt. Foote, as well as every other prisoner under his control, spoke most favorably. His kindness and forbearance towards all his American prisoners, was so universal, that he became quite popular with his enemies as well as his friends.

Of the British colonists, with whom he was compelled to associate, he did not speak, by any means, as favorably, for they annoyed him excessively, by their braggadocio insolence, and when, after his return to New York, he heard of the capture of the Guerriere by Capt Hull, in the Constitution, he said that he would have been willing to have remained a prisoner, in Halifax, six months longer, for the gratification of seeing how

the news would be received by some of his acquaintances there, who had annoyed him by their
boasts of the invincible prowess of the British
navy, and wishing that one of their sloops of war
could have an opportunity of displaying it by being matched with an American frigate. The captain of the Guerriere had, a short time previous to
her capture, endorsed on the register of a small
vessel which he allowed to go into port, a chal-
lenge to any one of the "*largest* American frigates,"
to meet him on the ocean. This register was presented to Capt. Hull, (it was shown to Capt. Foote,)
and is probably still preserved, being in the possession of the late Rev. Dr. Jarvis, his brother-in-law.

After a due course of imprisonment, Foote was
exchanged, and returned to New York, where his
brother had several vessels laid up, but not in
quite so hopeless and discouraging a condition as
during the embargo, the enmity of Great Britain,
not being as heavy an evil as that of our own government towards our commerce. The brothers
determined not to lie idle during the war, but to
risk further loss instead; for the decay, cost of
ship keeping, wharfage, etc., would be as ruinous
as capture. They, therefore, loaded one of the
vessels, of which Capt. Foote took the command,
and by avoiding the usual routes, which his accurate knowledge enabled him to do, arrived safely
at St. Jago de Cuba, where his cargo was sold, the
proceeds invested in sugar and coffee, and shipped
on board a Spanish vessel, in which he returned

to New York. He loaded the same vessel and returned to St. Jago, from whence she was dispatched, with another cargo, but was never heard of afterwards. Foote remained at St. Jago, in order to transact the business of several vessels, consigned to him there. Of two fast sailing vessels sent to him by his brother, for their joint account, one went and returned safe, the other was captured. He was making arrangements with some Spanish merchants for extensive commercial operations, when the news was received by them that the British Government had declared the whole coast of the United States, from Passamaquoddy to New Orleans, in a state of blockade. This was, manifestly, only a paper blockade, as it was impossible to make it a real one, with all the British naval force that could be sent to the American coast; and if there had been any court in existence competent to enforce the Laws of Nations, captures of neutrals, under such a decree, would have been declared piracy; but the laws of nations, like those of the Christian religion, have only served, in most cases, but as maxims, convenient to be quoted, when they assist one party to oppose the proceedings of the other.

This blockade, however, such as it was, defeated Foote's plans, as the Spanish merchants would not risk their property under such hazards as it caused. He, therefore, determined to return to New York, and took passage in an apparently Spanish brig, bound for some port from which a passage might be easily obtained to the United States. The captain at first declined taking him, as the danger of capture and condemnation, in case of being visited by a British cruiser, would be increased by having an American passenger on board. Foote assured him that no danger should be incurred in such case, by his presence, for he would not speak a word of English, nor would he take with him a line of English manuscript. He, however, warned him, that he had neglected many other precautions, of more importance, which was soon proved to be the case, for the brig was captured by the La Hogue 74, to which ship the crew and passengers were transferred, and the brig sent to Bermuda for condemnation.

The character of the captain of the La Hogue was in strong contrast with that of Byron, and still more so with that of Hardy, he being a drunkard, and coarse and brutal in his manners. Foote messed with the other Spanish prisoners, and described their rations as consisting of chocolate for breakfast and pea soup for dinner, their qualities being such that "you could not tell which was the chocolate and which the pea soup, except by the time of day."

As the officers and sailors of the ship did not seem to think it necessary to restrict themselves to the use of gentlemanly language in regard to their prisoners, who did not understand English, they were in the habit of using such complimentary remarks, seasoned with those hard words which are customary, and considered as appropriate among troopers and sailors, as would have tempted the Spaniards, if they had understood them, to use their knives for some other purpose than that of carving their meat. Foote was strongly tempted to resent in favor of his Spanish friends, some of the remarks on their nation, which required some self-control to restrain, but which his agreement with the captain of the brig precluded him from appearing to understand. This state of durance, however, did not last long, they were all sent on shore, and he returned to New York.

On his arrival, he found that his brother had, during his absence, in connection with some other merchants, purchased a prize vessel, one of the Guernsey cutters, as they are called; vessels of such peculiar rig that they are known at sight by all the British sailors, and on that account considered more safe in running the gauntlet of British cruisers, than a vessel of any other class. This vessel was sent to Charleston for a cargo of cotton, and although that port was really blockaded, she went in safely, took on board her cargo, sailed for France, and arrived at Quimper, where she took on board a cargo of French goods, and returned in safety. Being equipped with letters of marque and reprisal, she took two or three small British vessels from the West Indies, and went in with them to Newbern, North Carolina, where the whole adventure was sold. Capt. Foote (his brother being ship's husband,) was dispatched to

Newbern, to transact the business: and at the
present day it is difficult to conceive the possi-
bility of such a state of things, in relation to
the intercourse of different parts of our country
with each other, at that time. The coasting trade
was of course destroyed, and the roads were in
such a condition, that transportation by land was
so enormously expensive, that no merchandize
could afford the charges incurred thereby. All the
banks south of New England had failed, and no
bills of exchange could be obtained in any of the
southern cities, on Philadelphia or New York.
Under these circumstances, it was, of course, a difficult matter, after all the sales had been effected,
to transmit the proceeds. The best plan that could
be adopted for this purpose, was to obtain bills of
the banks of the city of Washington, for which a
considerable advance was paid, and it was supposed that by paying another large advance, New
York bank bills might be there obtained.

On his arrival at Washington, Foote found that
city in the possession of the British army, under
Gen. Ross, and Admiral Cochrane, who had been
amusing themselves by making bonfires of the
Capitol and the President's house—a display of
Vandalism which disgraced the British with all
civilized nations. But this, disgraceful as it was,
was not so really infamous as the employment of
their savage allies, in their armies in Canada,
and saying that they could not prevent them from
torturing and murdering their prisoners.

All our government officers, and with them all the officers of the banks, had fled—most of them to Frederick, in Maryland—the President to his seat at Montpelier, Virginia, and others of less note, to different places in the interior. The British army had returned to the ships, and while waiting for the return of the fugitives, Foote took up his residence at Crawford's, in Georgetown, at that time the principal hotel in the district. He had remained there two or three days, when he attracted the notice of a gentleman—an old bachelor—of the Virginia F. F. V's, a brother of one of the original proprietors of the District—whose only vocation was gossipry, and the exercise of a philanthropic watchfulness over the conduct and demeanor of its inhabitants, not only those of our public servants, living there in official dignity, but also those in the humble walks of private life. His object was—like that of Columbus—to make important discoveries, for the benefit of his country and mankind. His success was exemplified in his researches respecting the affairs of Capt. Foote, of which the following is "a full and true account." He one day came to Crawford's, and inquired of him, "Do you know that man who is walking along yonder?" "I do not recollect his name," said Crawford, "but you may see it on the register." "Well," said the other, "I know him; he is Admiral Cochrane, and he has come here again in disguise, with other spies, to see

what further mischief they can do."   "Pooh,"
said Crawford,"I have seen Admiral Cochrane, and
know that that man is not him. What has put
such a notion into your head?" "Why," said the
other, "he always looks very grave, talks to nobody, spends all his time, when in the house, in
writing, and when out of it, in thinking," adding
some other circumstances of equal importance,
and verifying his suspicions by the important in-
quiry, "If he is not Admiral Cochrane, who can
he be?" Crawford's testimony, however, was not
satisfactory to so profound an investigator of the
historical details of public and private events,
their causes and consequences. He, evidently,
thought that as the necessary precautions for
guarding the city had been neglected, previous to
its capture, a double quantity of unnecessary ones
adopted after it, would be the proper remedy for
the misfortune.

It was curious to see and hear the great number of profound tacticians, whose talents were
called forth—into conversation—on this occasion,
and the variety of their plans. They agreed,
however, in but one point, which was, that if the
enemy had been beaten at Bladensburgh, instead
of our army, the city would not have been captured—if the British had been driven to their
ships, our government would not have been driven
to Frederick.

It was, undoubtedly, a great consolation to
these men, to be able to find a safety valve for

their patriotic feelings, in cursing both parties;
the British for their Vandalism, and our defenders
for their incapacity and cowardice. The gentleman in question, however, who had taken up the
subject of spying out the British spies, was not
satisfied, like the others, with a due exercise of
the "*cacoethes loquendi*," but was, besides, active
and efficient; for he harangued and wrought upon so many minds of a similar calibre to his own,
that it was determined by them, in council, that
something must be done. In order to determine
what that something should be, they appointed
a committee of two, to examine the room of the
dreaded spy, in his absence, and make the necessary discoveries to authorize their taking him into custody. This committee—who may perhaps
have been of the number of those brave men who,
with "victory or death" inscribed in letters of
gold on their caps, threw down their guns and
fled as soon as they were near enough to the British soldiers to see that they had not discretion
enough to throw down *their* guns and flee—went
to the room designated, and finding the door ajar,
peeped in, and seeing the dreaded enemy at his
writing, with a sword and pair of pistols lying before him, concluded that it would be best to proceed no further, in a matter which assumed an aspect so threatening. They, evidently, thought it
best, not "to fight and run away," but to run away,
without fighting—as the "victory or death," vol-
unteers had done—proving that to be the surest

method of being enabled to live another day. Their recommendation to proceed no further, in so dangerous an undertaking, was adopted, and the committee discharged.

A German, however, who occupied a room adjoining that of Foote, was not so easily satisfied. He thought that this singular stranger must be, if not a spy, a Mephistopheles, or at least, one of the various species of wizards manufactured in Germany, and sent abroad in their modern literature. He might not only set the city on fire, but the Potomac also, and not only carry off the officers that had already ran away, but all that they had left behind. What could be done in the matter, was the puzzling question with him; for it was too dangerous to meddle with a potent enchanter, and still more dangerous to allow him to go on weaving his accursed spells and enchantments for some future awful catastrophe. However, before that point was settled, the government returned from its travels into the interior, and resumed their protective functions.

Having fully protected that portion of the country that was in no danger, they could rely on their experience in that department of their duties to claim the entire confidence of the citizens of the District. The bank officials returned with those of the government, and with them a brother of the suspicious character, together with a brother of the author of the suspicions, a president of one of the banks on which were his demands. He had left New York at about the time of the landing of the British forces, and was proceeding to Washington in the mail stage, and when near the city, was met by a messenger who gave the information that the battle of Bladensburgh had been fought, and that the enemy had marched into the city, and was then enjoying the amusement of burning the public buildings, and destroying whatever they pleased, and that the government was taking a·jaunt into the country. As all the passengers had some business to transact with the fugitives, it was determined to be necessary to tread in the footsteps of the guardians of their country's honor and glory—if they could be found—and they therefore directed their course to Frederick. At this place, all the highest dignitaries of the country, except the President, were assembled, and seemed to be in a situation very undignified, and looking as if Oliver Cromwell's speech to the long parliament had been addressed to them, and they felt they had deserved it, viz: "Get ye gone, ye rascals, and give place to honest men." Their deliberations, during their visit to Frederick, did not appear to be more effective than their warlike operations for the defense of the capitol, and after a few days delay, intelligence being received, that the enemy had evacuated the city, they all returned, except Gen. Armstrong, the Secretary of War, whose conduct had been so outrageously inconsistent with his duties, that accusations of treachery, cowardice and treason, were in the

*6

mouths of all the inhabitants of the District, and it would have been unsafe for him to have been seen there, where stories of his misconduct were being continually repeated and generally believed. It is probable, however, that many of them were inventions, yet some circumstances of his life— such as the Newburgh letters at the close of the revolutionary war, and his treatment of the claims of his countrymen for French spoilations, while he was minister to France, were such as to seem to justify the suspicion, that he was capable of any act of treachery to which he might be tempt- ed.   He was another instance of the folly of put- ting into office men who do not possess the quali- fications of ability and integrity.   Of the former, he was possessed, but without the latter, was only thereby more disqualified for office.

The most valuable qualifications for a states- man and a man of business, after those above named, are, to know, in any emergency, what is best to be done, and to possess the necessary ener- gy and determination for its accomplishment. These qualifications were instructively exempli- fied by Washington as a statesman, and the sub- ject of this memoir as a man of business.

Thus far the progress of the war had been strictly in accordance with such expectations as those of its opponents, and as would naturally be experienced by any sagacious mind, looking at the time and manner of its commencement, the characters of the men who governed, and the agents to whom they committed its management. The redemption of our country from its disgraces on land, where all the glory of the war had been anticipated by its partizans, had been begun on the ocean, all power on which they had proposed to give up without a struggle.

The brave men who began and continued to raise up our country's fame from the deep degradation into which it had been sunk by incompetent statesmen, had by them been treated so contemptuously, merely because they were Federalists, that when they were permitted to go forth upon the ocean, they were smarting with the wounds on their reputation, and were prepared to sacrifice their lives, if necessary, but never to add a new sacrifice of their country's honor.

The time for the restoration of our reputation on land had not yet arrived. The Harrisons, Jacksons, Scotts, and other brave and skillful generals, had not yet obtained the opportunity of redeeming our fame on land.

After making the best arrangement of their business affairs in their power, the brothers returned to New York, and in passing through Bladensburgh, stopped long enough to obtain some idea of the price paid for the glories of war. Although the battle at that place had been a mere miniature representation of a battle, in comparison with those of that period in Europe, through which the minds of men had been so long familiarized to the slaughter of tens of thousands on one field, yet a sight of its effects on so small a scale even, was sufficient to make any one with human feelings,

"Hang his head for shame, and blush to think himself a man."

The wounded were lying in a large barrack, "on their pallets of straw," where with groans and cries of distress, they were begging the surgeons for that relief from pain which it was not in their power to give. The smell from the battle field gave evidence that the dead had been carelessly buried, and the vultures and buzzards scented the field from afar, and were hovering around. Amputations were still called for, which, in the situation of the patients in the hot summer weather, seemed often to give only the relief of death, which in most cases appeared to be a welcome messenger.

They left this scene with feelings of deep distress, from the sight of suffering which they could not relieve—with feelings of shame and mortification for the disgrace of their country, and of resentment towards an enemy capable of inflicting wanton injuries on peaceful citizens, from whose enmity they had nothing to fear, and from whose distresses they had nothing to hope. The wanton outrages committed by an army sent over from a Christian nation, professing to be governed by the laws of civilized warfare, against a Christian and kindred nation, were a mark of backward progress towards the ages of barbarism, which it is to be hoped, have been repented of, and will never be repeated by the armies of Great Britain.

For France, after decreeing that Death is an eternal sleep, and there is no God but nature, it was in character to overrun Europe with her armies, and commit the atrocities and horrors to which such principles lead—to rob and murder innocent victims, and spread desolation over the most fertile fields of the earth—for such a people such a course might be consistent with the system of ethics adopted by them when they discarded the doctrines of Christianity. It was perfectly in character for that nation, after having abolished all worship but that of glory, to deify Napoleon, who bestowed so much of it upon them—(for men, when they abandon the worship of God will always make to themselves idols, first of flesh and blood, and afterwards of baser materials.) But for Great Britain—a nation containing a large proportion of Christian inhabitants, and professing to be governed by Christain principles—for Great Britain, which had so long held up the anti-Christian example of France as a warning to her people—for this nation to follow that example, in sending armies abroad, to commit ravages, which all Christian nations denounce—(and imitate when they consider it good policy)—and set an example in the deification of Nelson, of idolatry as gross as that imitated by her enemy, in the case of Napoleon—were inconsistencies too glaring to be justified by any nation professing Christianity.

And yet they were, although condemned in words, justified in acts, by the United States, in the invasion of Mexico, under a pretext so flimsy that it would have been more creditable to have said: "We want a portion of your territory, and we are the strongest and will take it." And it would have been an exhibition of frankness—such as civilized nations never exhibit—to have added: "We want opportunities for our political aspirants to distinguish themselves as warriors, and our nearest neighbor is weak enough to afford us such opportunity, without much risk, which we must improve."

Our armies, however, never committed any such acts of Vandalism as the burning of public buildings, dedicated solely to civil uses, nor committed any acts of wanton cruelty, and we are confident that none of the officers under Taylor, Harrison, Scott, or any other of our Generals, were ever guilty of that extreme of meanness exhibited by Ross or his subordinates, who dismantled the office of the National Intelligencer, and threw its types into the gutter.* As this journal from the period of its establishment to that time, (and down to the present,) had been remarkable for the courtesy and gentlemanly demeanor of its conductors, both editorially and personally, towards its opponents, (qualities very rare in public journals

---

*The writer picked up some of these types and preserved them for some time as specimens of modern modes of warfare.

at that period,) if singled out by the enemy, it should have been for the purpose of showing respect for those qualities, instead of contempt and disregard for them.

That doctrine of devils, which teaches that a *defensive* war may be made by sending armies to overrun and conquer a neighboring territory, to devastate the towns and fields of individuals engaged in peaceful pursuits—in such pursuits as are necessary to the existence of the very armies themselves—has not yet been superceded by Christian ethics.

Let us hope, however, that the time may come, when Christianity shall be a governing principle for nations and individuals, instead of a mere theme of discussion for polemics, and a political stalking-horse for governments.

CHAPTER VII.

PEACE.

" Hail sacred peace."—DWIGHT.

" Wine is as good as life to a man if it be drank moderately." *
SON OF SIRACH.

" Como el gran, Sancho Panza tomo possession de su insula."
DON QUIXOTTE.

On the return of peace Foote was in North Carolina, where he had in former visits, formed some friendships, which he cherished with characteristic warmth, and which were cordially reciprocated by the genial, kind-hearted friends residing there.   One of these friends, Wilson Sawyer, was an eminent merchant, in Elizabeth City, whose commercial operations had been successful, and therefore very naturally excited a willingness to extend them.   With this gentleman his friendly relations were very intimate, and each was alike enterprising and sagaciously observant of every circumstance in which their efforts for public or private advantage could be exerted with a prospect of beneficial results.

---

*And as bad as death to him if it be drank immoderately.

The deficiency of enterprise and industry in the natives of that region, was so apparent as to be one of the first subjects of remark, not only in relation to commercial, but to agricultural operations. To aid in remedying this defect, the two friends proposed to become benefactors of that portion of their country, in both of these departments.

The commerce of all that part of North Carolina, bounding on the Pamlico and Albermarle sounds, (the latter especially,) and the rivers which flow into them, has been rendered difficult and dangerous, by the closing of the inlet through which the ships of Sir Water Raleigh entered without any obstruction. This inlet was north of Roanoke island, opening directly into Albermarle sound. Its obliteration by the loose, shifting sands which constitute the sea-coast for a great distance towards the south, compels all vessels bound to the north-eastern ports of North Carolina to go round the dangerous Cape Hatteras, and enter the sounds by way of Ocracock inlet, a distance of some hundreds of miles out of their way in going and returning; requiring northerly winds to reach the inlet and southerly winds as soon as they pass it; not only causing delays and hazards, but much expense of lighterage, all of which might be avoided if Roanoke inlet could be again opened.

The two friends projected the improvement of this extensive coast navigation, by a restoration of the original channel through which Raleigh's ships entered, and by diking the other small inlets, to keep this one open continually. This undertaking being successfully accomplished, it was to be a matter of course, that a commercial city would be established near the northern point of Roanoke Island. The idea probably was not original with them, but they supposed the plan to be perfectly feasible, and its advantages so manifest, and the results capable of being made so profitable, that it ought to attract the capital and enterprize necessary to its complete success.

With this improvement these sounds would be (in some measure) to North Carolina what the Chesapeake is to Virginia, and it ought to have been carried into effect at a much earlier period. The enterprize of that region, however,—small in amount at any time—was at that period so strongly attracted towards making new settlements in Tennessee and Alabama, then newly opened to emigrants, that not enough of it remained behind to carry into effect any undertaking of importance. Much talk, and some newspaper paragraphs were expended on the subject, but very little or nothing else.

The agricultural plan for the improvement of the country, was the extension over it of the cultivation of the Roanoke Island vines, from which the natives were in the habit of making a wine, which they spoiled, by mixing with it whisky or peach-brandy, to check the fermentation which the heat of the climate rendered so rapid, that the real merits of the wine could not be developed. In that sandy region, which can not be cultivated to any profit with the usual products of agriculture, vines grow luxuriantly; and in that State there is found a greater variety of wild grapes, and those of better quality, than in any of the other Atlantic States.

The Roanoke vines are a strong exemplification of the influence of soil and site, upon their vinous products; such as is remarked and unexplained in the wine making districts of Europe. The inhabitants of the low country say that the transplanting of their vines to a distance even of fifty miles into the interior, changes their character entirely.

If cellars cool enough to cause the fermentation of the must to go on as gradually as is requisite for developing and preserving the true character of the wine, could be constructed, the product, doubtless, would be greatly improved. Foote had made many observations in the wine countries he had visited, respecting the methods of making, preserving and improving their wines, and supposed that some of the methods which he had observed might be applied to wine making in North Carolina, and that the introduction into that part of the State of this new branch of industry, would be of inestimable advantage there, and might encourage some of the listless idlers, which abound in those regions, to attempt the employment of their time in more profitable pursuits than drinking whisky as a prophylactic to fever and ague, or lounging about, and "for want of thought" weakening their mental and bodily faculties together.

Sawyer and Foote made a purchase, for joint account, of a piece of ground on Roanoke Island, with a view of making the experiments projected for an improved system of cultivation of the vine. It was planted with vines; and the European methods of cultivation commenced. But for the success of wine growing in the United States it was necessary that the patient perseverance and exhaustless capital of a Longworth should be devoted to it—that a Buchanan should collect and publish maxims for cultivation of the vines, and making the wine—that a Rehfuss, a Werk, a Mosher, a Yeatman, a Mottier, a Bogen, and others, should, some of them, bring to the aid of cultivators European experience, and others, the intelligent Yankee style of observation necessary to adapt it to our climate. This combination of advantages which has given to Cincinnati a fame for her wines, which promises to be as extensive as that which she has obtained for her pork, was wanting to North Carolina, whose sterile sands contrast as strongly with our fertile Miami vallies, as her lazy "poor white men" with the industrious, unwearying, cultivators of these vallies; and repulse immigrants as decidedly as our rich free soils attract them. Her best and most profitable staple products might have been made—and nature displayed it by unerring tokens—from the cultivation of her vines, for in the low country, along the coasts of her sounds and seas, they will grow luxuriantly on the sandy soils which will nourish scarcely any thing else.

A general belief has always prevailed in that region, that their native vines will not submit to the restraints of cultivation, but that like the human natives, they must be allowed to take their own course unfettered—not merely by too much, but—by any regulation.

It was supposed, however, that practical experiments would afford such a manifest refutation of this doctrine, that it would soon be ranked among the exploded superstitions of the past ages. The parties to this attempt, however, could not afford to devote the time, labor, and capital necessary to test the experiment, and it remains still a problem to be solved by some future cultivator. The appearance of the experimental vineyard, when seen by the writer several years afterwards, seemed to favor the original ideas of the natives, and to demonstrate that European modes of cultivation are not adapted to American climates.

These projects and experiments, however, could not be continued, for the inducements to improve the advantages opened to commercial pursuits by the return of peace, could not be resisted by the two friends, and they, therefore, turned their attention to their customary pursuits.

10*

They found in Norfolk a British prize brig of large tonnage for sale at a low price, and purchased her for their joint account, intending to load her in Charleston with cotton for Europe. Foote named her the Sancho, in compliment to one of his old favorites, Sancho Panza, she being like him, capable of stowing in her capacious bowels uncommonly large quantities of good things. This quality, however, as frequently happens with human devourers of great quantities of nourishment —was the cause of her ruin, for it rendered her like them, dull and heavy, not obeying her rudder with sufficient promptitude; in consequence of which, being attacked by a gale of wind in going out of the Chesapeake, she was driven on Bodies' Island, and lost. As in a former case, the letter ordering her insurance miscarried; in this case from Post office negligence; and was restored to its proper route only in time to arrive simultaneously with the accounts of the vessel's loss, consequently there was no trouble with the underwriters on the subject. A letter from Foote gives the following account of his disaster:

"You will be obliged to procure a map of North Carolina in order to discover what part of the world I am writing from, and even then, unless you get one upon a very large scale, I doubt whether you will be able to find me out.*

* Professor Bache, in his "Coast Survey," has brought this island into more extensive notice than it had ever attained before.

"It is a little uninhabited Island or sand bank, between Cape Hatteras and Cape Henry, where I was driven ashore in the night. in a gale of wind. Fortunately no lives were lost, and we have been able to save a part of the cargo, sails, rigging, etc. With our sails we have erected tents upon the beach, where we are now living in true Robinson Crusoe style—goat skin dresses excepted. Having fallen in with a company of fishermen, who are encamped on a neighboring island. catching herrings, I have dispatched several of them in various directions, to give the inhabitants of the neighboring districts intelligence of our being here, and of our wish to remove to a more northern climate, to spend the approaching summer—at the same time inviting them to attend a public sale of all our goods. wares and merchandize, on the 14th inst.

"We were fortunate enough to save plenty of provisions, so that we have no fear of starving, but having lost all our water, we have been a little incommoded on that account, having nothing to drink but the brackish stuff we can procure by digging holes in the sand."

This was the only instance of shipwreck suffered by Capt. Foote during his nautical career, and it may be, perhaps, attributed in part, to his opinion of the superior strength of construction in British built ships in comparison with those of our own country, and to his overlooking the great advantages possessed by the latter in fast sailing, and easier control. He spoke in a letter to his

mother of his vessel's being "British built," as
reasons for diminishing her apprehensions for his
safety. Her shipwreck, however, taught him a
lesson which he did not forget, and when at a subsequent period he built the Fabius, he had learned
to combine strength of construction with swift
sailing, so that that ship was the most perfect in
all her qualities that had been built up to that
period.

After his shipwreck he returned to New York,
and resumed the trade with Havana and Cadiz,
varying occasionally his voyages to other European and West Indian ports. The trade with
England having been so long interrupted during
war, was revived with so much spirit and energy
after the peace, that as usually happens in such
cases, it was overdone, as was all the regular business with most of the European and all the West
India ports. One of the commercial crises which
have seemed to be periodical in the United States,
took place in consequence of overtrading, and produced extraordinary distress and frequent failures
among merchants, which being caused by no great
public events, such as the embargo and war, seemed to baffle conjecture as to its causes. There,
probably, was but one—overtrading—which no
warning is ever sufficient to restrain. One or two
years of prosperous commerce seems to cause the
most prudent and cautious merchant to forget the
lessons of caution which he regularly receives, and
to tempt him to extend his operations beyond the

limit of prudence, and thereby suffer the loss of all the accumulations of his industry.

After terminating the business which the unfortunate Sancho brought to a close, Capt. Foote renewed his trade with Spain and her colonies. In the course of it, the following illustration of his character and habits occurred, which it may be useful and instructive to contemplate. That portion of the fourth commandment which required him to honor his mother was so deeply rooted in his feelings, that he thought he honored her—a widow—by a readiness to aid and assist any widow in need of aid and assistance whenever it was in his power.

He became acquainted with an English lady, of superior education, the daughter of a man holding the office of Governor of that princely commercial corporation, "The Hudson's Bay Company," in London: a gentleman whose conduct to his daughter might suggest the idea that the cold, sterile, inhospitable regions under his government, had lent him some of their characteristics.

She had, at his dictation, married a man for whom she had no particular preference, though as her affections were not engaged to any other man, her obedience did not cost her any extraordinary effort. To the same dictation, however, she refused to yield obedience when it required her to abandon her husband after he had wasted his property, and debased his character, by dissipation and extravagance: she did not recognize any principle that would justify her separation from the man whom she had (although thoughtlessly) bound herself to "love, honor and obey as long as they both should live." On the contrary, like a true woman, she devoted herself more deeply and exclusively to him in proportion to his need of her affection and assistance—in proportion to the dependence on her alone, to which he was reduced by the abandonment of all his friends and associates.

They emigrated to America, and she established, at Boston, a female seminary of the highest class, and was enabled, by its success, to maintain her family, and educate her children,—two daughters and one son. After a few years her husband died, and then her father allowed her an annuity sufficient for her personal wants, and her two daughters being married, and residing in New York, she removed to that city, where she became acquainted with Capt. Foote. Her son, the youngest of her children, resolved that his mother should not restrict her comforts by taking from her limited income the amount that would be necessary to qualify him for a profession. He determined at once to become independent, and rely solely on his own exertions for his future support and advancement in life. In pursuance of this determination he shipped as a foremast hand on board a merchant vessel, for the purpose of qualifying himself for the command of a ship in that service. He had made several voyages in that capacity,

when his mother became acquainted with Capt.
Foote, and thinking her son had served long enough
in the school he had entered, to qualify him to begin to rise in his profession, begged him to take
Robert (the son) on board his ship, in the capacity
of second mate. Upon examining the young man,
the captain liked him so well that he made him
his chief mate; probably perceiving in him some
of his own characteristic traits. His mother was
delighted to find her son advanced two grades,
when her highest hopes had been for a rise of one
from the forecastle, and she considered him now
as certain to attain the highest grade in his profession very soon.

The voyage, at that time in prospect, was to include Cadiz and Havana, but it had not been
determined whether to load first for the latter
port, and take a cargo of sugar from thence to
Cadiz, or go first to Cadiz, and take a cargo of
Spanish goods to Havana, and return with a cargo of sugar and coffee to New York. It was, however, finally settled to take the latter course, but
before the ship was ready for sea, intelligence was
received that the yellow fever was raging at Cadiz
with unprecedented virulence. A son of an eminent merchant in New York, in the counting house
of F. X. Harmony, to whom the ship was consigned, had died suddenly of this disease; and
among foreigners generally, it was peculiarly
fatal. Upon the receipt of this intelligence in
New York, great consternation was excited among

those who had friends in, or on the way to, that doomed city, as it was then considered, and Mrs. Field, mother of the newly appointed mate, had her joy for his appointment changed into horrible apprehensions, that he was on a forlorn hope bound to almost certain death. She came to Capt. Foote, in a state of uncontrollable distress, begging him to alter the destination of the ship, as well on his own account as that of those under his command, and to go first to Havana, where the ship would probably be detained long enough for the epidemic to have spent its force in Cadiz. before her arrival there. He replied to her solicitations with an assurance that he would have taken as much pleasure in granting her second as her first request, if it could be granted with propriety. But the ship was loaded, almost ready to sail, and her destination could not now be changed. He told her further, that his invariable rule of conduct was to determine on the course he intended to pursue, and to arrange all his affairs in conformity with that course, and then to press forward, and use the best means, and his utmost exertions, to bring about a favorable result. But in relation to those matters which belonged exclusively to the government of God, he left them in His hand, their results to be borne patiently if adverse, and received thankfully if prosperous. That if she dared not trust Robert (her son) in His hands, he could leave the ship without incurring any censure for timidity, or occasoning inconvenience or delay to the ship, as his place could readily be supplied. The struggle between her fears for her son's life, and apprehensions of his losing a situation he had been so anxious to obtain, was truly distressing. But Robert partook more of his Captain's trust and confidence than of his mother's fears, and could not endure the idea of relinquishing a berth which fulfilled his present hopes, and gave a promise for the future too bright to be darkened by apprehension of danger, to which he must expect to be always exposed, and which it was part of the education he was now acquiring, to learn to look in the face without shrinking. His mother, therefore, endeavored to be resigned, and allowed him to depart, with as little display of those feelings by which he would be as distressed, on her account, as she was on his, as possible, and he sailed in the ship for Cadiz.

Before their arrival at that port, the epidemic had ceased, and the effects of its ravages were only felt in the hearts that had suffered bereavements, not seen in the hurry and bustle of business that enlivened the city at the period of the Ocean's arrival. In the mean time the epidemic had made its appearance at Havana, and if the destination of the ship had been changed, in compliance with the wishes of the anxious mother, she would have arrived at the period when the disease was at its height, and peculiarly fatal to strangers.

11

The epidemic had disappeard from Havana previous to the ship's arrival there, and after accomplishing the business of the voyage, she returned in safety to New York, with all on board in good health. Mrs. Field expressed her gratitude to Capt. Foote, for refusing her second. as strongly as for granting her first request, and her hope now was that her son might become such a man as his Captain, and that she might have an opportunity of presenting him to her father, and claiming from him that pride in his grandson which she felt in her son. This hope was cherished for a considerable period, with bright prospects of its fulfillment. Robert soon became a respectable shipmaster, and at so early an age as to justify his mother in anticipating for him a favorable career, in which all her best hopes should be fulfilled—the hopes, namely. which a widowed mother always feels in the future of an only son. who has given such proofs of a dutiful and virtuous character, that she asks nothing more for herself. than to witness the prosperity and happiness which she thinks must. of course. attend him. But alas! these bright anticipations were destined to be of brief duration. Robert died at sea, soon after he attained the command of a ship, leaving his bereaved mother inconsolable, and when the writer saw her two years afterward. his memory seemed to be the only object of her thoughts, and her grief so fresh and deep. as to render her incapable of comfort.

CHAPTER VIII.

BUENOS AYRES.

———

" He left a name—
To point a moral."—JOHNSON.

———

The office of Sheriff of the city and county of New York, was one of the most valuable of the "spoils of victory" obtained by the Democratic, or self-styled Republican, party, on the successful termination of the struggle between that and the Federal party, in the year 1814. This office was bestowed on Ruggles Hubbard, a most active and efficient partisan, whose aid in obtaining the victory was very marked, and whose personal influence with the voters was seen to be so great as to entitle him to a most important portion of the spoils.

He was a man of restless, enterprising character, possessed of boundless ambition, and in a wonderful degree of those talents for acquiring popularity with the masses, which have always distinguished successful demagogues, and been the most efficient means for the accomplishment of the designs of the ambitious. These talents had

been successfully exhibited in the political struggles of the two great parties, into which our country was then, as always, divided.

He had, at the commencement of his career as
a politician, joined the party then styled Republican—afterwards, and until the present time, Democratic—which designation they assumed instead
of Anti-Federal, their style at the formation of the
two political parties, after those of Whig and Tory
had terminated. In this party he displayed a
boldness and confidence which were among the
causes of his success, and which were unlooked
for by his warmest friends.

The parties in the State of New York were so
nearly balanced, that it was in the power of such
a man to turn the scale. The struggle between
them had been carried on with such energy and
perseverance, as to give ground for the belief, that
the doctrine that "to the victors belong the spoils,"
was a deep seated principle with leading politicians; the period of such unblushing corruption
as permitted its avowal as a party dogma, in the
Senate of the United States, had not yet arrived.*

The county of Albany, and the senatorial district of which it formed a portion, was the most
decidedly Federal of any part of the State, and
Stephen Van Rensellaer, a Federalist of the
school of Washington, was the most popular man
in that district, and second to none in respectabil-

---

* Appendix No. 3.

ity of character in that State, or even in the United States. This man, in that district, Hubbard, a young and obscure lawyer, opposed as a candidate for the State Senate, and to the universal astonishment of all parties, was successful.

His effective talent for controlling the votes of the million consisted in being able to make them see and feel the genial, kindly disposition which characterized him, and which was perceived to be in his nature, not assumed—though used—to promote his ambitious aims.

Under the first Constitution of 1777, the State of New York was divided into four Senatorial districts, and from each of these districts one member was selected to constitute, with the Governor, a "Council of Appointment," as it was styled; a body which had the control of all the offices in the State. Hubbard was chosen a member of this body, and obtained the best office it could bestow.

This early tide of success did not satisfy but rather increased his ambition, as is its regular effect in similar cases. An opportunity for its display occurred during the term in which he held his office, (the appointment being for three years,) which impelled him to the adoption of rash and ruinous projects. and finally caused his early death.

The Spanish Provinces in America had for some time been in an anomalous, revolutionary state: some of them had attained their independence,

*11

and among these was the Republic of Buenos Ayres, which sent, in 1815, an ambassador to the United States, Don Martin Thompson by name. He was empowered to make some private negotiations with individuals, and in the course of them became acquainted with Hubbard, whose ambition was directed towards those Provinces which had not yet become independent, in which he proposed to take advantage of their disordered condition, and by some bold course of operations, raise himself to the dignity of a lawgiver and founder of a state, in which he might become a second Washington.

For the commencement of these designs, however, large funds were necessary, and his first object was to devise the ways and means for making a large and rapid fortune. With commercial operations and principles he was unacquainted, but he had seen that by them such fortunes had been acquired, and thought (as many persons do of farming) that no particular knowledge of the subject was necessary, but that genius and enterprise would stand in the place of every requisite for success.

The Buenos Ayrean Government was desirous to introduce the French tactics and discipline into their armies, but possessing no officers with the necessary knowledge for this purpose, Don Martin was authorized to engage a certain number of French officers, and send them out at the expense of the government, and give them their suitable rank in the armies of the Republic.

After the battle of Waterloo, the occupation of an immense number of Buonaparte's officers was gone, and many of them had emigrated to the United States, and were living in our large cities. They did not seem to possess that facility of changing their avocations with their change of circumstances, which distinguished their country-men who emigrated in the early period of the French revolution. Many of them were living in a state of great destitution—in obscurity and idleness—hard for such men to endure, and it was to them a manifest God-send to be offered service in any army of any country whatever. It was consequently a matter of no difficulty to engage as many as were wanted. Hubbard opened a negotiation with Don Martin for the transportation of these men, and also for the second object of his mission, which required his attention in New York.

The success of the introduction of steam-boat navigation on the Hudson river had been so signal and decisive, as to attract the attention of most civilized countries, and those who possessed rivers susceptible of that kind of navigation, were desirous to imitate the brilliant example of America, and introduce it into their territories. The Buenos Ayrean Government, just then emerging from their half savage state of colonial degeneracy, seemed desirous of showing themselves worthy of

the independence they had acquired, by introduc-
ing as fast as possible, those marks of improved
and improving civilization which were then in
progress in Europe and North America, and from
which they had been debarred in their colonial
state.   The jealousy of foreigners, which had
marked the Spanish Government from the period
of the establishment of its American colonies, had
restrained their enterprise, and thereby caused indolence and degeneracy.   Don Martin was authorized by his government to grant privileges, similar to those granted to Fulton and Livingston by
the State of New York, to any individual or company that might be induced to introduce steamboat navigation into their dominions.

The project was afterwards discovered to be—
like many other projects—planned, not because it
was likely *to be* successful, but because a similar
one *had been* successful somewhere else, and under
different circumstances.   And it is not strange
that such a notion should be adopted in that semi-
civilized country, when in the sharp-sighted, close-
calculating State of Connecticut, characterized by
the extreme of caution in public undertakings, the
people were so dazzled by the success of the New
York canals, which had been constructed when,
and where, and because, they were wanted, that
they supposed a similar success would attend one
in their own State, where it was not wanted; and
they built one from New Haven to North Hamp-
ton.   This they were fortunate enough to convert

into the bed of a railroad, after a few years, thus obliterating a memento of their folly, and making the best of a blunder.

Hubbard considered that he had achieved a great success in obtaining this grant of the exclusive privilege of steamboat navigation to himself and his associates, for an unlimited period, together with some commercial privileges which, together, he supposed would be the foundation of a great and rapid fortune, such an one as would enable him to undertake the higher object he had in view, with the requisite facilities for commencing and carrying it forward.

He had known Foote intimately from his boyhood, had been with him during his residence in Jamaica, and returned from that Island in his company, and knew his qualifications for conducting operations requiring energy, tact, perseverance and knowledge of men, better than he did his own *dis*qualifications for carrying out projects and plans so extensive and varied as those he now had in view. He therefore used all those powers of persuasion, which he possessed in so eminent a degree, to induce him to undertake the management of the business throughout.

Foote was far from being as sanguine in respect to the success of the undertaking as Hubbard, who, to induce him to bestow on it his time and talents, agreed to give him an equal portion in the profits, both of the steam navigation and the commercial grant of privileges.

He, however, was persuaded to undertake and prosecute the business; which he did with his accustomed energy.   He bought a ship for the joint account of Hubbard and himself, and immediately fitted her for the transport of the French officers.

The commander in chief of these men had been an aid-de-camp to Napoleon, and, as he said, had received from him. in acknowledgement of some daring act of bravery on the field of Waterloo, the title of Baron Ballina, of which he was very tenacious, so that his real name was scarcely known, and it being one of those unpronounceable Polish names, annoying to eye and ear, was well lost. His second in command was also a Pole, with an equally unpronounceable name.   Their military titles were General and Colonel.   The other officers were captains and lieutenants, all of them Frenchmen.   Most of these men were so totally devoid of all moral principle. that they appeared in their conversation to have no idea of, or capacity for. the slightest degree of that attribute of humanity; there were, however, a few exceptions, and only those were successful in their future career.   Moral principle had not been inculcated in the French armies, not being considered there an element of success.   Implicit obedience to the commands and will of Napoleon took the place, in those armies, which, in pious Christians, is given to the commands of God.

And if professing Christians in general would "serve their God with half the zeal" that these men served their Emperor, the histories of nations would not be such exclusive Newgate calenders of crimes as they have ever been. The worship of Buonaparte was combined with that of the bloody idol honor, which, with them—as with us—abrogated the moral law, substituting, in its stead, doctrines to which it is diametrically opposed.

Capt. Foote was not pleased with the prospect before him of making a long voyage in such company, but he determined to keep the control of them at all hazards. He was always strict and unyielding in his discipline with his men, and determined to be equally so with his passengers, requiring, in all cases, implicit obedience to his commands.

Of the necessity of this determination proof was given before the sailing of the ship. On the day appointed for her departure, the writer went on board to take leave of his brother, but learned that he was attending to some business on shore. He found the two Poles, the General and Colonel, at the dinner table, over their wine, engaged in a warm dispute in their native language, which no one on board understood but themselves. One of them at length became so heated with passion, that he seized a decanter and struck the other on the head with it, breaking it and the head of his adversary, who in return took up a carving knive and made a thrust at the other's throat with it, but missing his aim he struck the forehead, and the skull being too hard to be penetrated, the knife glanced around it, making an ugly gash, but doing no other injury. A great row and confusion very naturally ensued, the passengers all seeming disposed to join in the melee, some of them appearing willing to have a private battle, on a small scale, got up in order to prevent their warlike faculties from abatement by *non user*. At this moment Capt. Foote returned on board, and no one ever saw him roused to so vehement an assertion and display of his authority, nor ever before or afterwards heard him use those hard words which were formerly considered a necessary portion of a sailor's, as well as trooper's, vocabulary, and which were not then, as they are now, considered inconsistent with the language of a gentleman. He addressed them with a sternness of command and a fiery vehemence under which—insolent and overbearing as they had been—they quailed like whipped hounds; he ordered them to cease their disorderly conduct, and give an account of its cause. They explained it in the French language so that all could understand and judge the merits of the quarrel. It proved to be a dispute beginning with a matter of trivial importance, and proceeding until the explosion was caused by the application of one party to the other of an insulting term (*maurais siyct*) which could not be endured by one who had been an officer of the "grande armee" of Napoleon.

Capt. Foote then warned them that *he* was to be commander-in-chief during the voyage, and that they must all yield to him implicit obedience or go on shore immediately, and that he should not permit any such transgression of the laws of good-breeding as had just been exhibited, and would punish any such outbreaks of violence, without regard to rank or station, in the offenders. Their habits of military obedience were now manifested, and all agreed to submit to the Captain's authority, investing him with the arbitrary power to which they had been accustomed in the French army to yield unquestioning obedience.

The ship sailed, but in the course of her voyage, the quarrel broke out again, and Ballina would have killed the Colonel with a hatchet which he threw at him, if his aim had been as good as his temper was bad. The Captain was thereupon required to interpose his authority to restore peace and order. He assured the parties that any renewal of such disorderly conduct would be treated as mutiny, and the offenders put in irons, and kept so until their arrival at Buenos Ayres, when he would deliver them to the proper authorities. This threat of being ironed like common criminals was very hard of digestion by the proud commander-in-chief, but there were some on board who had sailed with Capt. Foote before, and were able to testify that the discipline of *his* ship was never relaxed under any circumstances, and that. in relation to it, whatever promises he made would be fulfilled at any hazard. No chance for a successful mutiny in resentment of the Captain's rigid discipline appearing, as all the sailors and some of the French officers were ready to obey his orders, whatever they might be, the General thought best to be quiet during the remainder of the voyage, and order thenceforth reigned in the ship, as remarkably as it once did in Warsaw.

After the arrival of the ship at Buenos Ayres, and the transfer of the command of the passengers to the constituted authorities, they were sent to their stations at Mendoza, where they very early displayed the need of a continuation of Capt. Foote's rigid discipline. The government soon discovered that the introduction of French tactics and discipline into their army by French officers, was not as brilliant an idea as they had expected, and that foreign teachers were not suitable instructors in their armies. The conduct of Ballina soon became so atrocious, that he was arrested and ordered to be sent back to the United States. The order was not, however, enforced; but what was the termination of his career was never learned.

Some of the young men who went to Buenos Ayres with him, were, Capt. Foote says, worthy young men, but one only ever attained any distinction. Capt. Foote met with him some years afterwards, at Lima, in the army of San Martin.

in which he held a high rank, and was of good repute for character and talents.

After finishing that portion of his business which related to his French passengers, he directed his attention to the other objects of his expedition, and first to that of the introduction of steam navigation upon the waters of the La Plata and its tributaries. This he soon discovered was a hopeless project, and that steamboats would have as little prospect of finding profitable employment there as canal boats had found at New Haven.

After making all possible investigations, and obtaining from the commercial members of the community all the details of the business of the country, and the manner in which it was conducted, as well as the course and manner of travel in that country, he was satisfied that an attempt to carry out the steamboat project would be a wild-goose chase, and the sooner all idea of it was relinquished, the more apparent would be his discretion. In his letters to Hubbard, after giving the information he had gained, he says that under such circumstances their commercial projects were out of the question, and steamboat navigation worse than out of the question, for in that country the travel was exclusively on horseback, and that the inhabitants must be brought within the pale of civilization (an event far in the dim distance of time) before they could comprehend the advantage of any other mode of travel than that to which they were accustomed.

A Buenos Ayrean, if he wished to make a rapid journey, would select from a drove of a thousand or ten thousand horses, such an one as he approved, mount him and ride at full speed a hundred miles or more, and if this trial killed him, the value of the hide was so near that of the living animal, that the loss was of no consequence; but if he was able to endure such a trial he was a most valuable animal, and became a favorite with his master, whose life is nearly all spent on horseback.

Among such a people, it was as hopeless to attempt to inspire any idea of the advantages of steam navigation, as it would be to give our law-givers in Congress a correct idea of the advantages of good-breeding, and to make them understand that killing a waiter for neglect of due servility to the representatives of the freest people on earth, is inconsistent with common politeness, and the laws of God, which ought to have the preference to those of honor.

Commercial operations in that country were conducted in the most dilatory and expensively tedious ways, and he says in his letters, "It would take more time than I can spare, to detail the toil, and trouble, and difficulty of purchasing and shipping a cargo, and I think I would hardly accept of $100,000 as a present if I were obliged to embark it in the produce of this country."   *   *

"You are *obliged*, if you have any cargo, to employ the launches of the country to discharge it, and run the risk of losing one-half, and having the other half damaged, for which you pay a greater price than you would for carrying it from America to Europe." * * "If you happen to be in want of any thing on board, there is no ship-chandler to whom you could go and supply yourself, and your only resource is to take a horse, ride round the city and country until you find some out-of-the-way kind of thing which may answer your purpose, and for which you have to pay five times as much as it is worth—then get a permit from the custom-house—then leave from the Guarda—then to be examined by the Resguarda—then go to the Mole for a boat—and then wait for good weather to take it off. If the river be low, a small boat cannot come within half a mile of the quay, and, in this case, carts are employed to communicate with her, and if you happen to get belated, or the weather proves bad, you are obliged to drag her up on to dry land, turn her over, and set a guard over her, and wait till morning or good weather returns."

The commercial privileges granted by Don Martin were not sufficient to induce a continuation of a trade with such a country, and it was abandoned, after taking two cargoes to Spain, from whence he returned to New York.

He found Hubbard, in pursuance of his original design, and undeterred by his want of success in

12*

raising a rapid fortune, planning a filibustering expedition to Florida. From this project he (Foote) endeavored to turn his attention, representing the disappointment he would experience even in case of success, from a want of knowledge of the Spanish character. But although Hubbard held a most enthusiastic opinion of Foote's judgment and talents, his heart had been so long and so deeply fixed upon this expedition, that he could not be persuaded to relinquish it. All his powers of exhortation, on the contrary, were exerted to induce Foote to join him, and all the visions of a bright imagination were themes of persuasion : but they could not dazzle the strong common sense, nor overcome the principle which repelled the feelings of Foote from an undertaking so lawless and dangerous.

No arguments, however, nor any representations of the probable result of his project, were powerful enough to induce Hubbard to relinquish it. He had held a correspondence with some of the inhabitants of the province, and with Aury, a kind of freebooter, who had, or pretended to have, a commission from one of the South American revolutionary governments to cruise against the Spaniards. He had several vessels under his command and was styled commodore. Hubbard was encouraged in the belief that he could take possession of the country without resistance, and that Aury with his fleet would furnish a navy sufficient to guard against any force that Spain,

in her then depressed situation, would be likely
to send for the recovery of the territory.

A Scotchman, calling himself Sir Gregor Mac-
Gregor, was at the same time planning a similar
expedition, pretending to have authority, and
assurances of support, from the governments of
Mexico, New Grenada and Florida. He had the
advantage of a prepossessing appearance, his
figure large and commanding, and his bearing
that of one accustomed to command, but that was
all.

Hubbard was decidedly inferior to him in personal appearance, but superior in every other quality.
He determined to be in advance of any operations
on the other's part, and, collecting a body of such
desperate, unscrupulous men as usually constitute
the troops employed in filibustering expeditions,
he embarked them on two vessels which he had
purchased for this object, and, resigning his valuable office, sailed for Amelia Island. He arrived
there after a short and easy passage, landed his
troops, and took possession of the Island without
resistance, and raised the standard of independence for Florida.

The inhabitants of the province generally were
tired of Spanish domination, and ready to join
any leader that offered himself as a chieftain to
lead them on to freedom and independence, which,
like all the other Spanish colonists, they thought
would bring them happiness and prosperity, not
being at all aware how unfitted for self-govern-

ment centuries of colonial subjection had rendered them.

Hubbard's popular manner and talents immediately attracted the favor of all the inhabitants of the Island, who, soon after his arrival, unanimously elected him their Governor. Three days after this he was attacked by the yellow fever and died, and all his plans died with him.

This termination of one of the earliest filibustering expeditions from the United States, afforded one of the many unheeded warnings against such expeditions—expeditions which have since been so often repeated, and, in most cases, terminating in still stronger demonstrations of their folly. This piratical spirit, which was so early directed against the Spanish colonies in America,* seems to have sprung up anew in this enlightened nineteenth century, and forms a prominent feature in the lawless proceedings by which our country has been disgraced.

Hubbard, at the commencement of his political career in New York, was the rival of Martin Van Buren, and while a member of the council of appointment, the strife between them for mastery in

---

* The Buccaneers of the Seventeenth century were the precursors of our modern filibusters. They, however, had suffered heavy wrongs from the Spaniards, for which they sought redress and vengeance. Those of the present day have no such pretext. They possessed the daring, courage and enterprise of men in a state of desperation, which the moderns do not. Their conduct after a series of successful raids and robberies, and the commission of atrocious barbarities, is an exemplification of the moral results of successful piracies.

the party was violent and bitter. Hubbard was successful in the struggle, and if he could have submitted to be governed by Foote's advice, might have retained his ascendancy, and perhaps been equally successful in the struggle for the Presidency of the United States. The fable of the dog and the shadow never had a better illustration, and the pointing of a moral by the termination of his career was as decided, though not of as world-wide fame, as that of "Swedish Charles."

Hubbard's death left the field open to Mac-Gregor, who, says Hildreth,* "Having collected a band of adventurers in Charleston and Savannah, took possession of Amelia Island, at the same time proclaiming the blockade of St. Augustine. In the hands of these desperadoes, this Island was soon converted into a resort for buccaneering privateers under the Spanish-American flag, and a depot for smuggling slaves into Texas."

Whether MacGregor's career was stopped by death, or by his want of power to lead his desperadoes to new undertakings, is not known; he never emerged from the obscurity into which he sunk, as soon as lawful measures were adopted for the suppression of his piratical course.

* History of the United States.

CHAPTER IX.

MADAME BALLINA.

" And Hope attends, companion of the way,
  Thy dream by night, thy visions of the day.
       *   *   *   *   *   *
  While Memory watches o'er the sad review
  Of joys that faded like the morning dew;
  Peace may depart, and life and nature seem
  A barren path, a wilderness, a dream."—CAMPBELL.

WHEN Gen. Ballina came from France to America, he was accompanied by his wife, a Spanish lady of great beauty, whose short history had already been very eventful. She had been one of the celebrated "heroines of Saragossa," having belonged to the corps of ladies, organized by the Countess of Burita, to aid in the defence of the city, by services in the hospitals, and wherever else their services might be made available.

Madam Ballina was not only beautiful, but possessed of "that grace of Spanish women which all recognize and none can describe, for mere form and feature does not explain it."* Her manners

---

* Urquhart.

and general bearing gave the idea rather of a Titania than a Clorinda or a Britomart—of a sylph or fairy rather than a heroine. She had, however, taken a very active part in the female corps to which she belonged, and which during the seige had exhibited an extraordinary degree, as well of patient endurance of labor and fatigue, as of daring enterprise and courage, by which they were so exposed as to be sometimes engaged in skirmishes with detachments of the beseiging army. In one of these she had been engaged, and was slightly wounded in the neck by a French soldier, who was about to finish his barbarity by killing her, when she was rescued by Ballina. From gratitude for this deliverance, she married him and followed his fortunes. He carried her to Paris, where her beauty and romantic adventures made her a personage of extraordinary interest, and the most polite and friendly attentions were bestowed on her by the ladies of the court, and by the imperial princesses especially. Belonging to a family of the highest order of the ancient Spanish nobility, she was on that account, probably, more caressed and petted by the parvenu nobility of the imperial court than one from a humble origin would have been with equal celebrity and beauty.

When her husband, during the hundred days, obtained favor with his master, Napoleon, sufficient to be made one of his aids, he left his wife with the imperial princesses, and followed the

Emperor to Waterloo,* expecting to return with the spoils of victory—with honors and nobility—and her expectations pointed to the enjoyment in France of a rank equal or superior to that which she had renounced in Spain. These hopes and anticipations were destined to a grievous disappointment by the result of the battle, which condemned Napoleon to perpetual Promethean torture on the rock of St. Helena.

Ballina, with many other officers of the French army, emigrated to the United States, and had resided sometime in a state of poverty and destitution hard to be endured, in the city of New York.

The expedition to Buenos Ayres awakened new hopes—hopes destined to meet a still more severe and bitter disappointment than those crushed by the Battle of Waterloo.

On this expedition Madam Ballina could not accompany her husband, as the Buenos Ayrean government only provided for the transportation of the officers engaged by Don Martin, and they had no private funds to enable them to provide passages for themselves. Ballina was therefore compelled to leave his wife in New York, promising to send for her as soon as suitable provision

---

* Capt. Foote speaking of Ballina, in one of his letters says : " One of the officers who came out with Carrera (Gen. Lavasse) knew him in France, and says he has always been every thing that is base, villainous and cowardly, and that only the interest which the Empress and Princess Pauline took in his wife raised him to, and maintained him in, the rank he held under Buonaparte."

could be made for her passage, and for her comfort on her arrival at Buenos Ayres. The writer saw her for the first time on board the ship in which her husband was to sail the next day. She was inquiring about the comforts provided for the passengers on the voyage, and the dangers to which they would be exposed in crossing the equinoctial line. and other perils of the torrid zone and hurricane latitudes. Like a young school girl, she enquired whether they poured oil on the waters in these modern times in case of a tempest. and whether there was a supply of it on board. She had no foresight of the tempest that would be awakened the next day. on board the ship. while in port, requiring the oil of commanding authority to control, as related in the last chapter.

She was left at New York in a situation very little suited to her habits of life. with a very limited provision for her support until her husband could send for her to join him in Buenos Ayres.

On Capt. Foote's return to New York, after his voyage from South America to Cadiz, he made inquiries respecting her, and learning her situation, which was, in fact, that of a deserted wife, he called on her for the purpose of communicating such intelligence respecting her husband as was in his power. softening it as much as he could consistently with the advice he intended to give. This was to seek a reconciliation with her father, who. being a Spanish nobleman, and still wealthy.

13

notwithstanding the devastation of his country and the sack of his city, would doubtless relieve her pecuniary distress.

In the state of feeling which existed in Spain during, and after, the French invasion, no greater or more unpardonable crime could be committed by one of her daughters than marrying a Frenchman, and especially one of the invaders, whose unrestrained barbarities were, like those of the Indians of our country, marked by such deep and damning outrages as could never be forgiven or forgotten. Notwithstanding the existence of that feeling, however, Capt. Foote believed that if her father could be made to understand her true situation, and should be appealed to with the display of a penitent spirit, and with a filial humility, it would be impossible for him to resist such an appeal. Even if he should refuse to be fully reconciled to her, he surely would not refuse to grant her pecuniary relief. He recommended her to write a letter to him, giving a full account of her situation and of her wish to be reconciled to her parents. She said that she had already written such a letter, and also one to one of the French princesses at Paris. From her father she had received no reply, but from the princess a very pleasant, friendly answer had been immediately returned. It invited her to return to Paris, where a situation should be provided for her which would secure her future comfort. This invitation she was desirous to accept, but had not the funds necessary for her outfit and for the payment of her passage to Havre. Capt. Foote, therefore, immediately interested himself in her behalf, and secured a passage for her in the first ship that was to sail for that port. He also made such provision for her comforts, and the necessary facilities for her proceedings on her arrival in France as he would have made for a sister. But at almost the last moment, when she had only to embark, having all her affairs arranged, and Capt. Foote was ready to see her safely on shipboard, she informed him that she had received a letter from her father with a remittance of two thousand dollars, and had, in consequence, changed her determination respecting her return to France, but instead thereof had resolved to go to her husband at Buenos Ayres. This step he foresaw would destroy every chance of happiness for her future life; though the banishment of Ballina had not then been carried into effect, if it had been decreed; yet his knowledge of the man's character taught him that his wife must necessarily be miserable with him, since the indulgence of his evil passions had rendered him almost insane.

The triumph of womanly affection and confidence in the man on whom her earliest affections had been bestowed, over discretion and experience—of hope over warnings and disappointments—was as complete as it was mistaken and unfortunate. She went to Buenos Ayres and joined her husband, who, when he had obtained the money sent her by her father, made her life so miserable that it could not be endured. Hope was so completely subdued that it could shed no gleam of brightness on the path of her future life. She left America in a British ship for Europe, but whether she went to her friends in France, or returned to her family in Spain, was not known.

CHAPTER X.

PERU.

———

—————" Why those various toils,
Those wanderings o'er the wide-extended main."—POTTER.
—————" They ride
Over ocean wide,
With a hempen bridle and horse of wood."—OLD BALLAD.

———

IN his commercial operations, and the course of his trade with Cadiz and Havana, Foote had formed intimate commercial and friendly relations with Peter Harmony, a very eminent merchant of New York, and also with his brother, Francis Ximenes Harmony, of Cadiz, an equally eminent merchant of that city, which lasted during their lives, and controlled or influenced all that remaining portion of his life which was devoted to navigation and foreign commerce.

These gentlemen were of the historical family of Ximenes, which gave to Spain its greatest statesman, in the person of the celebrated Cardinal of that name, Prime Minister to Charles V; and their commercial talents were not inferior, in the pursuits they had chosen, to those of the statesman in that higher vocation, in which suc-

13*

cess confers fame, preferring that in which it confers wealth. Their name, in consequence of its initial being one of those unpronounceable gutturals introduced by the Arabs into the Spanish language, was Anglicized by Don Pedro into Harmony, which name was added to that of his family by Don Francisco.

Various mercantile adventures had acquainted these parties with each other's talents and business qualities, and, in consequence, established a well founded confidence, which was never shaken, and a firm, enduring friendship, such as men of worth and integrity are always disposed to cherish.

They built for their joint account a beautiful bark, in which Foote introduced some improvements in the rigging, which were adopted as soon as seen in all square-rigged vessels. He made several voyages in her to Spain and the West Indies, but she was soon found to be too small for the views of the owners. They therefore resolved to build a ship of the largest class, and, accordingly, built the Fabius, a ship which at that time was of that class; ships of one to two thousand tons had not then been thought of as suited to any branch of the commerce of our country. The Rhinelanders, of New York, had, about the beginning of the century, built the Manhattan, of near six hundred tuns, but she was built for glory rather than profit, being too large for any trade that was carried on at that period, and could never be made profitable.

The Fabius was as beautiful a corvette as had ever been built, and her ownership was equally shared by Harmony, Foote, and Eckford the celebrated ship-builder, who was afterward sent for by the Sultan of Turkey to superintend the building of ships for his navy at Constantinople. By the exercise of his talents in the construction of her hull, and those of Foote in the arrangement of her rigging, she was probably the most beautiful and perfect ship in the commercial marine of the United States, which already included some of the best specimens of naval architecture in the world. Her first voyage was to Cadiz, carrying as passengers, Mr. Forsyth, American Ambassador to the Court of Madrid, and his family. At that port the ships of all the commercial nations of the world are seen, probably, in greater variety than in any other, London not excepted, and there the Fabius excited universal admiration, and gained the palm of superiority in beauty, in capacity for easy management, and in that combination of sailing and carrying qualities united, which had always been the greatest desideratum in the construction of merchant vessels.

Soon after her arrival, Mr. F. X. Harmony obtained, from the government at Madrid, permission for her to trade with the Spanish colonies on the Pacific, for which trade she was better adapted than any of the Spanish ships that had formerly been employed in that trade, being better qualified for rounding Cape Horn with safety, as well as for making her voyages in much shorter periods—qualities of which her subsequent performances gave sufficient proofs.

She was loaded with a cargo of upwards of six hundred thousand dollars value, shipped chiefly by different Spanish merchants who had had experience in the trade with those colonies, and knew what kinds of merchandise they required. There was probably, at that time, no trade with any country in the world, where a knowledge of that kind was so useful in directing the articles suitable for its commerce; a curious exemplification of which was given by some British merchants in one of the earliest of their adventures to Peru. The English are not exceeded by their Yankee descendants in their eagerness to be the first in carrying supplies to any new market that may be opened to their trade.

These merchants, in their anxiety to take advantage of the trade with the Spanish colonies on the Pacific, did not wait to ascertain what articles were suitable to their market, nor what would be the proper mode of transacting the business of this new field of commerce, but made up a cargo for Lima which might have been suitable for Calcutta, but was very unsuitable for Peru.

This cargo seemed to be selected under an impression (not uncommon with John Bull) that British goods comprised every thing desirable in any market, and that such goods were more desirable than any other in all markets. Their cargo. being made up in accordance with this opinion, consequently included a quantity of London porter, a liquor which it was taken for granted every body liked, and would drink if it could be obtained. This opinion, however, proved to be as groundless as that of the Nova Scotians respecting the comparative prowess of British and American frigates. London porter could not be sold at any price in Peru; indeed, it could scarcely be given away. The consignees, therefore, very judiciously concluded that the most suitable disposition that could be made of this liquor would be to drink it themselves. Acting in conformity with this opinion, they obtained a profit equal to the expectations of the shippers by selling the empty bottles at a dollar each, although they could not have been sold at half a dollar a dozen when they were bottles of porter.

The Fabius made her passage with the usual experience of stormy weather in rounding Cape Horn, and arrived safely at Callao, the port of Lima, six miles distant, at a period more stormy and dangerous on shore than any of the storms she had encountered at sea. The period of her arrival was one of great public calamity and extensive and deep private distress.

The province had been conquered by an army under Gen. San Martin, from Buenos Ayres. This army had first marched to Chili, conquered

and revolutionized that province, and established
an independent republican government there.
San Martin then proceeded to Peru, which province also was subdued with very little opposition.
He was proclaimed Protector of the Republic, and
was a dictator with despotic power, as every con-
quering general is in the region he subdues. In
all countries, and especially in the Spanish-American provinces during their struggle for independence, in revolutionary periods the peaceful pursuits of commerce are not held in as much respect
as at New York or Cadiz in ordinary times; great
difficulties were, of course, experienced in the
transaction of commercial business. Private
property was esteemed rather as a raw material
which might be converted into the "sinews of
war," than as a matter subject to individual control. It was regarded rather as a means of affording facilities for furthering the operations of
the conqueror, than as means of contributing to
the comfort of its proprietors. This doctrine being one of those established by prescription and
general approbation in all invading armies, was
exemplified in faith and practice by both parties.
as power, subsequently, passed from one party to
the other.

The obstacles to the prosecution of a peaceful
commerce, and the difficulties in the conduct of it
when thus forced out of its usual channels, may
readily be imagined. The talents, the vigilance
and sagacious industry necessary to transact com-

mercial business, and bring it to a successful result, under such circumstances, are very rarely united in any individual, and the plan and manner of education adopted by Foote, as recorded in our third chapter, were calculated to form such a man as those circumstances required.

He, however, possessed some extrinsic advantages which were more accidental. Some of the officers in the army of San Martin (one of them holding a high rank) had been of the number of those carried by Capt. Foote to Buenos Ayres, and, of course, held him in high regard for his character and talents, and, probably. gave him influence with San Martin. His character, also, of a citizen of the United States, gave him a higher standing than any other would have held, from his nationality, among the revolutionists. This estimation was probably strengthened by the presence, in the harbor of Callao, of the United States ship, Franklin (74). commanded by Capt. Stuart, whose energy and decision of character no one of any party would have desired to see exerted for the protection of any of his fellow countrymen from any wrong.

The influence which it was perceived was possessed by Capt. Foote with all parties, subjected him to many solicitations for the exercise of that influence in behalf of various oppressed and suffering individuals, to which he always responded promptly, and. in most cases, effectively.

And not only individuals, but public institutions, sought and obtained his assistance. A valuable diamond was presented to him in acknowledgment of his services in protecting a convent of nuns from military license during the most lawless period of the occupation of the city by the enemy's army. Other services which he rendered to the exposed and the suffering, obtained less costly, but, to the heart, not less valuable, testimonials of his efforts in the cause of humanity. The blessings of many who were ready to perish came upon him, and among them were some of the poor priests, who, in the license of the times, were not spared from reverence for their office.

To the pure and Christian-like character of many of the Roman Catholic clergy, he bore testimony, although his early life and education had been calculated to excite in his mind strong prejudices against that order of men. In that city, so long famous for the corrupt and licentious manners prevailing there, men who, from the influence of their religion, could preserve purity in life, were entitled to a high degree of respect, and some such men were found there.

The acts of kindness which he was happy in performing for them, he considered such as begin and end with the occasion that calls them forth—to be thought of no longer; but, on his return to Spain, he found that they had given him a reputation such as he had never expected to obtain.

and such as no *heretic* had ever enjoyed in that region before. One lady expressed a great desire, and strong hopes and expectations, that he would be converted to the true Catholic faith, in which case she expected he would become a saint. Others also expressed the most sanguine hopes of his conversion and consequent salvation.

But the conduct of his own affairs, and the judicious management of the business confided to him by others, required incessant vigilance and labors such as were not often seen in that region of indolence and self-indulgence.

The disordered state of affairs, however, and the delays consequent thereon, caused him a detention of eight months at Lima before his business could be closed. But this to the Spaniards, accustomed as they were to the slow progress of commercial transactions in the South American provinces, did not seem so extraordinary a delay as it would be to a hurrying, driving Yankee, whose motto is, that "time is money," and money the one thing needful. The whole of this period was one of incessant labors, cares and watchfulness. wearisome alike to body and mind. To protect the property entrusted to him by his Spanish friends, in such times of military license and revolutionary misrule, required talents as extraordinary as the circumstances that called them into exercise. and a wearisome vigilance more trying to the constitution than the night and day watches on shipboard when passing the stormy cape.

The settlement of his commercial affairs at Lima was, however, at length happily effected, and the Fabius sailed for Guyaquil, where she took a return cargo for Cadiz, at which port she arrived in safety without damaging a spar, sail or rope, although in rounding Cape Horn the ship was exposed to the tempestuous weather which seems to be almost perpetually prevailing in that latitude.

The voyage terminated profitably to owners and shippers, and having been effected at a period when, in addition to the ordinary dangers of commercial adventures, the extraordinary ones arising from the disordered state of the South American provinces were added, it was considered an achievement which could only have been accomplished by the exercise of a rare combination of talents. The special protection of the saints, also, had, in the opinion of some of the pious shippers, been granted to the prayers of the poor priests, who had received benefits for which they had nothing else to give in return.

The success of this voyage, under the difficulties which threatened a disastrous termination, and which had been happily surmounted by the exercise of discreet vigilance and a capacity to create and direct circumstances, seemed to inspire Capt. Foote's associates and friends with the idea that *he* could accomplish any object that he might undertake, and they immediately proposed a second voyage to the Pacific, from which they hoped that the knowledge and experience gained in the first would aid in producing a still better result. The physical and mental fatigues and sufferings which he had undergone, however, made him hesitate and dread a repetition of them. He represented to his associates that they ought not to expect a second adventure to terminate as successfully as the first, and that it would be wiser to be content with what they had gained than to risk the loss of it by trying to gain more. They, however, would not be convinced that there could be any doubt of the success of any undertaking confided to his management, and assured him of a profit to himself in any case, whatever might be the termination of the adventure and its results to themselves, and that his reputation should not be lessened by any result however unfavorable.

Although he could have retired at that time with the modest competence to which he had looked forward at the commencement of his career, yet circumstances had since occurred which made it desirable to enlarge his demands upon fortune, and he was, therefore, more easily persuaded to try another adventure. This was to be a repetition of the previous voyage, the cargo to consist of merchandise similar in kind and amount. A considerable portion of the cargo consisted of articles suitable only to the trade with the Indians—a traffic which yielded large profits, but

which the state of the country rendered difficult
and extra-hazardous. Another portion consisted
of such Spanish fabrics as the colonists had been
accustomed to use and to pay high prices for, the
policy of Spain in requiring her colonies to contribute to the prosperity of the mother country,
by consuming her manufactures, having been as
decided as that of England. This system had
been so long in operation, that substitutes for
Spanish fabrics, similar in kind, and even if better in quality, could not be introduced. Those
articles which they had been accustomed to use,
and to pay high prices for, they would continue
to use, and pay, if necessary, still higher prices
for, even if better articles were offered them at a
much lower price.

On this second voyage, the license from the
Spanish government was, from unforeseen circumstances, occurring previous to the arrival of
the Fabius at Callao, probably of more value
than on the former voyage; and the experiences
of that expedition aided Capt. Foote greatly to
overcome some very important and unexpected
difficulties in the transaction of his business,
which had arisen among the recent changes of
the state of affairs in Peru.

The ship passed Cape Horn safely and without
any accident, although she encountered terrific
storms, with more than the usual quantity of
perilous fatigues and apprehensions on the part of
the officers and crew. The care which had been

bestowed in causing the construction of the hull to be as perfect as knowledge and skill could make it; with the provision of every thing in rigging and tackle likely to be wanted in any event, was found to be an insurance against loss of which the underwriters share the benefits with the owners.

On this voyage, while going down the coast toward Lima, the Fabius had occasion to stop at a very obscure port, the name of which had scarcely ever been heard on this side of the continent. After casting anchor, when the captain was preparing to go on shore, he said to his mate, "Well, there is one novelty I shall certainly find here—a place without a Yankee inhabitant." Observing, however, a boat coming from the shore, he awaited her arrival, and on her coming along side, a young gentleman came on board from her who, at sight of the Captain, exclaimed:

"Why, Capt. Foote, is this you?"

"It surely is, if you are Eldridge, about which I can hardly believe my senses! But how came you here, and what are you doing in this out-of-the-world place?"

"Oh, I have been drifting along down, and thought I would stop here and see if something could n't be done in a place where there are no Yankee competitors—hav n't done much yet, but expect something will turn up that I can take advantage of; they are so lazy in this country that there is n't much danger of competition if any thing should offer." And in the changes and chances which in those revolutionary times were taking place, it is probable that something did turn up, but of what nature is not known. The right or wrong of the occurrences of those times were not easily comprehended by the million, most of whom were ready to follow any leader in any enterprise he might propose, the labor of thinking for themselves being too heavy a task.

After transacting some trifling business which had caused her delay, the Fabius sailed for Arequipa, and, not being long detained there, proceeded to Callao, where she arrived after a passage of ninety-three days from Cadiz.

At the time of her arrival there on the previous voyage, San Martin, with the revolutionary army, had captured the city, and was punishing the royalists, including in that class all on whom he chose to lay contributions.

At this period, Canterac, with the royalist forces, was in the ascendant, having reconquered the province. He was, as a general, superior in talents, courage and skill, to San Martin; but no talents or skill could restore permanently the Spanish dominion. In a letter of 23d of June, 1823, Capt. Foote says: "We have been in a most terrible state of alarm ever since our arrival, and have at last been fairly driven into the sea by the royal army, which is now in possession of Lima. They entered it on the 18th inst., without firing a shot, and are now amusing themselves in levying contributions, shooting the inhabitants and robbing the houses. It is thought, however, that they will not remain here long, and we have hopes of their returning to the mountains as soon as they have satisfied themselves with the booty they are collecting. *We are safely lodged on board our ship, but it is a sad thing for the poor inhabitants, thousands of whom have fled from the city, and are wandering about the shore without shelter and without food. Those who remain are subject to all the violences and exactions of a wanton soldiery, and are perhaps more to be pitied than those who are starving along the coast. * * * My ship is full of people who have fled from the town."*

A portion of the cargo of the Fabius belonged to a person in very bad odor with the royalists, and Foote had some difficulty in saving it from their clutches. He, however, succeeded in preserving every thing under his care, but found his situation, if possible, still more exposed to annoyances and vexations than on his former voyage.

In a letter to his friends at Nutplains, dated 19th July, 1823, he says: "I wrote you a short time since, advising you that we had all been driven out of the city by the royal army, and were shut up in Callao. On the 17th, the royalists evacuated the city, after having squeezed near two millions out of the inhabitants, and we are now returning. In a month we may, probably, have to fly again, as the enemy has it in his power to come back whenever he chooses. This state of uncertainty has put an entire stop to business, and I am no further advanced in my affairs than the day I arrived. * * * A short time since we had a shock of an earthquake, but, fortunately, its motion was undulating, and, therefore, did but little damage; had it been vibrating, it would have shaken the teeth out of our heads. The undulating earthquakes do not shake houses down; the ground only opens and swallows them up, which you know is a mere trifle. In the one we had, the earth opened about a mile from the city, so that we all escaped with a little fright and a great deal of dust. * These are strange countries, and you may tell G. that those who come here for dollars buy them as dearly as in digging potatoes: for my part I think I shall, in future, seek for them somewhere else."

In a subsequent letter, dated 23d of September, he says: "The city is entirely drained of its wealth, and as the inhabitants are too cowardly and indolent to give the enemy the least uneasiness, we are enjoying all the security of poverty and insignificance. The sad situation of the country has been the cause of my long delay, and I have yet no prospect of getting away in less than two or three months. * * * You cannot imagine how sick and tired I am of these long voyages, and I am every day making the strongest resolutions in the world that I will never undertake any more of them. Will you

give me a berth at Nutplains if I will promise
not to go to sea any more, and will tell you long
stories about these strange countries? Well, we
will see when I get home."

The state of poverty and destitution to which
the city had been reduced by the alternate exactions of patriot and royalist armies had reduced
many of his friends to great distress. He spoke
of one whose wealth had been so great, and with
whom the precious metals were formerly so plenty
that the cornices of his rooms were of solid silver,* and whose command of wealth seemed
boundless, who had been driven from home and
forced to leave his wife, bred in the enjoyment of
every luxury that wealth could give, in a state of
poverty and destitution of which she had never
dreamed. Capt. Foote was enabled to be of service to her, as well as many others, and one of the
turns of fortune, frequent in that country, restored
the family to a more comfortable condition, though
not to its former opulence.

The churches had been stripped of a great portion of their gold and silver ornaments, and the
clergy were obliged to share the sufferings of the
laity. Under such circumstances, to make a safe
and profitable voyage required no ordinary talents, together with a laborious and sleepless vigi-

---

* The mention of this circumstance was to illustrate the luxury and extravagance which prevailed in the city previous to the revolution, and the
want of good taste in its display. These cornices were fastened to their
places with coarse iron nails, the heads of which were visible.

lance, so fatiguing to body and mind as to elicit the complaints in the above extracts from his letters, and to fix steadfastly his determination never to expose himself to such wearisome and exhausting labors and cares again; a determination requiring strong efforts to adhere to, as will be seen presently.

The settlement of his affairs at Lima, requiring five or six months instead of the two or three spoken of in his letters, being at length effected, the Fabius sailed from thence, and after proceeding to Payta, Piura and Guyaquil, where her return cargo was completed and shipped, she passed the stormy Cape and arrived safe at Cadiz, having never in her four passages suffered any damage or lost a man.

Capt. Foote was warmly welcomed by his Spanish friends, to whom the detail of the difficulties he had encountered, and the manner in which they had been conquered, seemed so wonderful that they were confirmed in their previous idea that he must be under the special protection of the Saints or of Nuestra Señora herself, and that it was possible for *one* heretic to be saved. They urged him very strongly to undertake a third voyage, offering to guarantee twenty thousand dollars profit to himself, whatever might be the result of the adventure, and assuring him that the reputation he had acquired with them should not be lessened by any misfortune or evil casualty that might occur. He, however, was fixed in the de-

termination expressed in the extracts from his letters above quoted, and resisted the solicitations of
his friends, who were convinced that the favoring
care and protection of him by the Saints had been
so strikingly manifested in so many perils and
dangers, that they indicated very decidedly that
he was destined to be brought, eventually, into
the true Church, and saved among the company
of the faithful.

He was not only unwilling to resume those cares
and labors which anticipate the march of time,
but was satisfied with the gains he had already
acquired, and was anxious to begin a life of greater
quiet, in which he might indulge those feelings,
which having been gratified in one object, (that of
seeing the world as it appears in different countries,) turn to other objects for new sources of
gratification.

All the objects of his life beyond the acquisition
of the means of support and comfort for himself
and those dependent on him, were for the further-
ance of such designs as are intended to promote
the welfare of the community, and increase the
progress of refinement and civilization. In doing
this, however, he never displayed any ambition
to become conspicuous or acquire fame; but he
recognized the duties which devolved upon him as
a member of the community, and fulfilled them
faithfully.

In the subsequent events of his life he experienced a portion of the dangers and hazards of the

land, and overcame them as happily as he had those of the seas, and by a similar exercise of industry, discretion, and forethought.

CHAPTER XI.

CINCINNATI.

"The end and the reward of toil is rest."—BEATTIE.

Although Capt. Foote, at the termination of his second voyage around Cape Horn, was in the full tide of a successful career, and urged with very strong inducements to continue it, he felt that the cares and labors of body and mind which it required, were too great and exhausting to be compensated by any amount of success. He, therefore, persisted in his determination to abandon a career of life which would inevitably anticipate the march of time, and bring on premature old age.

The period to which he had looked forward for the enjoyment of the fruits of his labors and cares seemed to have arrived, and he determined not to continue the pursuit of wealth, until the desire of gain should swallow up those feelings of benevolence, charity and loving-kindness, for the indulgence of which wealth is chiefly to be desired—before every feeling and principle should be subjected to the desire of accumulation.

15

In 1827 he married Elizabeth, daughter of Andrew Elliott, Esq., of Guilford, and as he had always determined never to have the anxieties respecting the welfare of a wife and family on shore added to those which must necessarily weigh heavily upon him at sea, he resolved to exchange its dangers and toils for those of the land. Being provided with the means of averting such of those last as are most dreaded in prospect, he resolved to look around his own country, and select such a place of residence as should appear most eligible under all the circumstances which it was necessary to take into consideration in making such a choice.

After spending some time in visiting various parts of our country, he determined to relinquish his character of a citizen of the world, and become a citizen of Ohio and of Cincinnati, to which city his elder brother had emigrated some years previous, and had made some investments there in real estate for his account.

Being established there, he immediately began to take an interest in all matters that affected the prosperity of the city.

The first of these objects that was presented to his consideration, was "the Louisville and Portland Canal," for the construction of which a joint stock company had been chartered by the Legislature of Kentucky, with ample powers and privileges. Its object was to remove the obstruction to the free navigation of the Ohio, occasioned by the falls—as they were styled—of that river, they being dangerous rapids, and impassable by boats except during a few days in the year, when the river was raised by the annual freshets. This work, which was one that ought to have claimed the attention of the National government among its earliest cares for the commercial prosperity of our country, had been disgracefully neglected: most of our Eastern legislators probably thinking the taunt of John Randolph, that the Ohio was a river "dry in summer and frozen in winter," must have some grounds for its justification; and our Western men were then, as they have ever since been, too ready to submit to the dictation of Southern statesmen, and surrender the interest of their constituents to the (supposed) necessity of following in the train of party leaders—even in matters in which party principles were not concerned.* The removal of this obstacle in the way of the commerce of so large a portion of our country— the only course in which its products could find their way to suitable markets—for railroads had not then been invented, nor our canals to the lakes constructed—was manifestly one of the greatest requisites for the free trade of the Ohio Valley.† It

---

* We had some honorable exceptions from Ohio, some whom modern degeneracy had not tainted.

† That portion of the duties which we require at the hands of our National Legislature, consisting of the regulation of our commerce, including therein such provision of all the facilities for its operations, as the nation alone can give—has been exercised, not only unequally, but unjustly toward that large proportion of the inhabitants of our country, the citizens of the

was universally considered to be one of vital importance to the prosperity of Cincinnati; but notwithstanding this admission by all its citizens, very great efforts were required to induce them to further the object by becoming stockholders in the association. To this stock every one thought it the duty of *his neighbor* to subscribe, and of *himself* to commend that duty to others; just as every one thinks it the duty of his neighbor to practice the Christian virtues, and that his own duty is to censure him for his short comings in such practice.

Foote's subscription was the largest in Cincinnati, but few others, and those of small amounts, having been obtained in that city, to which it was

---

Great West. The internal commerce of the country is not only far greater in amount than our foreign commerce, but is of more importance to the progress of our country in improvement; and its comparative value is constantly increasing.

The aids of government toward that most important work, the Canal around the falls of the Ohio, doled out at different times in subscriptions for its stock, and making the tolls pay all the cost of the work, contrast strongly with the liberal disbursements of public money at the Pea-patch in the Chesapeake.

The taunt of John Randolph respecting the Ohio river may be laughed at as the senseless rhodomontade of a boy—of a boy so flattered and petted during his boyhood, that he was thereby continued a boy, mentally, all his life; a smart, sharp, and intelligent one, indeed, but only the more troublesome on that account.

The ridiculous idea put forth by Calhoun, that the government had no right to make improvements in rivers, unless they passed three States, is a specimen of special pleading too intricate and too much above popular comprehension for practical use in a popular government. The remarkable metaphysical talents of this gentleman could not be sufficiently appreciated by the people, and were never of any use in conducting the affairs of government, during the period in which he was the master spirit of a large party.

acknowledged to be of the greatest importance. and those few were most of them sold or abandoned on the calling in of the second and third instalments. The largest and most persevering stockholder was John Shackford, of St. Louis, whose aid was so essential that it, probably, saved the work from being abandoned, as a previous project of building one on the Indiana side of the river had been. This project (the Jeffersonville canal,) had been so far carried forward as that a competent engineer had been procured to superintend the work. He had made the necessary surveys, and directed a commencement of the excavations; and then the work was abandoned for the want of funds. In order to avoid such a catastrophe in the case of the Louisville and Portland canal, a deputation was sent to the East, to invite capitalists there to embark in the undertaking, and the work may be considered as indebted to Messrs. Shackford, of St. Louis, Ronaldson, of Philadelphia, and Hulme, of New York, for its completion. The former of these gentlemen embarked all his fortune and his credit, and the others not only invested large amounts in money, but gave much of their personal exertions and superintendence, until the work was completed. Some aid from government was obtained, but its grants were on a very contemptible scale, compared with those for the aid of foreign commerce, on our Eastern coasts and harbors. They were in the form of subscriptions to its stock.

15*

At an early period in the history of Cincinnati, when its future growth and prosperity appeared to be fully established, the need of a regular supply of water was seen to be necessary, not only for family purposes, but for supplying the wants of manufacturing establishments, which were beginning to be requisite for the supply (especially) of those heavy fabrics, the transportation of which from the seaboard imposed taxes too heavy to be borne by the early emigrants to our Western towns and farms. This want, a most energetic and accomplished man of business, Col. Samuel W. Davies, undertook to supply. He raised a substantial building of stone and brick, at low water mark of the river, for the accommodation of the lifting and forcing pumps, necessary to convey the water of the river to a reservoir, on a hill immediately north of the building. This reservoir was about three hundred feet above low water mark, and was near the eastern boundary of the city, and higher than its highest levels. He laid wooden pipes for carrying the water through the principal streets of the city, but its rapid increase soon showed that such pipes were insufficient to supply even a small portion of its requirements. The growth and extension of the city being chiefly to the westward, iron pipes, and those of larger calibre than would have been necessary, had the growth of the city been upwards on the river, as had ever been the course of our river towns, were needed.

Col. Davies, when he had devoted all his means
—his capital and credit—to the work, found that
he had but made a commencement, and there was a
necessity for a much larger amount of capital than
any individual in the West, at that time, could
furnish. He, therefore, proposed to put the works
into the hands of a joint stock company, and obtained a charter for the formation of such a company, which he endeavored, with his characteristic
energy, to organize. He found, however, the vis
inertia of the citizens in regard to public improvements, proportionate to their efforts for the increase of their individual fortunes. As in the
case of the canal stock, there was found a sufficient
number of citizens who considered it a public duty
of *others* to carry out Col. Davies' undertaking,
which was the extent of their public spirit in this
case. The prevalence of this opinion, however.
did not produce the desired practical result, and
the plan was on the point of being abandoned for
the want of funds. Under these circumstances
the following named gentlemen undertook to unite
with Col. Davies, and carry on the works; these
were Davis B. Lawler, Wm. Greene, Samuel E.
and J. P. Foote, and N. A. Ware, who, however,
soon sold his share in the establishment to George
Graham and Wm. S. Johnston. These gentlemen
constituted the "Cincinnati Water Company."
Samuel E. Foote was appointed its secretary, and
served in that office during its existence, without
compensation. In this office he brought into ex-

ercise that knowledge and capacity for business
by which he was always distinguished. All his
accounts and plans are models of correctness and
adaptation to the interest of the institution. The
company made extensive improvements, substituting iron for wooden pipes, in those streets that required the largest mains, establishing improved
pumps, enlarging the reservoirs, and generally
adapting the progress of the works to that of the
city. They, however, became weary of well doing
in the cause of the public, for which their returns
in money were not enough, and in reproaches and
abuse for demanding payment of water rents,
too much, for the comfort of their lives. They,
therefore, made an offer of the establishment to
the city, for a sum which—judging from the cost
of subsequent improvements—was less than half
what it would have cost to begin and carry forward the works to the state in which they then
were. The offer was submitted to a vote of the
citizens, and accepted, though similar, and, perhaps, more favorable offers had been previously
rejected. The water rents have been increased 50
to 100 per cent. since the sale, but they are, perhaps, not now too high, though as long as they
were much lower, and collected by a private company, they were intolerably oppressive.

The elegant mansion, built by Mr. Foote, on the
corner of Vine and Third streets, was for many
years, and until the fatal commercial crisis of 1837,
the seat of a liberal hospitality, where the visits

of relatives and friends formed a prominent portion of the enjoyments of social life.

Those pleasant reunions, established under the title of the Semi-Colon club, held their sessions there, and alternately at the adjoining residences of Charles Stetson and William Greene. At these meetings, a number of persons of both sexes, of the highest order of intellect and cultivation, assembled for the enjoyment of evenings of social relaxation, and rational amusement. Their mode of proceeding was to read such literary contributions as were sent in for the purpose, by the members of the club, after which such discussions ensued as might be elicited by what had been read. or by any other literary matter of interest at the time; music, sometimes alternated with readings and discussions, generally closed the sessions.

Among the founders of the club were the Rev. E. B. HALL and his highly accomplished lady, who had jointly and severally contributed valuable aid to the educational literature of our time, and also Judge TIMOTHY WALKER, whose contributions to educational, mathematical and legal science, contrasted strongly with his humorous contributions to the literature of the club. His death, in the prime of a most useful and laborious life, disappointed high hopes of future usefulness, and was considered, like that of JAMES H. PERKINS, a few years afterward, a public calamity. NATHAN GUILFORD, also the distinguished advocate of popular education, whose exertions in the cause of the public school system obtained for him the designation of the father of that system. Other contributors included names of high eminence, among them HARRIET BEECHER, afterward STOWE, whose papers have since been published in a volume entitled "The May Flower," and dedicated to the club. Judge JAMES HALL, whose reputation was already established, as an author of high and varied talents. His articles were published in the magazine, of which he was at that time the editor. Miss CATHARINE BEECHER, whose fame and literary works have been widely disseminated before and since, some of whose contributions to the Semi-Colons have been published in annuals and magazines. Professor HENTZ, an accomplished naturalist, and his wife, Mrs. CAROLINE LEE HENTZ, who became a very popular novelist; Rev. Professor STOWE, already celebrated as one of the most learned scholars of our country; E. P. CRANCH and U. T. HOWE, some of whose very amusing articles were published in a newspaper which they conducted, but the best and wittiest of which are still inedited: some of them had their attractions increased by exquisitely humorous illustrations from the pencil of the former; Professor O. M. MITCHEL, now of world-wide celebrity as an astronomer; CHARLES W. ELLIOTT, historian of New England, and author of various other works of merit; Dr. DANIEL DRAKE, of extensive and established fame as a medical author and professor; BENJ. DRAKE, his brother, author of the lives of Tecumseh and Black Hawk, and other works. mostly on Western statistics and history; E. D. MANSFIELD, his associate in his statistical works. and author of many biographical and other works of great merit; Professor JAMES W. WARD, poet and naturalist of fine and varied talents; DAVIS B. LAWLER, JAMES F. MELINE, Judge CHARLES P. JAMES. Dr. WOLCOTT RICHARDS, D. THEW WRIGHT, JOSEPH LONGWORTH, J. NEWTON PERKINS, EDWARD KING, CHARLES STETSON, T. D. LINCOLN, WM. P. STEELE, GEORGE C. DAVIES, and some other gentlemen whose contributions are still in manuscript. JAMES H. PERKINS, whose extraordinary and versatile talents were as much admired as their possessor was beloved, and whose untimely death shed a gloom over the city —over the poor to whom he was a missionary, carrying in his visits temporal relief and spiritual instruction—as well as over an admiring and extensive circle of friends in the highest classes of society; WM. GREENE. eminent as a political writer, and expositor of the principles of our Constitution; CHARLES D. DRAKE and C. B. BRUSH, whose poetical contributions graced some of the periodicals of the period; three Misses BLACKWELL, two of whom have since become eminent M. D's., and all of them valuable contributors to the literature and science of the age, three other ladies, whose names have since been changed, with others distinguished for intellectual qualities, constituted a literary galaxy which could scarcely

have been equalled at that time in any city of our
country.   The cultivation of musical taste and
talent has always been a prominent portion of
female education in Cincinnati.   From the earliest
period of its history this has been remarked by
travelers and visitors, and among the Semi-Colon
ladies, it was a matter of course that there should
be those whose excellence in that department was
equal to that of the best of the literary contributors.

These reunions began and terminated at early
hours, and expensive luxuries in food and drink being rigidly prohibited, the health of the members
was not endangered, (nor the reputation of their
neighbors);—intellectual food of a quality superior
to any thing afforded by the highest style of cook-
ery, and more wholesome than personal gossip, not
only for the mind, but for the body also, being
served up.   Visitors of congenial minds and talents were frequent guests, the members of the club
having the privilege of inviting friends to accompany them to the meetings.   Among those visitors
who gave and received much gratification by their
attendance, HOFFMAN, the highly gifted and unfortunate, is remembered as one whose company was
peculiarly pleasing, who gave no reason from any
peculiarity in his actions or conversation to apprehend the approach of the melancholy calamity
that afterwards destroyed the early promise of a
mind of talents, and of accomplishments of the
highest order, and overwhelmed one who had

given testimony of his desire, and power to aid in
the elevation of the literary reputation of his
country, with the heaviest of human calamities.
Other visitors of varied talents and accomplishments were occasional guests, and added to the
amusement and instruction derived from such
meetings.

Sumptuary laws, it was well understood, could
not be enforced by private associations any better
than by governments and lawgivers: it was, however, understood to be one of the principles of the
club to discountenance extravagance in dress, and
luxury in entertainments, both by example, and
by avoiding discussions in which they might form
a prominent subject.

In one of the papers, giving an account of the
objects and intents of the institution, it is stated
that "semi-colonism acts upon the *public* welfare,
by increasing the amount of the *private* and domestic virtues, by extending the influences of
kindly feelings, and the intercourse of friendship.
and of the knowledge that public prosperity is
better promoted by the exercise of private virtues
than by acts grounded on maxims of political ex-
pediency." These remarks were contained in an
article written to prove, among other equally important matters which seemed to call for proof.
that "fist-fighting in the Halls of Congress, and
meetings by its members at Bladensburgh, to commit murder—which at that time constituted a dis-
tinguishing portion of Congressional proceedings

16

—were not essential to the public welfare, and that
members of Congress were not necessarily required to be bullies and brawlers in order to be qualified for the duties of their stations." These arguments were perfectly convincing—being addressed
to those who were already of the same opinion,
like political speeches to partizan assemblages—
but unfortunately the club neglected to send missionaries into "the District," to propagate their
doctrines, and in consequence the heathenish darkness which prevailed in that benighted region, at
that period, still reigns there with scarcely dimin-
ished gloom. "Murder" has been "one of the
fine arts" of the late Congress, applauded and
approved as well when an Irish waiter was its subject, as when an adulterer in high life gave it more
eclat. The influence of the club, though lost to
the nation's representatives, was not equally un-
profitable to the morals and manners of the higher
classes of society in Cincinnati. For from that
period to the present, there has not been, in those
classes, any examples of murders, duels, breaking
the heads of gentlemen while sitting quietly at
their desks, nor any of the other Congressional
proceedings of that kind, by which members occasionally exhibit their talents and fitness for the
office of legislators for a free people, whose free institutions can only be preserved by virtuous principles. Had the club sent missionaries to "the
District" at the proper period, and had they exercised their functions in a Christian spirit, it is

probable that a commencement of civilization might have been made in that semi-civilized region—some lives might have been saved, and some characters—among them that of our country —been preserved from many of the foul stains that grieve the hearts of the good, and give courage to the vile, by lowering those to whom they ought to look for good examples, to their own level.

The club continued in existence many years, and until the fearful commercial catastrophe of 1837 swept like a flood over the country, and occasioned a domestic revolution proportionate in its effects to those crises, as they are styled, which, since 1789, (and before,) have been historical events in the annals of commerce, both in Europe and America. The losses and misfortunes inflicted upon individuals and families at that period, were no respectors of persons, like hurricanes, earthquakes, and conquerors, they carried desolation very impartially to all in their course, especially to all commercial cities. The banks failed, and individuals were compelled to follow their example.

Although Mr. Foote was not concerned in any business except that of the Water Company, he had lent his name so freely to his friends, that he thought it incumbent on him to make important changes in his manner of life. He sold his elegant mansion with its adjoining buildings, (one-third of the price of which would have paid all

his own debts,) gave mortgages on the other portion of his real estate, to cover all his liabilities,
and directed his attention to the object of dis-
charging them as soon as possible. The banks
granted him all the indulgence he asked, and he
directed his attention to the sale of property for
this purpose. After the sale of the Water Company property, he accepted the office of Secretary
to the Whitewater Canal Company, and afterward
the same office in the Ohio Life Insurance & Trust
Company, which office he held until he had so
regulated his affairs as to be free from all liabilities, and in the enjoyment of an income equal to
his desires. He then resigned his office, and determined to return to his native State, and pass
the residue of his life in the neighborhood of the
scenes of his boyhood, and among his early associates, of whom a large portion still remained
there; some had emigrated, but few had died.

One of the reasons assigned by him for his desire to remove from Cincinnati, was his disagree-
ment in the opinion which he thought too prevalent in the West generally, and in this city particularly, of the superiority of the rights of children to those of parents. He did not object specially to the modern doctrine of the rights of women,
if carried into effect consistently with other rights,
and desired to have them recognized and increased
as far as reasonable and proper. But he thought
that *men* ought to possess some rights, and especially
that of directing the education of their children, and

keeping them under suitable restraints during its progress. In Connecticut the old English system of keeping children in a state of slavish submission to their parents, had been sufficiently relaxed; in the West it seemed to have been reversed, from an idea often acted upon, that the reverse of any wrong is right. In New Haven, the institutions for the education of youth of both sexes were of the highest class, having received as many of the modern improvements as sound judgment and discretion could approve. In addition to the long established seminaries, a semi-military school for boys had been founded under the direction of competent teachers, and in which the discipline bore a softened resemblance to that of West Point. as well as the modes and themes of instruction. Mr. Foote approved of this system, and the education of his son was commenced under it.

In addition to the educational advantages of New Haven, he believed that the climate of New England would be found more salutary to his family than that of Cincinnati, there being no consumptive tendencies in any member of it.

He purchased a beautiful situation on Whitney avenue, of about twenty acres, formerly the property of General David Humphreys, of revolutionary and poetic fame; afterward purchased by a Scotch gentleman from the South, who improved it considerably, and gave it the Scottish name of "Windy Knowe," which was found to be sufficiently characteristic. But the keen sharp winds of New

16*

England were found too severe for a constitution adapted to a southern climate, and Mr. Campbell, the proprietor, was obliged to abandon it. Mr. Foote immediately on taking possession began that system of improvements in ornamental horticulture, which caused it to be reckoned among the most beautiful suburban villas in that city of beautiful villas. He also commenced that system of agricultural experiments which he supposed might be made useful to the farmers of that region, some results of which will be found in extracts from his letters in another chapter.

CHAPTER XII.

HORTICULTURE AND AGRICULTURE.

———

" And thy sea-marge steril and rocky hard.

My bosky acres and my unshrubb'd down,
Rich scarf to my proud earth."—SHAKESPEARE.

———

During his residence at New Haven, Mr. Foote was distinguished, as he had ever been, by an extensive and liberal hospitality. This virtue was with him the cultivation and display of a strongly developed native taste, which his extensive knowledge and genial nature, combined with a peculiar vein of quiet humor, rendered exceedingly attractive to his associates. It was also in connection with his horticultural and agricultural operations and experiments, a means of supplying that need of excitement which is generally felt by persons who have retired from active business, for the enjoyment of that ease to which they look forward during their period of anxious toil and restless activity. The promises of increased happiness in retirement they, however, generally find as delusive as they have often found "promises to pay" in the course of their business.

The disappointments so common in such cases are generally caused by a neglect to educate the mind and heart in the love and true appreciation of the beautiful in nature, and the cultivation of good taste, which is its fruit. The success of this cultivation is as soon and as strikingly manifested in the improvement and adorning of garden and park grounds, as in any mode of its display. "Windy Knowe" was a specimen, not only of good taste in that portion of the grounds devoted to horticultural and floral embellishments, but of success in demonstrating the power of scientific agriculture over soils apparently almost barren, and as farming land considered nearly worthless.

The ungenial climate of New England can not be changed by any amount of scientific skill, but the products which can endure that climate, and flourish under its influences, may be made as remunerative to the farmer as those of more favored climates, if the necessary knowledge be obtained in regard to their cultivation, and only those which are well adapted to soil and climate be cultivated. In a letter giving an account of his success in his agricultural experiments, Foote says: "I have just dug 253 bushels of potatoes, from five-sixths of an acre of ground, and shall have 80 bushels of corn from an acre, and 800 bushels of carrots from three-fifths of an acre, and that is as well as you can do in Ohio with only common cultivation."

His experiments in this department were not made with any view of profit to himself, but were undertaken for the purpose of exhibiting the advantages of an improved system of agriculture to the farmers of New England, the need of which the recollections of his early youth, when he was one of them, was deeply felt. And this he considered one of the methods of paying the debt due to society from all its members. The other methods of paying this debt by contributions to useful public institutions, he did not neglect, nor did he ever seem to consider, (as some appear to do,) that, as a member of the community, he was entitled to receive as much as he was required to pay.

The following extracts from his letters during this period, are characteristic, and show that the genial, pleasant humor, which made him so delightful a companion, was not confined to his social conversation. His letters abound with the same light and easy humor, intermingled occasionally with paradoxes similar to those which he liked to propound for the purpose of exciting discussion. It is a matter of regret, that many of his most interesting and characteristic letters have been lost. None of them were written like Horace Walpole's, Pope's, Swift's, and other eminent authors, for publication, or with any idea that they would ever be seen except by the friends for whom they were intended. In consequence, all his characteristic traits contained in them, are so mixed with private individual circumstances, that only short extracts can be given from any of them.

In reply to a letter from his intimate friend, Dr. Ramsey, containing complaints of the various disasters in his pomological labors, and his agricultural experiments, he says: "Of course the leaves fall off the pear trees, and the fire-blight kills them, and the pears crack; and the peach trees have the yellows, and the cherry trees burst the bark, and the plums are all stung by the curculio. The apples are all stung by insects, and the trees killed by the borer. The wheat is eaten by the weavel, and the corn is killed by the frost, the potatoes rot, and the carrots have the August blight, and the bagworms cover the forest trees, and the melons have no sweetness, the raspberries shrivel up, and the gooseberries mildew, the red spider kills all the flowering plants, and the green fly eats up the roses, and the mealy bug covers every green thing. I might go on all the morning with the pests we farmers are subject to, and yet farming is considered such a very safe business, and a farmer's life exempt from care and anxiety. Why the anxiety a farmer has on the subject of rain or no rain, is greater than that of the merchant* or mariner, or Wall street stock broker, in all their operations."

---

* He seems to have forgotten the anxieties complained of in his letters from Buenos Ayres and Lima, or rather, this may be considered one of the paradoxes he took delight in.

His hospitable feelings were in constant operation, and nothing was so gratifying to him as to have his house filled, and his table surrounded with friendly faces. Invitations to his friends were frequent in his peculiar vein of pleasantry, of which the following are examples:

"Are you aware that there are in this region vast numbers of clams, lobsters, blackfish, and oysters? which are all living in the highest state of surprise and wonderment, that you do not come on, and brighten the chain of friendship that formerly bound you together in such loving intimacy, and the more especially that your unhappy fresh water country appears to be now threatened with another visitation of cholera, the just punishment of those foolish and reckless persons who hew out to themselves cisterns which will hold no salt water. I wish you would take the matter into your serious consideration, and let there be an 'effectual calling' upon you to visit the home of your fathers, and sit down upon the clam banks, and feed from the lobster pots that gave them strength in the day of trouble, to extirpate the savage from this land, and drive back the civilized invader of their liberties." * * "You Western people put off coming to the sea shore too long; I wish you and M. were here now, for the country is exceedingly beautiful in the spring, when every thing is bursting out fresh and green, and our sweet-fern and bay-berry, and sweet-briar, and honey-suckle are so very fragrant, and seem so healthful, and we have so many beautiful flowers, too, and the birds sing so sweetly, that it seems strange a sensible man can waste his life on Pacific railroads, and public improvements, and all the modern contrivances for destroying the happiness, and shortening the lives of the poor dupes, who are running from one end of the earth to the other, with as little purpose as a kitten runs after its own tail."

On the following spring he writes in a different vein.   *   *   *   "We have had such a long dreary, rain storm, that we are all in the dumps; our spring is entirely behind the age: trees have scarcely begun to show that they intend to have any leaves, and there is not a blossom in the fields.   *   *   *   We begin to have a faint hope that gooseberries may ripen between this and October: luckily I pulled up all my peach trees last fall, and thereby saved them from being winter killed. I do not perceive that the cold winter and late spring have had any material effect upon the trap rock in our vicinity, but I know of nothing else that has escaped injury.   I have not yet planted my corn, and the crows and blackbirds who were waiting to pull it up, have got tired, and gone off to some more genial climate.   *   *   *   I have not seen K. since she came on, but understand that she is getting on as comfortably as can be expected at a watering place, where every possible inconvenience is condensed, and you are in the focus. The moral and physical energy required to contend against the inherent evils of hotel life, give

a stimulus to the system which I suppose is beneficial, but like sea-bathing in winter, requires more
resolution than I can command." * * * *
"We have at last a few days of real spring weather,
and are beginning to hope that the angels have
not been skewing the world out of its proper
sphere, as Milton says they did after the 'Fall.'
Since the Dred Scott decision of Judge Taney, I
have had my fears that it might be considered as
a kind of second 'Fall,' and that these same angels
might have been tampering with the world's axis
again. * * But I am beginning to recover my
confidence in the stability of the present arrangement of the seasons and climates of the world.
* * * In short, every thing in nature seems
to intend to go on in the old way, just as if Judge
Taney had never made the astonishing discovery
that men of African descent have no rights which
white men are bound to respect."

The cold winter of '55-56 is alluded to in the
following extract, 6th February: "It is now ten
o'clock A. M., with a very bright sunshine, and the
thermometer in my back porch stands at 2° below
zero, and I suppose the mercury would go much
lower if it were not afraid of freezing. We are
satisfied with it, however, as long as the sun shines
so brightly. If it were cloudy, we would not
mind letting it go down as low as 20° below, which
we think is as far as any respectable thermometer would wish to go. 7th. The thermometer was
so pertinacious in its determination to go steadily

17

downward during the whole day, yesterday, notwithstanding the brightest kind of sunshine, that I thought I would wait and see where it would go to; at sun down it was 12° below zero, at sun rise this morning it was 15° below, where it was during night I do n't know." * * "We have not made up our minds whether we shall starve or not, after eating our cows and chickens. We all feel so dreadfully sorry for poor old Buchanan, who has got himself into such a tight place, (or rather has been driven into it by his Southern masters,) that we have little appetite, and therefore our stock may last longer than we feared, and especially so if we should be obliged to swallow Robert J. Walker, and Stephen A. Douglas, with our cows and chickens, as I fear we shall have to do." March 6. * * "You ought to have been here this winter—it has been such a real old fashioned one—eight weeks of fine sleighing—thermometer below zero—trees all broke down by ice and sleet—people all starving with cold and hunger—horses all ruined by overdriving—next year's fruit all destroyed in the bud—Kansas proclamations by Pierce—Southern domination established—dough-faces bought and sold—every thing in a nice way expects to be nicer."

"You will have seen by the papers, that we have recently lost our two most eminent divines, Dr. Croswell and Dr. Taylor, and I much fear that neither you nor I will live to see their places supplied; for I am satisfied—as all other men of

ripe age since the flood have been—that the world
and the people that inhabit it are growing smaller
every day, and, if possible, more dishonest.   *   *
Our 'Know Nothing' brother is getting on very
well, and I expect to see him this morning on his
way to Hartford, to resume his legislative duties.
But I am afraid that legislating is a business that
does not suit him.   Once before when he tried it,
it made him sick, and it ought to have that effect
on any one who is accustomed to the honest simplicity and sweet breath of oxen and cows.   *   *
The world has been so long governed by men who
did not know anything, and yet made much pre-
tension to superior wisdom, that I think it rather
a good omen they are now openly assuming their
true character."   *   *   *   "Some of our old companions in Guilford have died lately.   J. T. and
Mrs. G. L., both at the early age of sixty-five, and
I should not be surprised if the climate of Guilford, and the habits of its people, should become
so corrupt, that the average age of the inhabitants
should not exceed seventy-five years."

The agricultural experiments to which we have
referred, were made in pursuance of a resolution
adopted in the early portion of his life, to devote,
if successful in his career, some portion of his
time to improvements and experiments for the
benefit of that class of men among whom the first
part of his life had been 'passed, the farmers of
New England.   Their indifference to improved
systems of agriculture, and book farming, as it

was styled, has since that period, happily, been repented of by the intelligent and industrious among them, and the want of neatness: good order, and systematic management is not so marked a characteristic of our farmers as it was formerly. Good order and good taste, he considered two of the cardinal virtues in farming, which were most uniformly neglected, through which neglect much of the distaste of young men for a country life devoted solely to agriculture is generated. It is true that most of those who leave the farm for more exciting and more hazardous pursuits, generally intend to return when they become rich, and to spend the last years of their lives in making agricultural improvements. But of the few who are successful enough to be able to fulfill their intentions, scarcely any can find happiness in being relieved from the excitements and cares which they think are sources of unhappiness when they are obliged to suffer them in their business operations. Haste to get rich, which since the time of Solomon—and probably long before—has been the besetting sin of young men, and a theme of warning for old ones, generates tastes and habits which prevent riches from yielding the happiness that is expected from them. Fortunately for themselves, very few of those hasty young men ever succeed, and being obliged to struggle continually, are happier in their struggles than they could be in the fulfillment of their hopes and wishes.

Hope, if properly based and directed, is the healthiest of mental excitements. It forms the quiet, peaceful enjoyment of the farmer in preparing his grounds, and planting them for the future harvest, as well as of the merchant in planning his voyages, and sending forth his ventures. Hope deferred, however, seems to be a heavier burden for Americans to bear than for any other people, an overweening anxiety to see the result of whatever they undertake, being one of their strongly marked characteristics. That restless activity which flows from it seems (especially to foreigners who are frequently remarking it as one of the defects of our national character,) inconsistant with the true enjoyment of life. It has, however, had a marked effect on our history, and been the stimulant of our rapid rise as a nation, from almost insignificance to the highest rank among the powers of the world in little more than half a century. A rapid extension, not only of territory, but of every kind of improvement demanded by the progress of civilization, unparalleled in the history of the world, is among the consequences. But, on the other hand, one of the results to individuals is, that whenever their railroad rapidity in the career they are pursuing is checked, they become unhappy, and are very apt to try to keep up their excitements by stimulants which hasten their progress to the grave.

The New Englanders who stay at home, and cultivate their farms quietly, are generally very

17*

long lived.   The emigrants from New England, a much larger class, are not remarkable for this characteristic.   They, however, accomplish more during a short life than the others in a very long one, and more than the natives of any other country.   This is strikingly manifested in our Western States and Territories, where towns and cities rise "like exhalations," and railroad locomotives "shine like meteors," and seem to be chasing away the original forests; becoming, with other modern conveniences, regular institutions in those regions settled by New Englanders, within periods so short as to be unexampled in the history of human improvements.   The will of a despot, who could command the labors of hundreds of thousands of men to build such cities as St. Petersburgh, in modern times, or the Egyptian or Assyrian cities in remote periods, could raise up palaces and cottages with marvellous rapidity, but could only fill them with masters and slaves.*   They could not build up such cities as Cincinnati and Chicago, and provide for all their inhabitants such systems of universal education, as would make them all understand their rights and duties.   They could

---

* De Tocqueville considers a (political) aristocracy one of the most effective means of protecting the people from the encroachments of the despotism to which democratic governments have a natural tendency.   That this s true in relation to democratic governments which are centralized, may be believed from the testimony of history, as well as from personal observation.   In the United States, however, the federal principle of a union of states, with separate governments, gives us the protective advantages of an ristocracy without its oppressive tendencies.   But universal education is

not substitute the ballot box for guards to protect their persons, nor dispense with standing armies, from a reliance on the intelligence and patriotism of the people.

---

the only effective preservative of such a federal union as ours. In communities in which there is an educated and an ignorant class of population, as in most countries, the power of numbers is controlled by the power of intellect, and a feeling on the part of the latter class that they are oppressed by the former, is very apt to be felt, and generally with reason, for the love of power, like the love of money, grows with what it feeds on. But freedom to acquire knowledge and wealth will always restrain a people from violent measures for the acquisition of objects desired. " The Union " will be preserved, if the educated class in the South are sufficiently numerous to retain the ascendancy, and the ignorant (including " fire eaters " and demogogues of all kinds) kept in proper subjection.

CHAPTER XIII.

NEW HAVEN.

"———— whatever day
Makes man a slave takes half his worth away."—POPE.

The opinions of the citizens of New Haven on the question of negro slavery, were more nearly equally divided than in almost any other of the towns of New England. They, therefore, supposing that the stability of the Union was endangered by the intemperate discussions which convulsed the country, determined to invite two gentlemen, each holding opposite opinions on the question, to give their different views on this subject in public lectures.

On the pro-slavery side of the question, Mr. Fitzhugh, of Virginia, who had written a book to show "The failure of Free society," was chosen. His opponent was Mr. Wendall Phillips, extensively and favorably known as an anti-slavery advocate. Each of these gentlemen accepted Mr. Foote's invitation to become his guest at Windy Knowe, during his stay at New Haven. The former was a person of pleasing manners, and genial

disposition, bred in that region where the best
aspects—the least repulsive features—of negro
slavery are exhibited, and who evidently had full
faith in the doctrines he promulgated. Mr. Foote,
who held these doctrines to be political and moral
heresies, undertook to exhibit his arguments for
their refutation in the form of facts—facts which,
like figures, don't lie—the inference from which
he considered must be decidedly opposite to those
contained in Mr. Fitzhugh's book, and he entertained that respect for his guest which gave him
confidence in the result of their influence upon his
opinions.

He rode with him throughout all the streets of
New Haven, and directed his attention to every
thing in its vicinity, showing him that it contained
no abodes of squalid poverty—that nearly every
dwelling of even the poorest of the laboring classes,
had a neat, comfortable appearance, that, literally,
no cases of suffering from want of the necessaries
of life existed in the city, and that no poor-tax
was assessed on its inhabitants. This was exclusively the result of free labor, and nothing else,
for the commerce of the city was small, and had
declined (most of it having been transferred to
New York,) with the increasing prosperity of the
community, the lands were not naturally fertile,
but required much care and labor for their cultivation, and no government works brought any of
the public expenditures to New Haven. Attention
was especially called to the beautiful suburban

village of Fair Haven, established and supported entirely upon the cultivation and traffic in oysters brought from Virginia, and planted in the flats of the Quinnipiac river, near its mouth. These flats extend two or three miles upwards, and the grounds under water in that locality are subdivided among different proprietors, with the same care and attention to ownership as the dry land, and they yield as profitable crops, which supply the interior towns with a luxury of which the consumption is constantly increasing. The wealth of Fair Haven is also continually on the increase, for the oyster crops depend entirely on the industry of their cultivators, they never fail for want of rain, or from late frosts, or severe winters.

These "proofs and illustrations" appeared to have their proper influence on the mind of Mr. Fitzhugh, and he remarked that he must modify his opinions upon the subject of free labor. He had evidently acquired some new ideas on the subject of the superior benefits of slavery, by his visit to New Haven.

Mr. Phillips, whose fame as a zealous anti-slavery advocate, was as extensive as our country, was also a gentleman in private life, whose society was peculiarly pleasing, and his talents, although chiefly directed to labors for the extension of human freedom, were such as would command respect and fame in other departments. He possessed the advantage of a more extensive popularity than his opponent in New England, though the minority that adopted the views of that gentleman, was very large in Connecticut, for in that State the repulsive features of negro slavery had never been exhibited, and it was one of the States of the North where it lingered so long that it may be said to have there died a natural death.

The result of the public discussions was similar to that which usually follows such discussions, on any controverted subject of deep interest;—like that, for instance, between Robert Owen and Alexander Campbell, on the social system of the former, and the Christian religion as upheld by the latter, or that between the Rev. Mr. Hill and Daniel Roe, on the Roman Catholic and the New Church (Swedenborgian) doctrines—and like every other public discussion of deeply interesting subjects, furnishing each party with supplies of arguments for strengthening the previous belief of the hearers, but seldom changing the opinions of any of them.

The following extracts from letters written at subsequent periods, give strong expression of his sentiments and feelings on the slavery question, as the events of the period called them forth. That question had become the dividing theme of the two great parties into which our country always has been and probably is destined always to be divided. The danger of the dissolution of the Union has been so often made a theme of ambitious demogogues, for use in stump speeches, that he regarded it as one of those dangers which have been impending over the country at the time of almost every Presidential election, and which have subsided immediately after the story has been told by the ballot boxes, which like figures, and unlike stump orators, do not lie. His sentiments on this subject were deeply felt and strongly expressed. Although he had many dear friends among the slave holders, whose situation he could appreciate correctly, he never disguised his sentiments on the subject with them. But he was ready to do them justice, and in conversation with Northern abolitionists he would sometimes appear to them to be the advocate of slavery.

At the period above referred to, he expressed his feelings very freely in his correspondence, specimens of which are given in the following extracts:

* * * "It is all idle to think of putting down the pro-slavery feeling in so religious a community as that of New England, and I do not intend to fight against it any longer; Moses and the Prophets are against me, and the Apostles are not on my side—'the glittering generalities' that you shall not oppress your neighbor, and that you shall 'do unto others as you would they should do unto you,' have not a feather's weight against the *direct* authority of Moses, that you *shall* buy slaves of the heathen, and leave them as an inheritance to your children, and that you may whip them to death without being answerable for it, *because they are your money,* etc., etc. * * We have been

much edified by the late decision of the Supreme Court in the Dred Scott case, and think that after Kansas has been admitted as a slave State, and the Lemmon case decided in our favor, (as they certainly *will* be,) we shall be able to take higher and more *Constitutional* ground, and after Virginia has replenished her treasury by the sale of all her free negroes, I see no good reason why she should not be authorized to replenish her population by sending it into the free States, and buying or stealing such of the young men and women of the lower order—"greasy mechanics," etc.,—as she may find desirable, either for home consumption, or to send South for sale. There cannot be the slightest question as to the Constitutionality of such a proceeding, as it is evident that the true meaning of the clause "to secure the blessings of liberty to ourselves and posterity," means, to secure them to all born white south of Mason and Dixon's line —the universal opinion of the civilized world, that the "greasy mechanics," and other laboring classes, are an inferior class of beings, can't be disputed— and the idea that the framers of the Constitution, being of the FIRST FAMILIES OF VIRGINIA, or other Southern States, should have thought of guaranteeing them the same rights and privileges claimed by themselves, is too preposterous to be thought of for a moment. This argument might be continued after the manner of Judge Taney, and made equally satisfactory and conclusive, but I think it unnecessary, and every right-minded person who

18

is a friend to the Union, will see at a glance that the framers of the Constitution never had the remotest idea that the cotton fields of the South should be deprived of laborers by the shallow pretence that the Constitution was intended to guarantee the blessing of liberty to persons born north of Mason and Dixon's line, and especially those of the lower orders—and should a doubt ever arise on the subject, I think it will be set at rest by the uniform practice of Southern politicians, of buying and selling Northern dough-faces ever since the government has been established."   *   *   *

*   *   August, 1856.   "We are at this moment firing a grand salute in honor of the glorious victory of the Slave-Power over those d—d Abolitionists that infest the House of Representatives. A clean army bill is passed, and there is nothing now to prevent Gen. P. Smith from driving all those infamous Free State men out of Kansas, and establishing our beloved *peculiar institution* on a firm and solid basis.

*   *   *   Are you going to elect Fremont? and is it best that he shall be elected? I am rather disposed to think not; for I have a strong desire to have Mr. Toombs boast of calling the roll of his slaves under the shadow of Bunker Hill monument, literally verified, and I do not wish to have any invidious distinctions made respecting color, as I am perfectly satisfied that the whites will make just as good slaves as the blacks, if you only give them a chance.   *   *   *   I am

afraid it will take a great deal more cudgelling
than we have had yet, to convince New England
that she can sell her tin-cups and wooden nutmegs
to the Southern chivalry just as well *after* they
have dissolved partnership, as *before;* until this is
done, we have only to take patiently whatever insolence and scourging it may please our Southern
friends to vouchsafe us. The Legislature of Connecticut is now sitting here in New Haven, and
every morning Mr. Toucey has a larger number of
votes for U. S. Senator than any other man. So
long as such a state of things continues, it is to
be hoped that one or more Free State Senators or
Members will be assaulted and thoroughly beaten
every day—that a Yankee school master will be
shot down, or tarred and feathered, at least three
times a week—that all Free State women living
in a Slave State will be imprisoned and kept without fire and clothes or bed to sleep on, more especially if in weak health—and that any respectable
New England man, found in any Southern city,
will be immediately expelled therefrom by mob
violence, even should he be there in an ambassa-
dorial capacity from a sovereign and friendly State.
I think of selling my place here, and going South
to engage in the negro breeding business. I could
no doubt make it profitable, and it is becoming so
highly respectable that it would be worth a man's
while to enter into it at merely a moderate profit:
will you join me?   *   *   *   But enough
of this—I am sick and tired of it—and E. has be-

come so excited and nervous about Kansas and
Sumner affairs, that I have had to take her to New
York, until thought and feeling should get into
the channel of new silks and bonnets, and become
quieted.

*   *   *   "I hope you compromise people
will feel comfortable when Douglas gets his Ne-
braska bill through, as I expect he will. If I were
in the place of Chase and Sumner, and the other
Abolitionists, I would not only vote for Douglas'
bill, but would introduce a new one, which should
compel every State hereafter admitted to the
Union, to be a Slave State, whether they *would or
not*. The policy of such a movement is so obvious
that I am surprised the Free Soil party has never
adopted it. Had it not been for the curse of slavery, the States of Virginia and Kentucky would
now have had the supreme control of the whole
Union—the port of Alexandria would have been
the New York of the country, the cotton mills of
Massachusetts and Rhode Island would have been
on the Potomac—New York would have remained
a Dutch Province, and Pennsylvania a German
one, and Ohio would still be a wilderness. What
folly then for the Free States to put it in the power
of their neighbors to take the bread from their
mouths. I believe if this ground were taken and
stoutly maintained by the Free Soil and Compromise parties, that in five years the politicians
of the Southern States would be as clamorous for
Abolition as they now are for *Extension*."

The visit of Kossuth to this country, of course, excited his attention; and the following extracts from his letters exhibit the feelings and opinions called forth on the occasion. White slavery in Europe did not seem to him to require so much of his attention as negro slavery in the United States, but human freedom, generally, was always a subject of interest to him.

The besetting sin of the people of this country is to overdo every thing which is supposed to accord with the feelings of the people generally, and to atone for our want of a sufficient number of stated holidays for the people, by giving occasional ones, whenever circumstances are favorable for them.

*   *   *   "I suppose no one is aware of the amount of suffering he can bear till he is tried. I was perfectly satisfied some time since that reading all the speeches that Kossuth had delivered in England and America—and some of them capital good ones—together with all he had yet to deliver, would exceed the utmost limit of human endurance, but I find I was sadly mistaken—the little finger of the Morgan, Hodge and Long correspondence is thicker than Kossuth's loins, and yet one is obliged to read it or find himself behind the times. Our friend C—— is a raving Kossuth man, and like all other young men who are good for any thing, is perfectly satisfied that the world is about to be regenerated—that we must put our shoulders to the wheel, and the thing will be done;

18*

all that is necessary is to put down Tyranny and Oppression, and imbue the world with true Christian principles of doing as we would have others do to us—in short, he has adopted our friend L——'s theory, and insists upon it that the destiny of the world is in our hands, and that it is a shameful deviation from our imperative duties to suffer wrong and injustice any longer to show their heads on the face of the earth, and therefore we must fall down and worship Kossuth, and be led by H——. Should you not be able to perceive the necessary sequence, go to C—— or G—— and they will enlighten you. I suppose you wonder what all this has to do with you or me; with *you*, perhaps, it has little in common, but it makes it necessary for me, if I would not be put down and trampled upon, to read all Kossuth's speeches, and the interminable correspondence of our Naval and diplomatic 'Reeds,' when they are 'shaken by the wind' of a French Prefect or a Hungarian Refugee.

  *   *   * "Are you all as Kossuth mad in Cincinnati as we are here and in New York? if you *are*, the Lord have mercy on you; for *we* are past praying for. I should like very well to be a friend and partisan of the cause of Hungary and Kossuth, and liberty, and all that myself, if everybody were not making such Judys of themselves, and running the matter clear into the ground—out of sight. I hope if Kossuth *is* to be killed for the gratification of our rage for man-worship, it

will be before he is made a fool of—for I am disposed to believe he is a very clever fellow, and one who may be of great service in upsetting such severe despotisms as those of Naples, Austria, and Russia, if he is not poisoned by the slime of popular adulation. His wife, too, I like much, and think she ought to have a statue erected to her, with her answer to the 'woman's rights' deputation for the inscription on the base."

Louis Napoleon's coup d'etat called forth the following denunciation :

*   *   *   "I have little domestic intelligence to give you, and am so bamboozled by the public and political movements of the outside world, that I don't know what will become of me. Kossuth is insisting with an eloquence seldom, if ever equalled, that we shall commit ourselves body and soul to a crusade to redeem the down-trodden millions of Europe, from the iron rule of Despotism, at the same time, that one of its most enlightened nations, after an experience of many years of self-government in various forms, is allowing a trumpery 'Nephew of his Uncle' to assume and exercise over them a wantonness of despotism which would disgust the slaves of the Sublime Porte, or the Emperor of Morocco. I am perfectly bewildered with the idea that so poor a thing as Louis Buonaparte can, with a scratch of his pen, send hundreds of the best and most influential men in France to rot in the swamps of Cayenne, and thousands of them, including the high-

est and most popular of their military chieftains, to wander in homeless exile—that the whole people embodied as a National Guard, in precisely the form that one would suppose best adapted to prevent and put down such daring usurpation, should at his bidding quietly surrender their arms and uniforms, and break up a military organization which it has always been supposed was the only thing necessary to enable a people to resist any infringement of their liberties, or put down established despotisms, in short, all that Kossuth wants to establish freedom throughout the world—that an imbecile, twaddling bankrupt should establish himself in the Palace of the Tuileries, and send forth day by day, and hour by hour, decrees that Louis XIV. or the Emperor Napoleon would not have dared to think of—and all France seem to take it as a matter of course—that under such a state of things everybody should appear to be satisfied—that funds should rise and trade flourish—is it not enough to make one crazy?"

The long period of drought and hot weather in New England during the summer of 1856, is thus feelingly alluded to in one of his letters:

*   *   *   "Had you been here for the last fortnight you would have been fried brown. The hot weather in Cincinnati melts one down into a liquid pulp, here it fries us to a crisp, and I do not know which is the worst. For 67 years past the thermometer has told no such tales as during the last three weeks—so say the wise ones—in our

entry it has been between 80° and 90° every day but one, and it once rose to 91°. We have also had, and still have an unprecedented drought during the whole time. My potato crop is entirely ruined, and I shall not have half enough for my own use; my corn is nearly as bad, and I fear I shall not have enough to fatten my pigs; so you see that starvation stares us in the face, both on the animal and vegetable sides. Luckily the eating of horseflesh appears to be coming into use, and as I have plenty of hay, I hope to be able to get through the coming winter, and not in a coach, but on a horse."

As a contrast to this desponding state of feeling, we revert to the period of one of his early visits to Ohio, and give the following extracts of a letter written at the Yellow Springs, at a period when that delightful summer retreat was free from any of the contaminating influences of fashionable life, and when summer tourists had not lost that good taste which derives its enjoyments from what nature gives, and do not seek them in contentions and strife for superiority in dress, and in the various forms of the displays of wealth. The influence of the beautiful and fertile regions of the West, and their contrast with most of the countries he had visited, had a powerful influence in his selection of his place of residence.

July 16, 1828.—"Do you know where we are? why in the middle of the State of Ohio, in the most delightful place in the world—so cool and pleasant—such a fine healthy situation—such a romantic country—such lovely rides and walks—such a splendid chalybeate spring—such pleasant society—in short, the most beautiful summer retreat in the world. The country is like Connecticut, only pleasanter, and the people are many of them from thence—the choice spirits of the State picked out and congregated here to escape from the cares and bustle of life, and enjoy a few weeks of cool fresh air, and each other's society. We had a week or two of excessively hot weather before we left Cincinnati, and all got somewhat exhausted, and complaining, so we came up to lay in a stock of health and spirits to last us for the rest of the summer."

Some extracts of a more miscellaneous character are added. In a letter to a medical friend, he propounds one of his paradoxes on medicine.

"I am very much scandalized that you physicians, after two or three thousand years of study and experience, should be so utterly unable to cure any disorder that would not cure itself without you, and I verily begin to believe that the Homœpathists have the good sense of the matter in their practice, and a drop of camomile tea mixed with the whole water of Lake Superior is just as likely to cure any disease as the prescriptions of a physician.

Our children are very well; and they appear to be very happy, partly, I suppose, because they are well, and partly because we do not send them to school, or in any manner make old people of them. B. J. is very well, but has had a great deal of sickness in his family this winter, and Mrs. S. is still very far from well. Her husband being a physician, and all living in one family, would readily account for its general want of good health; but somehow or other the whole female population of the country seems to be destitute of any thing like good health, and it is almost literally true that I do not know a really healthy woman in the whole circle of my acquaintances. Can you give any good reason for this?"

Another specimen of the medical paradoxes which he liked to propound, is seen in the following extract:

*   *   "I have been quite edified by your address* to the homicides (that are to be) of Cincinnati and parts adjacent.   *   *   There is a matter in your address that I can hardly make up my mind to subscribe to. You assume that it is a more praiseworthy vocation to bind up the wounds and preserve the lives of soldiers than that of procuring them to be wounded and killed. The soldier hires himself out to be shot, and I think his employers are bound in good faith to perform their part of the agreement, and have him shot, and the surgeon who interferes in the matter is rather meddling with what does not concern him; unless he does it in the way of perfecting

* An address to medical students at their graduation

himself in his profession, in which case he should only be allowed to cut and carve in such a way as may be beneficial to himself, and not to his patient."

His opinions on the subject of railroad and steamboat accidents, and the dangers of the land, are given in his peculiar vein, in the following extract:

*   *   "I congratulate you on your safe arrival, without being ground up between broken railroad cars, or scalded, or burnt, or blown up on some steamboat. But you do not seem have kept up with the progressive age, in the matter of traveling. The idea that a man's comfort or even his life is a matter of as much importance, and to be attended to with as much care as the safe carriage and delivery of a package of goods, is altogether obsolete, and only referred to by persons who have become so old and broken down that they can amuse themselves in projecting, and endeavoring to make politicians assist them in making railroads across great continents, and through mountains so high that birds can not fly over them. I am afraid that you people of the olden time will never get over your prejudices respecting the value of the lives of men and women and children, and yet they would seem to have had a very proper estimate of them in the earlier ages of the world, when Timour could build a pyramid of skulls, or Herod send out and have all the children in Judea murdered in cold blood before breakfast, without

even having the matter alluded to in the morning papers. There is some comfort, however, in the knowledge that our 'fast' age is beginning to appreciate the soundness of the views of the men of old—not old men—and I see no reason why we may not, in the course of a few years be able to blow up a thousand people in a steamboat, or grind them up on a railroad with as much sang-froid as they used formerly to sack a city, and murder all the inhabitants."

Speaking of Jenny Lind, he says: *   *   * "I like her much, she has the only *good* voice I ever heard from a public singer, and if she would not be driven to execute these fantastic feats which *ought* to be impossible, she would be perfect. Personally she is exceedingly interesting."

"I have been much edified by your account of G——'s spiritual intercourse with his cook.   * *   * We have not been much troubled with spiritual matters lately except a small dab from C——.

*   * What a pity that you and I are so old that we cannot hope to see the time when our social intercourse will embrace the spiritual as well as the natural world, and when it will make very little difference whether our friends are dead or alive; with *some* of them, it is true, it makes very little difference *now*, but there are others with whom it would be a comfort to spend an evening occasionally.   *   *   *   *   * *   * September 4, 1854. "Our White Mt.

19

expedition was an entire failure.   *   *   S. and F. and L. made the trip, and had a very pleasant time. All such jaunts you know are very pleasant after you have got through with them, and have nothing to do but give glowing descriptions of all you have seen and heard and done, and make all those who could not go unhappy, in which they have been perfectly successful with E., but they will have to talk a great deal longer, and tell much bigger stories. before they produce much effect upon *me*."

CHAPTER XIV.

THE LAST OF EARTH.

"We cannot hold mortality's strong hand."—SHAKESPEARE.

During a residence of eight years in New Haven,—a period devoted chiefly to labors and experiments in Horticulture and Agriculture—the influence of an active life in pure open air doubtless had a tendency to preserve the health and energies of Mr. Foote unimpaired until the period of his last sickness, in October, 1858.

He had lived—in years—beyond the Scripture term of the ordinary life of man, and in acts and experience, a still longer period. For he not only began to be a man at a much earlier period of life than that in which boys are usually changed into men, but he performed a greater amount of manly labors in any given time of his early life, than any of his cotemporaries.

His time was seldom or never wasted during his early years; but the labors, anxieties, exposures and fatigues of that period necessarily affected his constitution, and rendered him less able to overcome disease in his old age. He had suffered two attacks of the diseases of tropical climates, (yellow fever in the West Indies, and a fever of somewhat similar character in Buenos Ayres,) and had been often exposed to the influences of sickly climates, which had been rendered innoxious to him through the exercise of prudence, temperance, and suitable precautions. But his system was necessarily so much worn as to render it incapable of resisting the attack of any violent disease, and that which terminated his existence was so violent in its attack as to cause great apprehensions of a fatal termination. As soon as the account of his condition reached the writer, he visited him, and found him in the condition described to him. After the first salutation, the sick man said, "I am an old man, my sands are nearly run out—I am going now, but you and George (his other brother) will soon follow,"—speaking as if he did not expect to be separated long from his friends, and exhibiting as much cheerful hope as his physical pain would permit. During his intervals of ease, his usual cheerful, pleasant humor, was so frequently exhibited, that although his excellent physicians, Professor Knight, of New Haven, and Dr. Rumsey, of Fishkill, (an intimate personal friend,) gave very small hopes of his recovery, his friends and family could not give up the expectation of a favorable change in the aspect of his disease, for it was hard to bring their minds to the belief that there could not be a longer period for their enjoyment of that social kindness, that easy, quiet humor, that sympathy with the suffering, and that general philanthropy by which he was characterized.

To his elder brother the idea had never occurred that he should be called to record the life and death of the younger. On the contrary, it was a consolitary hope with him that when called to depart, the paternal cares for those loved ones whom he must leave, would be continued for a while by a younger and more efficient brother.

On the morning of his death, the family were assembled in his room, some of them sitting and standing near his couch, when he desired to be raised up, but as soon as it was done he requested to be laid down again, and in the act a sudden painful spasm was seen to have seized him, and life was extinct in a moment. The painful expression of his countenance immediately passed off and was succeeded by a singularly beautiful expression of happiness, which, after a few hours, subsided into an appearance of a natural state of quiet, peaceful sleep.

The just appreciation of his character by his fellow citizens of New Haven, will be seen in the following obituary notices in the daily papers:

[From the New Haven News, Nov. 3d.]

DEATH OF SAMUEL E. FOOTE.—Another of our most respected citizens has departed. Mr. Samuel E. Foote, who died on Monday, Nov. 1, came to reside here some eight years since.

19*

After giving a sketch of his life, the following estimate of his character was added :

Few men, if any, whose time was not passed in public life, have ever produced in the community a profounder feeling of confidence and regard than Mr. Foote. It was so at Cincinnati—it was so here. His honor was above suspicion, and his intellect was clear and true as the diamond; while his sympathies for the suffering and oppressed were if anything too tender. Those who knew him least respected him, and those who knew him best loved him most. While then his family and friends mourn deeply their loss, our city too will regret the departure of one of her purest men.

The New Haven Journal gave a more extensive obituary, which is here copied in full :

Capt. Samuel E. Foote.—Within the memory of men now living, perhaps no year of general health has in New Haven been marked so much as this by the loss of so many of the most eminent and beloved of our older citizens. To the honored names of Dr. Taylor, Dr. Croswell, Hon. Henry E. Peck, John Fitch, Thomas Bennett, Thaddeus Sherman, Capt. Goodrich, Dr. Beers, Hon. Aaron N. Skinner, and others, must now be added that of Capt. Samuel E. Foote, who died of a disease of the heart, at his residence in this city, on Monday last, about nine o'clock, A. M., after an illness of about four weeks.

Capt. Foote was born in the town of Guilford, in this State, on the 29th day of October, 1787, and had therefore just finished his seventy-first year.

His early life was spent on a farm, from which like many others of the most enterprising and stirring young men of New England at that time, he passed to a life of peril and hardy adventure upon the sea. With such quickness of perception, such maturity of judgment, and such integrity as his he could not fail to make rapid advancement, and he accordingly was in full command of a ship before he had reached his twentieth year. His voyages were made to almost every quarter of the globe with which commerce was then carried on—to South America and the West Indies, to Africa, to the Mediterranean, and to the British Isles. He continued in this business for about twenty years, during which time his ship was once captured by privateers, and he lost the avails of his ventures.

About thirty-one years ago he retired from the sea, when he was married, and shortly afterwards settled in Cincinnati, where his character and talents soon placed him among the leading men.

He was a noble specimen of a gentleman. His personal appearance was striking. His snow-white beard so set off his fine expressive features, that the attention of every beholder was naturally attracted.

His nature was singularly sympathetic and kindly, and every way large. His sense of justice knowing no bounds of caste or party, made him deeply interested in all that concerned the public welfare, and all that interested the weak and oppressed. His thoughts were often busy with questions that most deeply interest the public mind, and to those who had the opportunity of profiting by his conversation, it was always suggestive and always delightful.

His intellect was acute and cultivated, and with sound, positive, almost dogmatic judgment, was joined a gravity, a depth of feeling, and a peculiar fancy, that made him sometimes seem to delight in paradox.

He rejoiced greatly in his labors in beautifying his home, which was indeed the center of a large and liberal hospitality. Thither were welcomed persons of widely different opinions and feelings. There Mr. Fitzhugh, who came from Virginia to tell us of the beauties of slavery, was invited to meet Wendell Phillips, with whose opinions of slavery Capt. Foote to a good degree sympathized—opinions always fully expressed, but never altogether popular. Such opposites could cordially meet within the circle of his genial influence.

We can hardly refrain from speaking of one thing that has always seemed exceedingly beautiful and illustrative of the character of this man. It is withal such "a good deed in a naughty world," that it deserves to be alluded to for the sake of the example.

Every one knows how a poor woman in New Haven, who had been highly educated and delicately bred, became, at the age of fifty-five, a mild religious monomaniac, and how, with others, she was arrested on a most serious charge and thrown into prison. She was utterly without money or influence. It is not probably known how substantial a friend she found in Capt. Foote. It is not necessary, in this world, to be known widely, how he interested himself to get a fair hearing for her case; and that when, after trial, she was remanded to prison, where she was likely to perish, how he secured her removal to his own house, where, cared for with every respect and attention, she remained about a year, till her death.

Oh! we know such things can not well be told, but they make the memory of some persons blessed forever. We think of them with a gratitude too deep even for tears. Indeed, a soul of rare tenderness has just passed on among the spirits of the just and good. Let us rejoice that we have seen and known him for a time.

This just and beautiful tribute to the memory of Samuel E. Foote, refers, in the two last paragraphs, to a singular act of benevolence—an act not singular as such, but for the circumstances that called it forth. A number of religious fanatics had formed an association for mutual enlightenment in religious doctrines and duties. They wished to perform some high, religious acts that should bear testimony to their zeal and devotion. In this idea they concluded that the highest performance of that character would be to destroy "the man of sin." One of their number was willing to be designated as that man, and to be destroyed. He was accordingly sacrificed, and the fact becoming known, the associates were immediately taken into custody, to be dealt with according to law. As their acts were sufficient proofs of insanity, they could not be punished as murderers. The woman above referred to, was rather a passive than an active agent in the proceedings of the fanatics, and during her residence in Mr. Foote's family gave no evidence of any return of insanity, but passed there a quiet peaceful life until its termination.

Many acts of benevolence, unknown to the writer, have been discovered since his death. Soon after that event he met a very respectable colored man in the streets of Cincinnati, who enquired so particularly, and with so much deep feeling respecting the circumstances of Mr. Foote's sickness and death, that he thought it necessary to give a reason for it to a companion standing near: "Why," said he, "he bought me!" This, however, unlike many others of his acts of benevolence, involved no pecuniary sacrifice: the subject of it not only paying the price of his freedom by his success in the vocation which he adopted as a free man, but becoming sufficiently wealthy to be enabled to retire to a farm in the country, where he continues to set a good example to his fellow freedmen of "industry, perseverance and success."

In this, as in many other instances, the reflection of the influence of a good character by exciting imitation, (although in circumstances essentially different,) was felt by many who were not aware of its extent. The personal exhibition of attractive virtues in the person of the subject of our memoir has ceased, but this record is intended to perpetuate the rememberance of them, and to stimulate those youths who are beginning their career in life, to go and do likewise.

APPENDIX.

I.

Eli Foote occasionally indulged a taste for expressing his thoughts in rhymes, which were generally easy and graceful. They were as unstudied as ordinary friendly letters, which, indeed, they were, being invitations to visit his house on particular occasions like the following, or playful remarks on some passing events of the time. They were not considered poetical, but merely rhyming effusions, and were not preserved with any care; in consequence of which the following specimen of the toryism of the time is the only piece that has been found, though some of his old friends used to speak of others which have been supposed to have been much more worthy of preservation for their pleasant humor and shrewd remarks on the circumstances that called them forth.

TO L. H., ESQ.

St. Pumpkin's Day* being near at hand,
When priest and people through the land,

---

* The New England Thanksgiving Day received the sarcastic appellation in the first line from the Churchmen, in retaliation for the Puritan denun-

E'en every rebel, saint like whig,
With carrot locks and powdered wig,
And coat well brushed, and shirt of linen,
Made new from yarn of good wife's spinning,
Leads little Joe and simpering spouse,
With solemn step to meeting house
To thank the Lord, whose goodness fills
His leather book with Congress bills,
Gives store of corn to fat his pork,
And makes his oxen strong to work:
But most of all, whose wond'rous power,
Aided our troops in lucky hour,
Led them by dint of hardy blows,
Quite on the bulwark of their foes
At Stoney-Point: for which they sing
Praise to their God, and damn their king.
    On that great day I mean to dine
On roasted goose and mutton loin,
And drink a health to George our King,
Who'll rebels to repentance bring.
    If tired with gloomy cares, and sick
Of dull retirement in East-creek,*
Your Toryship will condescend
To bring your wife and see your friend:
To what my table does afford,
You shall be welcome as a Lord.—ELI FOOTE.

His attachment to the Royal cause was not shared by any of the members of his family, and by but few of his personal friends.

---

ciation of Christmas. Minced-pies which had always been considered a necessary aid for the due celebration of Christmas, were considered as savoring too much of prelatism, and pumpkin-pies were raised to festive pre-eminence in their stead.

  * A district of Guilford so called.

It was rather a religious than a political senti-
ment that caused the distinction between the
Whigs and Tories of New England during the
war of the revolution. The Puritan fathers did
not come to America to establish free toleration
for the religious belief of others, but to establish
a supremacy for their own religious doctrines, with
freedom on their part to prevent all other doctrines from contaminating the minds and morals
of the members of their Commonwealth. They
intended to establish a Theocratical government,
as nearly on the principles of that of the ancient
Jews as circumstances would permit, under which
all freedom of opinion in religious matters should
be monopolized by the elders and rulers of their
Church. Full and free toleration of religious
opinions was not included in any system of government then existing in the civilized world. Its
value as an aid to the progress of Christianity was
a discovery of a later period. Its necessity to any
system of free government was understood as soon
as the United States were required to frame such
a government.

Previous to the revolution, the Episcopalians
considered that the circumstance of their's being
the established Church of the mother country, was
their only security from the persecutions which
the Quakers, and others of different denominations, suffered at the hands of the Puritans. They,
therefore, very naturally ranged themselves under
the banner of "Church and King," fearing to lose,

in case of the establishment of the independence of their country, the security they enjoyed for their worship after the manner of their forefathers. If the Puritans had confined their intolerance to that of the immoralities and vices cultivated by the Cavaliers, who, at the restoration, obtained an unbounded sway in politics and manners, as distinctive marks of their being the opponents of the late government, it would have saved their reputation from much obloquy on account of their religious intolerance.

The two cardinal virtues with them were rigid Sabbath observance and chastity. These will make any nation powerful and unceasingly populous, for they will give strength and power to body and mind, by giving necessary rest to the one, and necessary exercise to the other. The "Universal Yankee Nation" has acquired its preponderance in numbers, as well at home as among the settlers of all our Western States and Territories, more from this than any one other cause.

APPENDIX.

II.

Although all the relatives of Eli Foote were of different political and religious opinions from those which he adopted, and all his brothers were active patriots and opponents of the Royal cause, yet their brotherly love was not impaired by the political condition of their country.

Ebenezer Foote, the fourth of the brothers, imbibed the patriotic ardor of the times with all the vigor of youthful enthusiasm, and became one of a party of similar enthusiasts, all minors, who left their parents, guardians and masters, without staying to obtain leave; determined to show themselves men in action and patriotism if not in law. They took part in the battle of Bunker Hill, some of them wearing the " goodly leather aprons " appropriate to the employment which they left.

He remained in his country's service during the war, and attained the rank of major, which he held at its termination.

The whole of his pay he lost by the dishonesty of the man with whom he entrusted the certificate of the amount to which he was entitled.

He married during the progress of the war, and in addition to his other losses, sustained that of the chief part of the property of his wife, by the depredations of the skinners, tories and out-laws, on the border region in New York.

His labors, services and sacrifices in the service of his country did not protect him from the denunciations of the Democratic party, by whom nearly all of those disinterested and patriotic officers who were his associates, and who adhered to the party of Washington, were stigmatized as tories; an exemplification of party violence not excelled by that of any subsequent period of our political history.

The following communication, published in the New York Commercial of January 7th, 1830, gives an account of some of the sufferings which he shared, with many other American prisoners in New York, and which few of them survived.

"In your last obituary you take notice of the death of Ebenezer Foote, formerly first Judge of Delaware County. He was a man of excellent character, and great good sense, and was in the literal sense of the expression, a Revolutionary Patriot. I was intimate with him, and have heard him frequently relate the following incident of his life:

"He was taken prisoner by the British at the capture of Fort Washington, on York Island, in November, 1776, and was put in close confinement in the building now called the Bridewell, in this

city. The severity of the confinement induced
him, and eight or ten of his companions, to attempt
an escape. They succeeded in the night in getting out undiscovered, in the rear of the building,
and were then in the fields in that part of the city
lying north of Chamber street. They made the
best of their way to the Hudson river at Green-
wich, and adroitly eluded all the sentinels. After
running up and down the shore they found a crazy
boat, and attempted to embark in it, but it was
too old and leaky to be navigable, and the others
went up the Island, and were most of them re-
taken. Mr. Foote found a plank, and determined
to cross the river by swimming, though it was in
the month of December. It was a most dangerous and distressing attempt. He was several
hours in the water, and passed undiscovered a
British ship of war that was lying at anchor in
the river. He was floated down by the tide below
Hoboken, and when he landed on the Jersey
shore, was not able to stand, and it was near day
light.

He was enabled after a while to crawl up to a
house, where he got refreshed, and completed his
his escape, but his constitution received a shock
from which it never recovered; and this desperate
effort enfeebled his health through life. He was,
however, permitted by Providence to enjoy the
blessings of prosperity and universal esteem,
through a long and busy life: and I recall to mind
his beautiful mansion on the bank of the Western

20*

branch of the Delaware, in the midst of romantic and wild scenery; and his warm hearted and hospitable reception of his friends, with mingled emotions of tenderness and respect."

A brief memoir of Ebenezer Foote, by his friend Gen. Leavenworth, was published soon after his death, in a St. Louis paper. It was a well written article, honorable alike to the writer and the subject.

His nephew, Samuel E., he spoke of and introduced to his friends as his son so frequently that, at length, he apparently forgot their real relationship.

He was one of those gentlemen said to be "of the old school," because their bearing and manner were more refined than "modern degeneracy" requires.

He was many years a leading politician in the State of New York; had been speaker of the House of Assembly, Senator, member of the Council of Appointment, and chief Judge in the county in which he lived.

In the violent party struggles of his time he had been warmly engaged, and consequently had many bitter enemies among those of the opposite party. To these, however, he became reconciled, and the leaders of the Democratic party—such men as De Witt Clinton, Judge Ambrose Spencer, (with whom, in the early period of their political career, he had carried on a war of pamphlets, marked, on each side, by the bitterness which characterized political publications generally at that time;) Morgan Lewis, the Livingstones, and other gentlemen of the old school, were always his guests when visiting that part of the country in which he resided. In a more advanced period of life, it was pleasing to hear such men speak of him with warm friendly feelings, contrasting very strongly with party bitterness at an earlier period.

We are apt at the present time to imagine that the rancor and virulence of party spirit have increased to such a point as to threaten civil war, and dissolution of the Union; but the danger from this cause in the days of our Fathers was more apparent. Time had not then cemented the Union, and they had not had sufficient experience of the curative influence of the ballot box upon political diseases.

III.

The American permanent embargo is herein made so prominent, and dwelt on with such emphasis, because it was the first governmental measure of importance which indicated that the waves raised by the tempest of the French revolution had not spent their force before reaching our shores. The wisdom and patriotism of Washington guarded us from their influence during the period of his administration, and his lessons were not forgotten during that of his immediate successor. But the election of Jefferson was considered by the adherents of the French revolutionary partisans, as a triumph of their principles.

And they had a right, from many circumstances, and especially from his letter to Mazzie, to consider him a thorough adherent of the French revolutionary philosophy. The embargo was a foretaste of the practical workings of that philosophy which, proclaiming "liberty and equality," was intended to destroy all then existing governments, and all authority, including that of God. The leaders of the revolution did not, however, intend to *destroy* arbitrary, tyrannical power, but to *transfer* it to themselves. The arch-jacobin, Robespierre, aware of the influence of time in fortifying and cementing any system of government, intended, says Lerminiere, to produce the effects of time by spilling a given quantity of human blood,—to obtain the influence of centuries by cutting off human heads.* The tyranny of the Dantons, Robespierres, Marats, and other leaders, was far greater than that of the Louises; and the Jeffersonian embargo was a more oppressive and tyrannical measure than the stamp act, or the plan of parliamentary taxation.

But the shouting of political watch-words by the million, give more power to demogogues than the calm suggestion of reason and common sense can withstand; and the raising of liberty poles with inscriptions of "No sedition law," "No stamp act," "No alien law," gave strength and stability to the Democratic party that no reverence for Washington, and the prominent patriots of the revolution, and no reasoning or experience, could overcome.

The paramount evil of the embargo was its tyrannical restriction of the freedom of citizens. It

---

* "Robespierre concut de remplacer le temps qui lui manquait par un poids spécifique de sang humain : il crut en abattant des têtes se procurer des siècles ; il tua les hommes en l'honneur de sa religion politique ; il prenait leur sang pour les convertir : c'était outrager la raison autant que la charité du genre humain. Il se trompa en voulant retourner le sol avec la hache des proscriptions : il n'y a de fécond que le fer de la charrue et de l'épée."—l'Influence de la Philosophie du XVIII Siècle.

was not that portion of the surrender of individual liberty for the protection of society from the crimes of the vicious, which is voluntarily made by communities, but a prohibition of a certain class of citizens from pursuing those avocations on which they depended for subsistence. By its advocates it was proclaimed to be intended for the preservation of the property of individuals—the object of ordinary embargoes,—and besides this object, that of annoying European belligerents by withholding from them those supplies of the produce of our country which they needed, as a sort of reprisal for their acts of hostility towards our country.

Most of the tyrannical restrictions of freedom in despotic governments, had their inception in the real or pretended care of the rulers for the welfare of their subjects. Despotic power darkens the understanding in relation to the influence of restrictive measures, making the ruler feel like Napoleon in the height of his power, that he is the State. He cannot look through that darkness, and see how much more men lose by the privation of the free exercise of their faculties in lawful enterprizes, than they gain by the increased security thereby obtained; and thus sovereigns often become tyrants with good intentions. Thus subjects suffer not only the evils of direct oppression, but the heavier one of that deterioration of character which always flows from any restraint of freedom that is seen to be arbitrary. Any law restricting

the freedom of the citizen so much as to be considered intolerable, and excite evasions, is worse
than the evil it is intended to remedy, and this, it
has been seen, was the character of the embargo
law.   It was supposed by many of its friends that
it would avert a war.   Its actual influence was to
hasten one.

In saying that this law was a greater evil than
the war which followed it, we spoke of it political-
ly, not morally; (under which aspect many considerations might be presented not necessary to
be discussed here.)   It took from us more of our
most valued political inheritance—freedom—than
wo could afford to lose.   We may lose any amount
of our property, our ships may be captured or
burnt at sea, and our towns may be bombarded
and deserted, but by the exercise of our freedom
of action in our accustomed pursuits, we may re-
trieve our losses.   But if we patiently submit to
arbitrary and tyrannical restraints in our ordinary pursuits, our liberties cannot be regained until
oppression begets revolution.   If the embargo
could have been enforced according to its intent,
and the principles which dictated its imposition,
it would have proved a political opiate to the nation as destructive as narcotic poisons to individuals.

The war with all its evils and early disgraces,
roused that mental and physical activity which
characterises the American people, and which the
misrule of Southern Statesmen had a tendency to

suppress.   Among a free, an educated and intelligent people, activity of mind and body will produce those results that are seen in a more general diffusion of the comforts and luxuries of life, —in a rapid increase of population, and in the cultivation of good taste in relation both to public and private matters.

The predominant influence of the Slave States, since the period of Jefferson's Presidency, accounts for many unequal and tyrannical laws.   Any system of slavery recognized as a proper and suitable institution, is always at variance with the political freedom of any class of the population.   It takes from the slave the best principles of manhood, and from the master that due appreciation of the principles of justice and human rights, which are necessary to the preservation of political freedom.

Christianity, in proportion as its influences are felt and acknowledged, checks the downward tendency of slavery in a nation, by its effects on the master and the slave.   Most masters are willing that their slaves should be good Christians—it increases their own security, and the value of their property.   The greatest desideratum, however, is that the masters should themselves be good Christians.

It is a question with many persons whether it is a greater evil for men to be too much governed, and thereby enjoy rest and quiet, or so free that societies may some times be required to protect themselves, or redress their wrongs by Lynch law, or committees of vigilance.   This question would never have been mooted with us, if our rulers had been chosen judiciously, and in conformity with principles on which elective republican governments are founded, and which are necessary to the highest political welfare of any free people.

21

APPENDIX.

IV.

THE SEMI-COLON CLUB.

There was no restriction in the rules of the Semi-Colon Club as to the subjects offered for discussion. Poetry and prose were equally eligible for the expressions of opinions on politics and literature, manners and morals, which, together with any other subject that any member might choose to bring forward for discussion, were legitimate themes, and gave opportunities for the display of the tastes and opinions of the members. Some of those articles which were published have been referred to, and some others are here given as specimens of the different subjects and styles of other members. Two of the poetical pieces are by the lamented J. H. Perkins, some of the others by lady members of the club. Many excellent articles have been "lost or mislaid," some others have been preserved in archives of the members.

A renewal of the operations of the club was proposed several years after its dissolution, and a very pleasant and characteristic meeting was held at the residence of Mr. Lawler, at which some excellent contributions were read, but the institution had lost with many of its valuable members the power of revivification.

The first piece here given was one of the chapters of an "Essay on Man," each of which was devoted to a different subject, and consequently there was no special connection, or relation of the chapters to each other. The various topics in most of the other pieces, as in this, were temporary in their character, and except those referred to as having been published, have not been preserved. The political prejudices of the time are nearly forgotten, but this first piece is a specimen of them then.

ESSAY ON MAN.

CHAPTER V.

There was a time when it was considered quite respectable to be a wise man.   This, however, was a long time ago.

The seven wise men of Greece are spoken of in history as having been quite influential and important characters among their countrymen; but we have seven foolish men in the United States that are far more so.

It is recorded of these seven wise men, that they were assembled on a certain occasion at a dinner party, and after the cloth was removed, were enjoying their wine—and their cigars, would probably have been added by Plutarch, if they had been able in those days to obtain so great a comfort—but for cigars, for the invention of steam-doctors, and for Richard M. Johnson, the world is indebted to America, of which country those sages had never heard.

It is probable they felt some thing was wanting to their enjoyments, though they did not know it was cigars.   The consciousness of this want may have led them to discourse of happiness, and in the course of the conversation the following opinions were given by the seven wise men, each of which we shall compare with the known opinions of our seven unwise men, and make such reflections upon the subject as we trust may tend to edification.

Solon said that a Prince or Sovereign has no means of acquiring glory and happiness so proper as by making his monarchy a democracy.

Senator V. thinks it glory enough to change a democracy into a monarchy, and that there is no way so effective for this purpose as to bamboozle the people until they confound the distinctive principles of the two forms of government.

Bias said the Sovereign should be the first to subject himself to the laws.

Gen. J. said very little about the matter, and subjected the laws to the Sovereign.

Thales said he considered a great man happy when he lived to a good old age, and died a natural death.

Mr. C. thinks a great man cannot be happy unless he commits treason, and deserves to be hanged before he arrives at old age.

Anacharsis thought him a happy man who should be the only wise man—or the wisest man—in his country.

Senator B. thinks happiness is to be found in making himself more completely ridiculous than any other man in the country.

Cleobulus said that a man to be happy must not place any confidence in any of his associates.

21*

The Secretary of the Navy thinks that the officers of the navy are knavish officers, and ought not to have so much confidence placed in them as to be trusted out of sight of land.

Pittacus said that that Sovereign would be the happiest who should so conduct himself that his people should fear—not him, but for him.

The Secretary of the Treasury is happy in causing the people to fear—not him, but his interminable reports—not his dignity and power, but his rigmarole.

Chilon said that a Prince ought not to think of any thing transitory and temporal, but if he would be happy, must think of things eternal and immortal.

The Vice-President would be happy to have us think he killed Tecumseh.

These opinions will serve to demonstrate that although in a poor little country like Greece, they could get along very well with wise men, yet it was probably because they were so poor and ignorant that they knew no better than to be content with necessaries: but as for us, we have long been beyond that period of civilization. We have arrived at that point when the most expensive luxuries are most esteemed, and they are prized in proportion to their cost. Now there is no luxury so costly as that of having foolish men for rulers; in which we have been indulging ourselves for so long a time, that we have begun to discover that, in this, as in many other matters, we have been too extravagant.

England, an old and rich country, can afford to have fools for kings, but we cannot: we are becoming embarrassed by our extravagance in this point, for we have gone beyond our models, (as people who ape the extravagances of others are apt to do,) and not content with having foolish men for chief magistrates, we must go beyond the English, and indulge ourselves in having foolish ministers of State also.

Many people supposed that the "illustrious predecessor" would have satisfied the utmost desires of any people for this species of extravagance, but the treader in his footsteps is still more costly.

It is generally thought that we cannot go farther in this course, but we have proved in a former chapter, that M. V. and R. M. J. are not the two foolishest men in the country, and although few will agree with us in this opinion, yet we shall continue to maintain it; for we will not sacrifice truth to the vanity of having it supposed that we are indulging in the most costly extravagance that could possibly be procured, a foolish vanity that admits of no excuse for its indulgence; for when people make a great display of luxuries that it is notorious they cannot afford, it adds nothing to their reputation.

The fact is as respects us, that such costly extravagancies as unwise rulers, tax us so much beyond our means, that we shall be obliged to go back to the use of such plain wise men as our fathers were contented with: for to endeavor to keep up appearances by trying one foolish man after another, only adds to our embarrassments, and will reduce us to abject poverty if we persist in it.

NIAGARA.

Troubled waves in beauty rolling
   Stately to the rocky verge;
And with solemn voices tolling
   Ever your majestic dirge;
Still your echoes haunt my slumbers,
   Dreamily around they float,
Blending still in spirit numbers
   Peace with every warning note.

Pure and white your waters gleaming,
   Rocks in vain your course would stay,
White with foam in sunlight gleaming,
   Onward still ye urge your way;
To the dizzy height you're sweeping,
   Pausing never on the brink,
O'er the edge in grandeur leaping,
   In the depths below ye sink.

Floating soft in spray to Heaven
   Now ye soar in glittering dew:
But the sunbeams' ray hath given
   To each drop a rainbow hue;

Trembling now my heart rejoices,
   As I gaze with awe and fear;
And the echoing spirit voices
   Still are whispering, " God is here!"

Thus at night around my pillow
   Still they chant when none are near;
"So thy life, a restless billow,
   "Speedeth to death's brink with fear,
"Breaking oft on rocks of sorrow,
   "Foaming still with passion tost,
"Moaning on through each to-morrow,
   "Till within the grave 'tis lost."

"Keep thy spirit waves as purely,
   "Strong through suff'ring urge thy way,
"In the dread abyss securely
   "Thou mayst plunge, nor wish to stay;
"Brightly then in light ascending,
   "Clad in raiment white as snow,
"Hope, thy tears in beauty blending,
   "O'er thy grave shall arch her bow."

NEW ENGLAND.

Why do I love that rocky land,
   And that inclement sky?
I know alone, I love it—
   And ask not. care not *why*.

As round my friends my feelings twine,
  So round my native shore;
God placed the instinct in my heart,
  And I seek to know no more.

Then howl, ye inland tempests,
  For ye lull my soul to sleep,
And I think I hear the ocean wind,
  And the surges of the deep—
New England's cold and leaden clouds
  Sweep o'er Ohio's sky,
Her frost bound soil rings to my tread,
  And her snow goes drifting by.

My father's bones, New England,
  Sleep in thy hallow'd ground;
My living kin, New England,
  In thy shady paths are found—
And though my body dwelleth here,
  And my weary feet here roam,
My spirit and my hopes are still
  In thee, my own true home.
March 22d, 1843.   J. H. P.

HYMN.

That voice which bade the dead arise,
  And gave back vision to the blind,
Is hushed, but when he sought the skies,
  Our Master left his word behind.

'Twas not to bid the ocean roll;
  'Twas not to bid the hill be riven;
No—'twas to lift the fainting soul,
  And lead the erring mind to Heav'n.

To heave a mountain from the heart;
  To bid those inner springs be stirr'd;
Lord, to thy servant here impart
  The quickening wisdom of that word.

Dwell, Father, round this earthly fane,
  And when its feeble walls decay,
Be with us as we meet again
  Within thy halls of endless day.

J. H. P.

———

A LAY SERMON.

"Consider the lilies of the field."—Matt. ch. 8th, part of v. 26.

In this age and country in which the principles of Utilitarianism are too prevalent for the general good of society, there is a peculiar fitness and propriety in calling your attention to this precept of the author of our holy religion. As it is the part of duty to yield implicit and unhesitating obedience to all the commands of our gracious Redeemer, so it is the part of wisdom to enquire into the reasons and influences of those commands; for thus shall we strengthen our faith, increase our hope, and extend our charity.

Flowers are among those common bounties of our beneficent creator, bestowed upon his rational creatures, for the purpose of increasing the happiness of them all; for like air and water they are accessible to all; and they cannot be neglected without producing some of those evils, which a neglect of any of the common and universal blessings, bestowed on us by our Maker, always occasions. Amid the toils, the cares, and the vicissitudes of life, the heart is liable to become hardened, and the feelings callous, unless the softening and refining influence of objects of beauty and humility be frequently presented to the senses—objects which, like the flowers of the field, in the voiceless language of angels, reprove with gentleness and sweetness the selfish and evil passions of our nature, and call upon us for gratitude and thanksgiving to Him who clothes the lilies of the field with splendor exceeding that of Solomon in all his glory, and who has assured us that his care for us is in proportion to our superiority to these fading and transitory flowers.

When we are overcome by distress and sorrow: when affliction bows our heads to the dust, these simple, humble ministers of consolation meet our view, and teach us that as they have arisen from the dust in beauty and fragrance, so shall we be raised from our weakness and depression, in power and glory, if we obey the commands of our Heavenly Father, and place our trust in Him alone.

Pride, ambition, and covetousness, when they take possession of the heart, expel from it the desire for those pure and simple gratifications which spring from a love of the beautiful in nature; and in the same proportion they expel happiness.

The statesman and the warrior do not "Consider the lilies of the field," and they never enjoy happiness during their career of intrigue or blood, but if their hearts be not entirely hardened and corrupt, they may, perchance, be awakened to a new course of life, and be swayed by gentler impulses, then—like the patriot Kosciusko, the latter years of whose life were devoted exclusively to acts of humanity and benevolence, and whose greatest pleasure was in considering the flowers of the field—for, says his biographer, whether in winter or summer, he was never without his flowers—like him, they may be good as they have been great—like him, if they be so, they will also love flowers, and will increase the happiness of their fellow creatures.

Thus we see that the precept in our text is, like all the precepts of our Savior, calculated to increase the sum of human happiness; and it is expressed in such clear and unequivocal terms, that we can scarcely call him a Christian who neglects the cultivation of flowers—who refuses to "Consider the lilies of the field."

22

FLOWERS.

There is no place
  In this world of ours,
Where ye come not with grace
  Fair flowers! sweet flowers!

Your beauty is dear to the eyes that weep,
And without you who would a festival keep?
To the hero's proud triumph, the path of the
    bride,
Oh what could atone for your presence denied.

  With what perfect bliss
    The wandering child
  Doth merrily kiss
    Your petals wild!

And affection would wish that your hues, fair
    flowers,
Might betoken the joys of his future hours!
On the bier ye are laid—of sweet hopes to tell,
And oh how can ye light up the captive's cell!

  And where is the prize
    Like your fragrant bloom.
  To the darkened eyes
    In the dull sick room?

What gleams do ye bring from days that are gone,
To bid the faint spirit live happily on,
It might almost seem that your eloquent breath
Could call the life back to the pillow of death.

     As the radiance bright,
      In the tents of the sun,
     When he resteth at night,
      When his course is run,

So are ye to our toiling and work-a-day race,
A vision of beauty and glory and grace;
If e'er for you, love be lost in the world,
May the recreant planet to atoms be hurled!
But may blessings of friendship, of joy and of
     mirth,
Rest on all your true lovers, ye gems of the earth.

BABIES.

> " I heard a voice cry, 'sleep no more,'
> Again it cried—'sleep no more'—to all the house."
> MACBETH, (new reading.)

Dear Semi-Colons, I want some help, advice. and consolation.

I am a bachelor—not by any means an old one —but just in my prime—past the greenness and folly of youth, not feeling at all the weakness and infirmity of age, but arrived at years of sobriety and discretion. and know a thing or two. But here is one thing, or rather set of things, which I do *not* know about; or rather, I should say, *understand;* for I *know* too much about them.

Babies! At my boarding house there is a young couple whose room is next mine, and they have a baby, the delight of their hearts, but the destroyer of my rest. I suppose it is colic; but no one would suppose that any thing short of red-hot pincers could draw such cries from human lungs. The amount of solid noise that child can manufacture in one night is absolutely incredible. I come home at night; everything is quiet; I go to bed with the pleasant anticipation of enjoying that sound, refreshing sleep that ever attends on a good conscience and a sound digestion. Presently I dream horrible dreams. I am in the dungeon of the Inquisition, and the shrieks and screams of the unhappy victims fall on my ear with frightful distinctness. Or I am a captive among the Indians—my comrades being slowly tortured before my eyes while I wait my turn. Finally I awake and still hear the dreadful yells, and find it is that baby! that blessed Baby! Then for the space of about an hour there is a succession of ear-piercing shrieks and demoniac yells as of an insane locomotive in the next room. Then comes a lull—and just as I am dropping off to sleep, congratulating myself that there is a limit to every thing, even the powers of that child's lungs, the uproar is renewed with double force and fury, as though the little wretch had merely

been getting an increase of strength and vicious-
ness during the temporary pause. It is a perfect
cataract of cries, a tornado of yells, an avalanche
of shrieks, all at once, and I am deafened, stunned
and stupified, and so lie and wish for day. That
child has converted me to the doctrine of infant
damnation; for certainly there never could be
silence in heaven for the space of half an hour if
a baby was there. Yet these parents, these infat-
uated parents, actually seem to take great comfort
in the little savage, and talk about it with the utmost complacency, and say its a dear, sweet, lovely, amiable child, except it has a little colic now
and then. Little colic! now and then! Great
Heaven! I sit and stare at them in dumb astonishment, and they are in other respects intelligent,
well informed people. And what still more as-
tonishes, and I may say alarms me, is, that I have
reason to believe that other people are just as blind
with regard to their babies; it seems to be a sort
of epidemic monomania. They call them angels,
cherubs; when they do not in the slightest degree
resemble anything angelic, except that like the
cherubim and seraphim they "continually do cry;"
and moreover there is this fundamental difference
between cherubs and babies, that whereas the
former, according to all writers on the subject,
have no place for the proper application of Solomon's antiseptic, the latter by a wise dispensation
of Providence are well supplied in that particular,
and nature herself seems to enjoin us not to neg-

22*

lect the opportunity offered. But parents whose opportunities are greatest for availing themselves of such facilities, seem to think of every other duty but that.

But what is to be done? Babies, to a certain extent, are necessary no doubt, and have their uses; but is it absolutely essential that there should be so many of them, and that they should be so omnipresent? Can't they be put somewhere at least until they are old enough to go to parties, and consume cotton, crinoline, and tobacco. They are bad enough then—but before, *intolerable*. If *they* can't be put somewhere, *can't* I? The discoverer of a remedy for this *crying* evil will be deservedly ranked by posterity with Fulton, Columbus, Galileo, King Herod, and other discoverers, inventors, philanthropists, and benefactors of mankind.

———

The humble petition of the editors of the Cincinnati Chronicle and the Illinois Monthly Magazine, to the *Semi-Colons.*

Fair and gentle Semi-Colons,
Bright as Hebe, wise as Solons,
Famed for beauty, wit and learning,
Jeux d'esprit, and deep discerning,
Secret, social coalition—
Listen to our poor petition.

Listen, laughing, lovely woman,
Famed for pointed quick acumen,
Critics hear whose sterner ken,
Walker yclept ac-umen,—
Semi-Colons, one and all,
Hear the prayer of Drake and Hall!

Each whose footstep hither tends,
Philosophic forty friends,
"Favored and enlightened few,"
Champions of the stocking blue,
For your own, your country's sake,
List, oh, list to Hall and Drake!

Thinking man or thoughtless blade,
Matron wise or blushing maid,
Samuel Essence, Cherubina,
Oh, for honied words to win ye!
Long, too long your inspirations,
Like some misty exhalations,
In the lonely mountain glen,
Shunning every human ken,
Have distilled in gentle showers,
On a few secluded flowers.

We would see those treasures rise
Boldly up to mortal eyes;
Like the clouds, in grandeur sail,
O'er the mountain, o'er the vale,
Decked with beauty, clothed in light,
Touched with colors dark and bright,

Flashing meteors o'er the sky,
Giving rainbows to the eye,
Darting outward as they roll,
Streams of wit, from pole to pole.

We suggest, (to change the figure—
And we urge the point with vigor,)
That ye act the part of churls,
Witty men and pretty girls,
Thus to light the torch of pleasure,
And to hide it in a measure.
Thus ye act like him who lingers,
Moping o'er a glowing grate,
Thawing out his own cold fingers,
Leaving others to their fate.

Gentle demi-Semi-Colons,
Thus ye lock up *nolens volens*,
Wisdom's fire, Genius' taper,
Thoughts that boil like steamy vapor,
Bachelor's groan and beauty's sigh,
(Meet repast for critic's eye,)
Caleb Comma's work of art,
Pithy things from spry Joe Dart;
Pleasant fancies—*all* your treasure
Hide ye thus beneath a measure.

We, like knights of famed romance,
Fain would couch the quivering lance;
We would slay the giant guard,
Who keeps nightly watch and ward

Over mind, and over beauty.
Like a sentinel on duty.
We would throw the portals wide,
See the fetters all untied;
Till Semi-Colon thoughts should fly,
Like comets through the darkened sky.

Plainly to speak—we edit papers;
Our readers all have got the vapors,
We've grown so dull of late, we scare
Can round a period, pen a verse;
Nor knew we why that we, who once
Were neither of us, quite a dunce,
Beheld our pages thus become,
So melancholy and hum-drum;
Until we found that you, dear friends,
Had crossed our purposes and ends,
By hoarding up, like pirate's booty,
All the wit, and *all* the beauty.

Give, oh, give us then the book;
Think how fine we all shall look,
Chronicled in goodly pages,
Mingled up with saints and sages.
Think how all the world would stare,
Seeing Semi-Colons there;
How they'll wonder, how enquire,
How they'll guess, and how admire!
And Semi-Colons, through the nation,
Meet with notes of admiration!!

HOW TO OBSERVE.

An Englishman passing down Pall Mall, found another man's hand in his pocket. This was a phenomenon. *Strange* hand in *his* pocket! It occured to him that the fellow had intentions, and turning, he asked him frankly if he did not intend to pick his pocket, and if he did, to tell him. as a friend, what he had seen particularly soft or foolish in his countenance that had led to his being selected as a fit subject for the enterprise. Such frankness required a return, and the fellow in reply, with many apologies for his mistake, told him that as to the matter of his countenance, that was well enough, but he had noticed that he *wore white cotton socks, and thin shoes of a wet day*, and had thought from that that the thing could be done upon him. The thief was evidently a philosopher, and a man of genius. All people will fail some times. He failed here, but it wasn't his fault. He should have succeeded. Every one will allow that on the premises the man's pocket ought to have been picked with the most triumphant success.

The world is censorious. An undiscriminating crowd would not appreciate the brilliant qualities thus displayed—they wouldn't know *how to observe*. They probably hooted and yelled, and insisted on escorting the fellow to prison. And the artistical merit—the show of genius that would have graced any brotherhood of choice jolly spirits for the pro-

moting of thievery on genteel principles, meets
with a premature fate on the rounds of a tread-
mill. This is harrowing.

But this isn't half so bad as another case, which
has long been weighing on my mind, and which I
will take this occasion of relieving my feelings by
commemorating. When will the world learn to
be just? I will not say generous, but simply just.
Now I know not if any instinctive sense of injustice in the bosoms of any here present will lead
them to conjecture to what object I allude—but I
anticipate that it will. It is the much abused—
meekly suffering Quack—that important personage
in the modern social economy. Every age is distinguished for some thing. In one it is the mariner's
compass. In another the art of printing. In another it is the great plague. In another the fun
that was had in burning heretics. In another
the similar amusement in doing the same thing
for the orthodox. In another the long-peaked
shoes. Our own is the age of Dr. Brandreth, Dick-
ens, and the Vegetable Indian Balsam.

Witness the philanthropy of the Quack. Dr.
So and So's "real blessing," for every body, is to
be had every where, by the gross, dozen, or single
box. What a gratifying assurance! Good, kind
Dr. So and So! Almost a *perfect sugar!*

But, as I said before, the world is a censorious
world. The order is misrepresented. "Sir," said
Dr. Brandreth to me, the other day, in the course of
a familiar conversation we had together, "people

don't appreciate us—the fact is, sir, they haven't *learnt how to observe.* The age is a superficial one. It doesn't examine. It doesn't *plunge,* sir! Thus we are not understood. A Quack—what is a Quack? He may be called a biped who consults the *wants, tastes, and feelings* of the community. He is an *adaptative* animal. He is a philosopher, for he knows that Quackery goes down—that people have a natural taste for it. Don't it? Follow my nine and a half a million of boxes of the genuine article that have gone off within the last five years, and then say. This I call aptitude. It is more—it is philosophy, taste, science, poetry, and genius!

"Sir, a man down South advertised that he had beat me. He said he could rejuvenesce old age. That I could do too. But he went farther. He said he could make a young man out of an old one, and have enough left for a little dog besides. But I tried him, and he couldn't do it. *The little dog was a failure.* He had *some left,* but not enough for an ordinary sized kitten. I published him the next day—and also an advertisement of Brandreth's Pills.

"The great merit of our system is the quiet and order with which everything is done. The system of *tooling* in all its branches we have nothing to do with. Other men may use the knife and dagger, but we avoid them. We operate with more precision, science and system. *Neat*—but effective.

"What then to the Quack are triumphs, processions, pomps and vain-gloryings? Conscious of his own merit, he does not need them. He works not for temporal honors. Like Augustus, he is satisfied with the substance without the show of power. He declines an ovation that might be garnished with the endless processions, of the vanquished and the spoils of victory. Through persecution and scoffing he meekly exclaims with the great and virtuous Iago. "Work on. my MEDICINE, work!"

"Consider the names that have borne the title. A distinguished Ex-President has been designated (but by the uninitiated) as a Quack. A Mr. C. once wrote of him that 'he was a man whom, whatever other qualities he might have, posterity would not fail to set down as a great financial Quack.' Now if posterity do any thing of this sort, they will be doing a very inconsiderate sort of thing. It pertains to the perfection of the character, that it should never have been contaminated by the taint of a Literary Institution. This gentleman was L. L. D.'d at Cambridge, and, of course, incapacitated. But that, in spite of this, he was designated for the honor first alluded to, only shows how eminently worthy in other respects he was considered for it.

"It is a matter of pride," continued Dr. B., "that this, our order, is only of modern growth. It is only under the illumination of the nineteenth century that it could flourish. Columbus was three centuries in advance of us. He opened a new world to Europe. We open a new world to every body—and a *very distant one.* In fact, people that go *sometimes* don't come back."

Dr. B. paused. He was just getting animated. A pleasant flush was overspreading his countenance, and he was preparing to resume, when a man called who had a broken leg cured by setting it so that it stuck out at right angles with his body, and wished for some of the "universal panacea," to set it right again. The doctor went to work putting up sixteen gross of boxes of his pills for him, and I reluctantly went my way, deeply impressed with the views he had presented.

———

LETTER FROM ONE WHO KNOWS "HOW TO OBSERVE."

Cincinnati, February 20th, 1843.

I still date, as you see, from the Queen City, where I have been detained quite beyond my expectations, owing to the suspension of navigation. For several days the river was obstructed by floating ice, then it began to rain in torrents, swelling all the tributaries, which came pouring their muddy currents into the Ohio, till the water became so thick that no boat could possibly get through it. You have no idea of the turbidness of this famous river. It is as near the consistence of their hasty pudding as any thing, and I am told at some seasons they eat it with a spoon. The very thought of it almost chokes me. What do you suppose they call this river? "The drink." There never was a greater misnomer. *The food*, would have been much more appropriate. As we were coming down from Pittsburg, the steward took the cook's boy to the side of the boat, and told him if he didn't behave himself he'd "spill him into the drink." I could not but smile at the singularity of the expression, though I was very much terrified lest he should carry his threat into execution; for they say it's very common for the captain to throw the hands, or even the passengers, over board in case of any difficulty. I can assure you I minded my P.s and Q.s, and took off my hat to the captain as deferentially as though he had been the Emperor Nicholas, for the thought of being plunged headlong into such a mud puddle was absolutely suffocating. I would as lief be drowned in a soft custard. I am credibly informed, however, it is considerably thinner in summer, so that when diluted with rain water or brandy, it is quite palatable. Indeed, most of the Buckeyes, and some of the New Englanders affected to like it as it is; even giving it the preference to the cold, limpid springs of their own native home. But there's no accounting for fancies, as the man said to his wife, who imagined herself a powder magazine, and was mad because she couldn't blow him up.

I am very anxious to get away from here I assure you. They call it the "Queen City;" but for what reason I cannot imagine, for its the most democratic place I ever saw. There's no deference paid to rank whatever. If the great Mogul himself, or any of the family of *gulls* were to visit here, they could only receive common civilities. The principle of democracy seems to extend even into family government, so that children contend that the majority should govern, and *they* (being in most cases a very large majority,) hold a pretty tight rein over their parents, manifesting no more respect for their seniors than they do for *themselves*, which is very little. A man who lives in a small tenement, in an obscure street, considers himself on an equality with the proprietor of a splendid mansion, and were it not for the Dutch, who bring with them the polish and refinement incidental to a monarchical government, the manners of the people would soon degenerate into a coarse, vulgar freedom, which would be quite intolerable.

In *one* particular, however, Cincinnati bears the palm over all other cities in the world. It is the greatest piggery in creation. You know there is a population here of about fifty thousand, but the greatest proportion of these are within doors. Just suppose them all in the streets together, men, women, and children; and they would (to use a very common expression here,) make a pretty tall crowd. Imagine then a population of 230,000 hogs, which is the number supposed to have been killed this winter, and which, of course, must have *lived* here, and remember they all live out of doors, and you can form some idea of the consternation a stranger feels in being thrown, for the first time, in such an extensive four-legged society. I have myself seen the streets so thronged with this privileged order that horses and carriages were arrested in their progress, till the slow moving procession should pass by. But though respected in life, they all meet with a violent and ignominious *death*, the details of which would, I fear, prove too much for your sensitive nature, I therefore forbear. Suffice it to say, they are often promenading the streets in the morning, offending the sight of the fastidious, and at night they are tickling the palate of the same fastidious ones in the form of sausages. But I must bring my letter to a close. If I should be detained much longer I may write you again. I should take the stage for Wheeling, but I am told the roads are nearly as muddy as the river.

We cis-montanes, as a well known Colonel in town would call us, are a great people. We overshadow the whole world as the Cedars of Lebanon overshadowed the brambles under them, "and all that sort of thing." We do every thing better than any nation under the high sun. We see more, hear more, and more wonderful things happen to us. Now, for instance, when Ned. Hughes

21*

came back from Rome, what could rival his story about the procession of priests at Candlemas? "Yes," said Ned., "there were five thousand priests, each bearing a lighted candle in his hand." "Five thousand priests!" said his brother Peter, with an air of doubt. " *Yes, sir*, and every candle was as big as the pillars in front of Dr. Beecher's church, and fluted from top to bottom, *by George, sir!*" Ned. was born out at Hamilton.

But speaking of candles reminds me of Judge B., of Western Pennsylvania. Now the Judge must be allowed to tell his adventures in his own way or he wouldn't tell them at all. If his facts didn't hang well together, why, that was their lookout—not his—he did all *he* could for them. "One day," said the Judge, "the men were going out to the harvest field after dinner, and one of them had a colt that he was trying to break to the saddle. He couldn't manage him, and I got on him to try what I could do. Well, gentlemen, will you believe me, that colt threw me over his head thirty-four yards and a half—we measured it afterwards. And if it hadn't been that there was a foot of snow on the ground, the fall would have broken my neck." "But Judge," said one sitting by, "I thought you said it was in the harvest field." "Did I?" said the Judge, as he turned slowly in his chair, and gave the fact lover a look that was enough to drill gimblet holes through him—"*no, sir*, I'll be d—d if I *did*." The doubter declined joining issue.

But speaking of colts reminds me of music.
Now Jack Jones *was* a good musician: he played
on the piano admirably. But the strangest things
would keep happening to Jack, and Jack *would* tell
them. We were all gathered round a blazing fire
one afternoon, each behind a sixpence worth of
good tobacco, and sending forth volumes of smoke,
when Jack got on to a remarkably *tough* one.
"When I was out in Wisconsin," he began, "and
you know that snakes are rather too plenty there
for comfort. The summer rains had come on; and
I was kept in a miserable little log cabin for a
whole week, with nothing on earth to do to pass
away the time. Well, one morning I went into the
drawing room and sat down at the piano—a first
rate Vienna instrument, by the way—to amuse
myself. I *thought* that I heard a strange kind of
noise every now and then, but didn't mind it
much. Well, I hadn't been playing much more
than half an hour when I happened to turn round,
and there was the biggest rattle snake I ever saw,
coiled through the back of the chair, and looking
over my left shoulder, right into the music book.
There he was: licking his lips and picking his
teeth with his tongue every minute, as if he had
just come from dining with an alderman. And a
beautiful audience he was for a modest amateur
who had never given exhibitions to a promiscuous
assemblage in his life before. Well, gentlemen, I
saw how it was going to be. I knew if I stopped,
or made one false note, the varmint would bite me

sure. So, on I went, with that pestiferous reptile hanging over my shoulder, and blowing his infernal breath into my ear, and played every thing I ever knew or heard of, and when I was done, I played 'em all over again." "Well, how did you get away at last, Jack?" interrupted some one through the smoke. "Why, I'll just tell you how it happened. The snake was keeping time all along with his rattles: and by-and-by he got to doing it pretty well. He made use of his big rattles for the bass, and the little ones at the end of his tail for the high notes. I saw it kind of puzzled him to manage some of the passages: and when I got to *putting in my big licks* in the high parts of Norma, I got, of course, clear down to the end of the treble keys. I kept one eye on the snake, and t'other on the door; and suddenly, when I was farthest away from him, kicked the chair over, snake and all, cut and run, and have been traveling ever since." "Whew!!!" said some fellow. But he was only blowing out a mouthfull of smoke.

But speaking of snakes reminds me of Democrats. My particular friend, Thomas Jefferson Smith, is a Democrat: and Thomas has a theory, too, about the weather. He was favoring me with it one day last week somewhat after this fashion. "You know," so he was pleased to begin, "that these bloody aristocrats in town here wont have anything to do with us Loco-foco lawyers. Well, here I was, sitting in my office all spring and all summer, and taking in no fees except the old clothes that I got from the jail birds for defending them. That did for a while. My landlady took old clothes for board until she got two suits apiece for her children all round, and a winter frock for herself. 'Twas bright, 'twas heavenly, but it would n't last; as the poet says. And my landlady, says she to me one day, 'Look here, Mr. Smith, I can't afford to trade any longer! so you must fork up the hard every Saturday night, or your name's *Walker.*' Well, I saw how it was going to be: I must either raise the wind or break up my interesting domestic relations. The election was coming on, and I determined to stump it for the sovereigns, to see if any thing would come of that. Up I went the first night, with my speech all learned by heart for fear I should forget it. Says I to myself, the Lafayette is a gone sucker now; and the *Life and Trust* may just as well shut up as not. Well, I mounted the stand, and was just giving them a broad-side right into 'em, when a chap in the crowd sings out: 'Helloa! Mister, *vot's your name?* Tell us vere you got your *brought-in up,* and all about it—let's have the proper documents!' Here was a go! It felt like a shower bath. Well, I told them all about myself; but they kept on asking question after question for as much as ten minutes. I answered them all, and rolled up my sleeves to fire away, and just as I got fairly into *the Constitution* and the *Rights of Man,* a big fellow gets up right in front of me, and says he,

'My friend, one more question, if *you're* agreeable to it. It may be necessary for you to settle one fact of considerable importance before you begin. So will you have the kindness to inform this meeting whether or not your anxious mother REALLY knows you're out?' I didn't hear any more, sir. I pledge you my word I *didn't* run. But I *did* do some of the tallest walking that has ever been known in these parts."

"But the weather, Tom," said I, "how do you account for all the rain we've had lately?"

"Oh, yes. Why, the fact of the business is, that the sovereigns '*rent the air*' so with their shouts as I was leaving that it wont hold water any longer, and the showers have been dripping through the holes ever since."

———

GRAHAMISM.

> " Could a Tartar e'er grow cruel
> Coldly fed on water gruel?
> But fancy his ferocious force,
> If he first ride, then feed upon his horse!"

"The interests of humanity," says a modern reviewer exultingly, "are at last suspended on a pothook." The seething cauldron embodies the elements of the progress of society. The simples of the cabbage garden contain the true elixir of life. "All flesh is grass," as has long ago been declared, and if man grows it must be grass that expands him.

Such are the promises of the vegetable—now denominated the *saw dust*, now the *graham*, now the *bran*, now the *oatmeal and chips* theory. Vituperation is to be expected. Every great discoverer treads, of course, upon the toes of the millions of stupid fellows, who have gone before him. But it is not by vituperation that a theory is to be tested. It is by what it has done, its results, achievements, by truth, reason and philosophy.

Taken in this light, our motto affords a most convincing and enforcing proof. It is also triumphantly illustrative of the doctrine. Let me repeat.

> "Could a Tartar e'er grow cruel,
> Coldly fed on water gruel?"

Could he? The idea is preposterous. Fancy an Arab going to victory on a stomach full of oatmeal and water. I know, indeed, of one instance of a hero going to battle on, for aught that appears, vegetable diet. The renowned and redoubted Wouter Van Twiller, who went forth, as is stated, "brim full of wrath and cabbage," but it will be remembered that he had poor luck—very poor luck—as the historian goes on to show. What might it not have been, had he substituted for the cabbage, pork, or mutton, or even smoked ham?

Take again the other phase of the theory. The Timour, the Ghengis Khans, the Mahmonds, of Eastern history, evidently traced their conquests by means of their beef and goats milk. We know that they had both of these, and we are well warranted in the conclusion. The warlike qualities became transmitted. It is true an ox isn't generally considered very bellicose, but get him roused and he has the spirit of a warrior. Is there any gentleman or lady present, perhaps, who would face a mad bull? Goats are notoriously belligerant. They wait only for the slightest provocation. Just *shake your head at them*, and they are sure to come. It is only in the light of these facts that we understand history. We see how essential it is to the character of a good warrior that he be a good trencherman. We understand the picture of our own old Barons,

> " Who *cawed* at their meal
> With gloves of steel,
> And drank the red wine out of helmets barred."

These rude ages, savage, ferocious, meat eating. blood thirsty and voracious, are gone. We commiserate their unhappy state. But what an illumination has succeeded them! men have become peaceful, quiet, tame, submissive. No longer does the Tartar, in the impressive language quoted. "first ride, then feed upon his horse." Since the *Graham* advent, men repose in quiet under the protection of a bran pudding. They rest easy by

the vigor of saw dust.   They go on their course
of indefinite progress under the impulse of inspir-
ing oatmeal.   No longer does the milk of the herds
urge frail humanity to deadly loggerheads.   No
more the hind leg of a cow impel to kicking up
one's heels in frolicsome disorder, and assaulting
one's neighbors.   Happy age!   Exalted Graham!

BAGS.

"Provide yourselves with bags that wax not
old," says the Psalmist.*   I wish to know if here
is not a command as plain as words can make it,
and I wish to ask you all—you female semi-colons
(my wife among them)—how do you obey this in-
junction?   Can you reconcile it with your con-
sciences to buy such quantities as you have done,
of silk braid, and silk floss, and linen twine—and
as you are now doing, of cruels and things of that
sort?   I've gone on, paying and paying, why,
bushels would not measure the zephyr-worsteds,
nor yard sticks the white kite string that I have
paid for.

My mother and the women of *her* day, *they* provided themselves with bags (indigo and pudding)
which waxed not old—at least not *very* old, and
if they did, they were just as good if not better;

---

* Luke, 12th ch., 33 v.

24

but now-a-days, I should like to see an old bag. Look round among the semi-colons and see if an old bag is to be found; look at my wife and daughters—blue and salmon grounds with little flying arch-angels all over them; *there, there's* where my money goes to—I keep it in bags.

I don't like to see a woman's eyes open very wide, so I don't say any thing about this at home; and to have a woman talk loud about "niggardly" and "scrimping," and pounce down upon one so for smoking cigars, makes me glad to get one to calm my nerves; for I can't bear to see any one do so; it sets me all in a flutter, and I can't get used to it. I do hope they will not adopt the fashion that the women have in Paris—of wearing daggers at their girdles—if they do, I shall certainly leave my bed and board, and go somewhere else.

We used to say in Paris when things were not right, "Cui bono?" I say now where's the use and the good in all this? It costs money and takes time; positively I have not had my best wig combed for a month, but have been obliged to wear my old one, because there is not time for *me* to do it when I am dressing for Church. I can tell worse things than that; and if you'll go out with me into the hall, I'll show you a hole in my stocking that is really shocking. I do not say these things in a complaining spirit; I suppose we get along as well as most married people; but what does my wife want these things for? I don't care to have her look pretty to other men, but to me—me—and if I don't like new bags I should think that it was enough! "One thing at a time," was the motto of my friend; he drank first the alkali and then the acid of a soda powder—the effect was astonishing. I *might* go on and say that the spirit of the psalmist was intended to reach *other* things than bags—but one thing at a time. I ask all to reflect upon the *danger* of bags—Judas had a bag, and what did *he do?*

I shall go round to Mr. Shillito to-morrow, and tell him not to let my wife go over twenty-five hundred dollars a year; that I'm determined upon; and if my wife does not heed this gentle remonstrance, and sew me up neatly, but goes on getting more and more bags, why, I'll send her to—Bagdad.

"THE MISERIES OF AN ENGAGED MAN!"

Yes, thought I to myself the other night at Mrs. G.'s Semi-Colon, I suppose they are miseries; real ones; but they are not the only ones, nor the worst in this life. They are no more to be compared to the miseries of a *man that is expected to be engaged* (and don't desire to be, at least, not yet) than a quiet, peaceful death by chloroform or charcoal, is to be torn by wild horses or broken on the wheel.

This may sound extravagant to those who know nothing of my experience, and perhaps I had better illustrate a little.

I grew up to manhood with an unbounded admiration, affection, I may say, *adoration*, for the female sex; having no sisters, this is, perhaps, not to be wondered at. I have always felt it my duty, as well as my privilege, ever since I came to man's estate, (at 17 or thereabouts,) to be devoted to them *in* season and *out* of season—some of my friends say, *in* reason and *out* of reason, too—and my parents, unwisely as I now think, encouraged this disposition—indeed my dear departed mother always said she felt perfectly easy about her Augustus when he was out of her sight; for she was sure that he was not poisoning his hair and whiskers with smoke, but improving his mind and morals in the society of ladies. The dear woman was partly right—I certainly know many things *now* that I did not know *once*, and I learn'd them from women, but whether the knowledge has not cost more than it comes to, is a question still open for discussion.

In common with most other young Americans, particularly Western ones, I have been in the habit of devoting my summers to the study of nature*—going from Saratoga to Nahant, from Lake George to Cape May, from Rye Beach to Newport, or elsewhere as fancy or fashion takes me. One

---

* Quero, human nature.

or two summers ago I repaired to a watering
place, somewhat exhausted by a winter campaign
of more than usual severity, and surfeited by a
more than usual quantity of moire antique and
point lace. I sighed for repose, and sweet simplicity—ringlets and white muslin; and shortly after
my arrival, was attracted by the singularly sweet
and modest appearance of a young lady, who I
then saw for the first time. I was charmed, too,
with her unpretending toilette—so different from
those of the belles at all the places of fashionable
resort which I had hitherto frequented. I was
introduced—found her as charming as she appeared—became acquainted with her mamma, Mrs.
Brown, a dignified lady, who had known my
father or grandfather, or some of my ancestors—
and her married sisters, who were pleasant, chatty
women, rejoicing in all the diamonds and point
lace that Louisa (that was her name) eschewed.
They all made themselves agreeable, and to this
day I do n't know which of the four I liked best.
However, somehow, it seemed to be expected that I
should devote myself to Louisa, as the others were
older and women of the world, and able to take
care of themselves. So I walked to the spring
with her *before* breakfast, and on the piazza *after*
breakfast, and complied with all the rules and re-
gulations made and provided for the government
of the people at watering places. We used to
talk about scenery and landscape, and all that
sort of thing, and I found she had never visited
24*

any of the "lions" of the neighborhood. So I requested permission to drive her to visit a beautiful waterfall a few miles distant. She hesitated a little, which I rather liked, but finally said that if "mamma" didn't object, she would like to go. "Mamma" was graciously pleased to consent, on condition that I drove *very* carefully, as her Louisa was very timid. Of course I promised any thing and every thing. We set off—the day was heavenly—the road admirable—my companion lovely —my team unequalled, and if there is one thing I can do better than another, it is drive. This day I was quite inspired, and flatter myself I talked as well as I drove. We had a splendid time, and I came back quite satisfied with myself and all the rest of the world. That evening was the usual weekly "hop" at our hotel, and as in duty bound, I requested the honor of Miss Brown's hand for a quadrille—the evening was warm, and after our set was over I proposed a stroll on the piazza; insensibly our promenade extended itself down the steps, and into the grounds surrounding the house. Subdued by the influence of the glorious summer night, our conversation gradually subsided into silence, and we walked on without profaning the hour and the scenery by words. I was startled from a reverie by a half suppressed titter, apparently proceeding from the adjacent shrubbery, and when my senses had succeeded in bringing themselves to the level of earthly things, to my horror I found myself clasping a small white hand in mine, with a wild, vague, dreamy fear that I had actually pressed it to my lips. I had presence of mind enough not to release it too suddenly, and as just then a turn in the path brought us under the illuminated windows of the ball room, I gathered courage and words enough to ask my companion if we should rejoin the dancers; to which she assented. During the next schottische I reflected that I had committed no unpardonable sin—I had kissed fifty women's hands before, and was none the worse for it, and if there had been any threatening of a storm, it had blown over without damage.

The next morning as I was lounging in my room wondering what I should do and where I should go next, when I was startled by the sound of voices in the room adjoining mine, which had been vacant ever since my arrival at the springs—as it communicated with mine by a door, it was almost impossible to avoid hearing any conversation which was carried on within it, and it now seemed to be occupied by some new comers, whom the habitue's of the house were enlightening as to matters and things going on among us. "Mr. Delancy," said a strange voice, "oh, yes, I know all about him, though I never saw him—his father is a millionaire, and he is an only child." "Well," said another voice, "so we heard the first day he came, and I thought it must be true, for you know what a careful mother Mrs. Brown is." I whistled and sung, and made all sorts of noises to let my neighbors know my vicinity, but women never hear anybody talk but themselves when there is any gossip to be heard or told. "Well," said a third lady, "Louisa has improved her time well." "Yes," said a former speaker, "she has been well brought up. Mrs. Brown is an excellent mother, see what matches her other girls have made." "But," said another lady, "is it quite certain that it is a match? Because I've heard things said about Augustus Delancy before that never came to any thing." "Oh," said a fourth lady, "they *do* say he proposed during their drive yesterday, and my Tom saw him kiss her hand in the garden last evening." "Well," said another, "it is a very nice thing for Louisa—but my dear Mrs. Smith you promised me that pattern."   *   *   * I didn't hear farther—it was unnecessary—I will not attempt to express my feelings, but will only say that the next mail brought me letters announcing the dangerous illness of my mother, or my father's failure, or some other shocking news, and the 2 o'clock train carried me Westward, though I did not draw a safe breath till I got to Cleveland. I came home and recorded an oath against sweet simplicity and unsophisticated innocence, and, indeed, against all marriageable women whatever.

The next summer, of course, my health required the relaxation and amusement of travel. I sought the seashore, and made one of the throng at Nahant. I kept at a safe distance from all young ladies—especially those who looked as if they had just come out. I devoted myself exclusively to married women—respectable heads of families. There was one very nice little article there, with three of the sweetest children in the world, perfect cherubs. As a general thing I hate children, but these were such nice ones—never cried—never had dirty aprons or faces, and never were in the way when I wished to devote myself to the mother —she was a Mrs. Higgins, from Boston, and as her husband chose to be detained in town by business, like many others, and she seemed to have nobody in particular to take care of her and attend to her comforts and amusements, I got into the habit of lounging by her side, handing her in to dinner, walking with her to the different lions in the vicinity—Swallow's Cave—Spouting Horn, etc., and in fact, looking after her generally. I don't think I ever felt so well satisfied with myself as I did just about that time, I knew I was keeping out of scrapes—no danger of getting out of the frying pan into the fire; or rather, out of one frying pan into another, as I had so often done before. I was clearly in the way of my duty— making 'myself useful—I couldn't be better off than in the society of a lovely woman, not too young, and in no danger of expecting me to lay my heart and hand at her feet. She was evidently very much attached to her husband—referred to his tastes and opinions on all occasions—wore blue because it was his favorite color—(singular coincidence! it was also mine!) and never rode because she had once been thrown from her horse, and Mr. H. had made it a point that she should never mount one again. I was having a good time generally, with no more nonsense about it than Fanny Dorrit, when my very particular and confidential friend Frank Smith arrived. I found him in my room after I returned from a stroll on the beach where I had been helping Mrs. H. gather shells to take home. After our first eager greetings were over, he said with rather a disturbed look: "But 'Gus, what is this I hear about you? I thought you had sworn off from the fair sex forever." "Nonsense," said I, "I never intended to give up the sex—only the dangerous part of it—I've been a pattern of prudence since I've been here." "Oh, well," said he, "some folks think widows dangerous—I do myself—but if you like that sort of article, and don't object to the children, I don't know that it's any of my business." "Widows!" ejaculated I, "what do you mean? there's not a widow within fifty miles that I know of, and I'll swear that I never treated one with decent civility, except my respectable and excellent grandmother. I've kept exclusively with the wives since I've been here." Fred. gave a long, soft whistle. "What do you mean to say about your attentions to Mrs. Higgins," said he. "Say," replied I, "why I say that if her husband does n't find fault with them, I don't know that anybody else has any right to do it." "Her husband," said

Fred, "I dare say the poor fellow would find fault if he could—they say he did n't much like such things formerly." "Well," replied I, "if he do n't like it I'm sorry, but then why can't he come down at least once a week, and look after his family. I've only been following the instincts of humanity, and protecting his family, while he staid in Boston, absorbed, I suppose, in mercenary pursuits." "Stayed in Boston!" exclaimed Fred, "is it possible that you are such an ass as not to know that he has been staying in Mt. Auburn these three years, with a ton of white marble, and an inconsolable inscription over him."

Imagine my rage, "the deceitful wretch of a woman!" I exclaimed, "swindling me out of my attentions in such an unprincipled manner! What on earth shall I do? This is worse than the Brown affair, or the White, or the Green, or, in fact, any of the other scrapes I've worried through.

Well, I went to bed and sent for the doctor—he came, and couldn't decide whether I had small pox or scarlet fever. The inhuman brute of a landlord turned me out of his house at the risk of my life. I took the steamer next morning at six o'clock. Either the trip or some thing else was so beneficial that I was able to go on to New York the same day, and ended my vacation at Cape May."

APPENDIX.

V.

CAPTAIN SYMMES.

At the period of Capt. Foote's arrival in Cincinnati, the eccentric, the simple hearted, kind, and benevolent enthusiast, Captain John Cleves Symmes, was proclaiming his "Theory of the Earth" with such perfect confidence in its correctness that one could hardly avoid sympathizing with him, and wishing him success in his endeavors to make the world believe his "theory."

He drew his proofs and illustrations from every discovery in nature, and all the researches of travelers in all parts of the world. And if he had possessed the requisites of eloquence, except that of full and perfect faith in his own doctrines, (by the bye, its most important quality,) he might have become a heretic in physical science of sufficient importance to have equalled in fame many of those setters forth of strange doctrines in physics and metaphysics, who have made their names known in the scientific world, through the labored refutation of their doctrines.*

Capt. Symmes being at this time in the full tide of enthusiastic search, calculated largely on the aid he might obtain from one who had four times passed Cape Horn, and was a man of observation, thinking that he could obtain facts enough to convince the most skeptical. His enthusiastic desire to obtain facts from the Antarctic regions in support of his theory was so strong, that it was quite painful to Capt. Foote to disappoint his expectations, and to be able only to furnish facts which opposed instead of supporting his theory.

It was quite edifying to notice the ingenuity with which he would draw his proofs from circumstances, which, to common minds, could have no bearing whatever on the subject.

One of his disciples published a volume containing his† facts and inferences in relation to this matter, and another, J. N. Reynolds, who possessed the oratorical powers that Capt. Symmes wanted, traveled with him for the purpose of lecturing on

---

* Thomas J. Matthews, a profound mathematician, and a man of extensive general knowledge, published in the Cincinnati Literary Gazette, a refutation of Symmes' theory—a refutation which the personal character of Capt. Symmes—not that of his theory—seemed to require.

† It was an abstract of his arguments to establish the "Theory of Concentric Spheres," "demonstrating that the earth is hollow, habitable within and widely open about the poles." It was written by James McBride, late of Butler County, and a copy was taken by Mr. Hall, who lately went from Cincinnati on a Northern exploring expedition in search of relics of Franklin's expedition.

the subject, in order to obtain means to send out an expedition to make the necessary discoveries to verify the "theory." The parties, however, separated, and Mr. Reynolds proceeded alone on his tour, changing his subject from the investigation of facts relative to Capt. Symmes' theory to a recommendation of an expedition to the South seas, under the direction of government, for the objects of making discoveries generally, in the wide regions still unexplored. He succeeded in part, but did not carry out his project of going to the Antarctic "verge," as Capt. Symmes styled the commencement of the opening into the interior of the earth; but landed in Chili, and afterwards embarked in the Frigate Potomac, commanded by Commodore Downes.

Of the cruise of this ship he published quite an interesting account, in a thick octavo, which contained no allusion to Symmes' theory, but gave an account of certain chastisements of savages for outrages on Americans, which have tended to inspire respect for the ships and sailors of our country that were much needed.

Commodore Wilkes' expedition, subsequently sent out by our government, made such discoveries in the Antarctic regions as probably settles the question, that if a Southern polar ocean or continent exists we can not get to it.

The discovery of the Northern Polar basin, by the expedition under Dr. Kane, would have given to Capt. Symmes "confirmation strong as proof from Holy Writ," of the truth of his theory. If he could have lived long enough to have heard of this discovery, it would have proved a balm for all the evils of life, for he had announced its exis-tence, and indicated almost the precise locality of its position, namely: about 60 miles North of 82°.

His childlike guilessness was a remarkable trait in his character, and being combined as it was with a courage as indomitable as it was quiet and modest, occasioned some singular adventures in the course of his life, one of which was the following:

While in the army, his artless, unsuspicious manners and bearing, was thought by a subordin-ate officer to constitute him a suitable butt for jokes, that were so apt to be carried beyond the bounds of gentlemanly forbearance, that some of Capt. Symmes' friends remonstrated with him on the impropriety of submitting to them quietly. He, said he, had never suspected that any affront was intended, but if he had borne any remarks that a gentleman ought not to bear, he was ready to do whatever was proper in the matter, and asked his friends what he should do. They told him he must insult the officer publicly, and be prepared for a duel. Accordingly on the next parade he insulted him before the regiment, drew his sword, and told him to defend himself. The other being an unerring shot with a pistol, declined fighting with swords, and appointed a meeting to settle the affair with pistols. They met accordingly, and as they were to fire simultaneously, the accomplished duelist endeavored to be so much in advance of Capt. Symmes, as to settle the matter by hitting him in a vital part. His pistol was accordingly fired while Capt. Symmes was raising his, and the ball striking his wrist bone at the moment he was pulling the trigger of his pistol, gave it such a direction that the ball struck the other on the knee, and maimed him for life. He became afterward very poor, and Capt. Symmes maintained him several years, and until he died.

At the time when the settlement of the Russian boundary in North America was made known, it gave Capt. Symmes a shock of distress apparently as great as that occasioned by the battle of Waterloo in the Buonaparte family. He considered that our country had abandoned a portion of its territory, in which the verge was situated, by which a passage into the interior of the earth was practicable, and that within it the sun's rays were so refracted that the interior would be found much preferable to the exterior of the earth.

The Russian Consul at Philadelphia, Mr. Harris, transmitted to Capt. Symmes an invitation from Count Romanzoff to accompany an expedition then in contemplation, for making further researches in the Arctic regions; but his health had become too feeble to allow him to accept the invitation.

The Captain exhausted all his property in efforts to establish his theory, and died, leaving no disciple to continue his researches.

GENERAL HARRISON.

The references in this memoir to the necessity of understanding, and being governed in our choice by the characters of the men to be selected for our rulers, do not relate particularly to their moral, pecuniary honesty. The fears that there could be any danger of robbery of the public monies by public officers, are of comparatively modern date. But when the spoils of victory became an excitement to partisan efforts, those spoils were soon made to include the opportunities for plundering the public treasury.

In Ohio, and the West generally, the period of common honesty among government officers continued until a much later period than in any of the other States. Alfred Kelley and Micajah T. Williams received and disbursed some millions of the public funds without a suspicion entering the mind of any one that there was danger of any defalcation.

25*

General Harrison, when a candidate for the Presidency, was commended for his truthfulness, his kind-hearted benevolence, and unbounded hospitality, but no one thought it necessary to speak of his scrupulous honesty in relation to the public funds of which he had the control—that was a matter of course. The following circumstance it was not necessary to relate then, but now it may serve to show how much men and circumstances have changed, and how necessary it was for Mr. Van Buren to discover that it was possible to establish places of safety for the public monies, and to endeavor (unsuccessfully, however,) to make treasuries and sub-treasuries, thief-proof.

As Governor of the Western Territory, and Indian Agent, General Harrison had for many years large sums of money constantly in his hands, and unrestricted power to draw on the government to a scarcely limited amount.

On one occasion he wanted a sum of two or three thousand dollars for his private use, and he had at that time about thirty thousand dollars of government funds in his possession, but it never occurred to him that he could borrow from that fund.* He had a friend living at a distance of two or three days journey, (in those days of slow travel,) from whom he had reason to believe he

---

* In Hall's Memoir of Gen. Harrison it is said, "He had liberty to draw on the government for an unlimited amount. During the war he drew on the government for more than six hundred thousand dollars for public purposes, not one cent of which was ever directed to his own use."

could obtain a loan to the amount necessary for his purposes. He took the journey, borrowed the money, and during the entire continuance of the loan, it is believed that he had a large amount of the public monies in his possession, but not, as he supposed, under his control for any but public purposes. Perhaps if this had been known to the political demagogues during the electioneering campaign of 1840, it might have been used by them as proof of the unfitness of Harrison for President of the United States. It would have been as effective as the circumstance of his living in a log cabin.

APPENDIX
VII.

NOTES AND REFLECTIONS.

Memorials of the dead when inscribed on costly monumental marbles, are seldom regarded as objects which are to furnish lessons of life to the living. But those which are inscribed on the pages of our biographical literature, if they do not teach such lessons, are as false to their trust as those monuments, which have generated the proverbial sarcasm, to "lie like a tombstone."

To the young men of New England, lessons of industry, frugality, patience and perseverance are taught by their granite rocks, their stubborn soil, and their merciless climate, and these teachers furnish some of the inducements which tempt them to brave the dangers of the seas. For the fears which we might expect to be excited by the frequent desolating storms, and heart-rending shipwrecks of their rock bound coast, seem to have no restraining influence on their minds. On the contrary, the perils of the seas seem to be more attractive in proportion as they are dangerous.

Perhaps the restless disposition which sends young Yankees* into every part of the habitable world, may, in part, be generated by their climate —marked as it is by frequent and violent changes —and also by the varied aspects of the ocean along their shores. The seas, indeed, when exhibiting their bright. peaceful aspect in calms, or when gently ruffled by light breezes. are very alluring, and seem to give fair promises to the enterprising youth, of prosperous and happy voyages, and banish the remembrance of the experiences which in any other case would lead them to distrust such fair promises. For the bright ocean when in its state of quiet repose, gives them no intimation of the dangers from the rocks and shoals beneath its surface, nor of the reservoir of dreadful storms and tempests in the white clouds and blue skies over their heads; but rather seems to tell in Syren songs, of pearls and precious jewels in its depths, and glorious brightness and prosperous breezes above. They are like the bright aspects of slavery, as we have seen them many times exhibited in the South, where a patriarchial care

---

* The term Yankee is general abroad, including all citizens of the United States, but at home is specific, being restricted to citizens of New England.

and watchfulness over the temporal and future happiness of the slave, was repaid by a love and reverence more than filial.* These scenes of love and trust make us forget that slavery conceals rocks on which our most cherished possessions are in danger of being wrecked, and tempests of fearful portent, which call for the exercise of every faculty of mind and heart, to enable us to steer our ship of State to a secure harbor.

The dangers to seamen of winds and waves are not those which are most to be dreaded. The Syrens of the Mediteranean, who in the time of Homer's heroes, were accustomed to entice sailors into bad company, and then punish them for going there, are represented in our sea ports by those

---

* We have no doubt that in our Southern States many examples might be found, of attachment between masters and slaves, similar to one which remains very vivid among the recollections of the writer's boyhood.

In the neighborhood of Newburgh, near New Merlboro', a fugitive from St. Domingo, Mr. J. J. A. Robart, purchased a small estate, which he improved with such skill, and beautified with such taste, that it was among the curiosities of that region.

At the time of the insurrection in the above named island, a number of his slaves exhibited their love for their master and mistress, not only in providing means of escape for them, and saving as much property as could be carried away, but in refusing to be separated from them, although it required the abandonment of freedom, and their beautiful island, for the (to them) fearfully cold regions of the North. Mr. Robart's character was such as might be expected from such proofs of love by his slaves. His wife was a most beautiful and graceful woman ; such a one apparently as the Empress Josephine must have been from the accounts given of her.

who are quite as dangerous, who follow their example, devouring the sailors' earnings, debasing their vocation, and unfitting them for any other pursuit. The example of the subject of this memoir is that of one who was never seduced into bad company in pursuit of pleasure, though often compelled to be associated therewith by the requirements of business.* He never was disqualified for any pursuit which circumstances required him to adopt, by youthful follies and careless neglect of the opportunities of extensive observation, which teach lessons more effective than those of the teachers who profess to teach languages and sciences in a few easy lessons without a master.

Among the plans of that class of benevolent Christians, who, in modern times have been making exertions to ameliorate the character and condition of seamen, the first idea very naturally and properly was to provide boarding houses for them, where they might live exempt from the temptations that more easily beset them.

---

* At the period in which Mr. Foote was embarrassed by pecuniary difficulties in Cincinnati, his characteristic straight forwardness and unreserved truthfulness, confirmed the character he had always sustained. "So great," says a gentleman who was President of one of the banks at that time, "was the confidence in Mr. Foote's honor and integrity, and in his anxiety to free himself from debt, that no requisition as to time or amount in the reduction of his indebtedness, further than suited his own convenience, was required of him by the directors. Their confidence in him was perfect, nor was it disappointed."

The same gentleman adds: " he suffered a loss of about one thousand dollars rather than implicate an individual who might possibly be innocent," one who had a family dependent on his labors for support.

Examples of *success* by the due exercise of industry, with patience and perseverance, combined with economy and self-control, will aid as a safeguard against many of the temptations to which they are exposed, and can not be too often placed before them. Hope with all seafaring, as with most others, is constantly gaining victories over fear, but disappointment too often conquers patience and perseverance, generating in their stead intemperance and carelessness of the future.

One consequence of the heedless disregard of the teachings of experience by seamen, and of its warning by merchants, has been the ruin of a great proportion of the latter class; men whose talents and enterprise, have been probably the most efficient causes of the rapid progress of their country in that career, which in little more than half a century has raised it from the lowest to the highest rank among nations.

When in high political party times our merchants were accused by Southern politicians of being bought by "British gold," and John Randolph sneeringly asked in Congress, where else they got the capital for the purchase of their ships and cargoes—as if no wealth could be created but by negro slaves—he was answered by Mr. Lloyd, of Massachusetts, that they obtained it by honest and honorable industry, and successful commerce. He did not give any exemplifications, but he might have given many like the following:

The ship Neptune was owned by a number of merchants of small capital, and mechanics, of Hartford and New Haven, and was fitted out for an expedition around Cape Horn. She carried nothing but young men,* (some of them fresh graduates from Yale College,) with their provisions and equipments. With these she proceeded to the South Sea Islands, where by the labor of her men alone, she obtained a cargo of seal skins, carried them to Canton, where they were sold, and the proceeds invested in teas and silks of the value of four hundred thousand dollars in New York, to which port she returned in safety.

Other voyages, some to the North-west coast of America, in search of furs for the China market, and others to various places in the Indian and Pacific oceans, brought great additions to the commercial capital of our merchants, and aided in giving fresh impulse, and opening new regions to their trade.

The pretext for the robberies of neutrals by the European belligerents, by which they were made

* Capt. Andrew Mack, formerly of this city, and afterward Collector of the Port of Detroit, was one of them.

26

to differ somewhat in appearance from the old fashioned system of piracy and buccaneering was, on the part of the British, by a paper blockade of nearly all the European ports, and on that of France by Buonaparte's "Continental system," followed by the British "Orders in Council," were by each party designed to obtain the spoils of successful war.

An English political writer of the time spoke of the robbery of neutrals as a source of "plunder for our brave tars," which had begun to fail for the want of enemies' vessels on the seas, with a glow of patriotism like that excited by fresh conquests in India; and the French Government seemed to desire to excel their enemies in this incident of belligerent operations as much as in killing, burning and destroying in the established modes of honorable warfare. America had been a field for plunder to the nations of Europe from the period of its discovery; and as it now failed to supply the usual gold and silver for this purpose, it was like a new discovery to find in that country a people who had acquired wealth which could be taken from them as easily as it had been taken from the Aborigines, and with as little regard to the rights of the owners. The British government trusted to their ships to find and appropriate their share of the spoils, but the French, being by the English naval supremacy rendered powerless at sea, contrived to obtain their share by offering inducements to neutrals to trade at their ports, and making prizes of them on their arrival.

The infamy of those proceedings has since been shared by our own government, for the French, by a treaty with us, made reparation in part for those spoliations, paying to our government certain sums agreed on for this purpose, which to this day have not been transferred to their rightful owners.

The enmity of both parties of belligerents, together with that of our own government, which our merchants had to encounter, it might have been supposed would have annihilated the commerce of any nation, and especially of one possessing such boundless agricultural resources as the United States. And this would probably have been the case in any nation in which the love of freedom and of commerce, its parent and offspring, had not been so early and strongly developed. In the United States it might be modified by circumstances, but could not be entirely suppressed.

The fearless enterprise of our merchants contributed to raise up that indomitable host of seamen which no other nation has ever equalled. The fame of our whalemen became at an early period so great that the French government, despairing of ever being able to raise such seamen themselves, invited our whaling ships to sail to and from their ports, and special privileges and immunities were granted to induce them to accept tho invitation, which some of them did, but it was an unnatural course, and soon terminated.

Our trade with China became at one time so extensive that we supplied not only our own country with Chinese teas, silks, etc., but also some portions of Europe, especially Holland, to which country some of our ships made direct voyages from Canton, although she had been formerly so tenacious of her trade beyond the Cape of Good Hope, that the struggle to render it exclusive to herself, was the commencement of the decline and downfall of her commerce forever.

The course of our commercial prosperity operated on us as a nation in the same manner that success too often operates on individuals, being followed by reverses which could not be retrieved by men of weak minds among merchants—nor among nations, by those under the rule of weak statesmen; such countries as Venice, Holland and Portugal for instance.

The opposition to a commercial policy for our nation began with the transfer of political power to the anti-federal party, led by Jefferson, whose political education was finished in France, where hostility to England was nourished as the first duty, not only of statesmen, but of patriots in all classes; and England being considered the nurs-

ery of commerce, inhabited by a "*canaille mar-
chande*," it was regarded as one of her attributes
to be held in inimical contempt. The enmity of
Southern politicians toward England led to a similar course, when they lent their aid to suppress
American commerce.

———

The variety of denominations and sects which
the Christian religion has awakened among those
nations where freedom of religious discussion is
permitted, has been one of the causes, and a very
important one, of the more rapid progress of civilization and improvement in all the arts of life,
among Protestant Christian nations than in any
others.

The efforts which have been made to establish
uniformity of religious belief, have retarded mental
growth and progress in all matters. In the United
States, where a greater variety of Christian denominations, and more perfect freedom of religious
opinion exist than in any other country, greater
progress is made in one generation than in pagan
and idolatrous countries in centuries. And in those
Christian nations where uniformity of belief in
creeds and dogmas is required, and dissent punished, a proportionate difference in progress is observed. Compare the progress of improvement in
the arts and sciences in Spain, Portugal and Italy

with the same in England and the United States, and the contrast will be found striking. Every sect and denomination in endeavoring to make proselytes by reasoning and not by force, contribute to mental progress, not merely in metaphysical and theological knowledge, but in that exercise of mind which generates improvements in matters of which theological disputants make no account. When ever it is attempted to propagate the Christian religion by any other mode than that of counsel and reasoning, and instruction, it destroys its most distinctive characteristics, which are comprised in one little word—LOVE.

———

Success is always deified by nations, and generally by individuals. For want of it, Byng was hung, and through its influence Nelson was raised to the rank of a demigod, and allowed to commit with impunity more sins than any extent of charity can cover. It enabled him to blind the British nation to their atrocities so completely, that he felt as if it made him so superior to the influences of virtue or vice on character and reputation, that he dared to recommend to the care and protection of the British nation, the harlot by whose wiles he had not only been induced to abandon the wife of his youth, but to commit one of the most atrocious murders on record.

By recommending examples of success to the consideration of the young, we endeavor to make friends of the mammon of unrighteousness, in hopes that they may be received into the houses of their minds, accompanied by industry and prudence, patience and perseverance, and that the illusions generated by the success of criminals in stations so exalted as to be above human punishment, may be dispelled by the lights of truth, of sound judgment, and just appreciation of the nature of those acts which confer reputation independent of character.

www.ingramcontent.com/pod-product-compliance
Lightning Source LLC
Chambersburg PA
CBHW020927120726
47905CB00008B/2408